THE GOLDEN SCARAB OF
BALIHAR

THE TALES OF ZAHRA 1

MICHAEL GRAYFORD

The Golden Scarab of Balihar

The Tales of Zahra 1

Cover design by Gina Gonzales

Edited by Tarryn Thomas

Sveva font copyright and trademark of astype

ISBN: 9798861463614

Library of Congress Control Number: 2023918332

Produced in Los Angeles, California, the United States of America

ACKNOWLEDGMENTS

This book would not have been possible without the support and feedback of my local writing group, The Inklings, with particular thanks owed to Seth Wagerman and Gina Gonzales for extensive story notes. I also give a heartfelt thank you to my beta readers: Dan Nichols, Steve Rousseau, Alicia Parker, and Ellie Race. You each gave wonderful feedback that helped improve the book. Additional thanks to my online writing group, the Westering Mastermind, for being a fantastic source of inspiration and information.

Finally, an extra special thanks to Michael Legg, for the inspiration to write this story.

CHAPTER 1

Z ahra promised herself that this time she wouldn't get into trouble. All she had to do was stay focused on the task at hand—finishing the preparations for the night's feast.

Easy.

Yet she couldn't help but stop and gawk as the performers for the evening show strolled by. The nearest entertainer bore a flag identifying their troupe, emblazoned with a sun in the corner and red and yellow rays spreading out, a simple design but brightly colored.

As the group progressed through the hallway, Zahra stepped from beneath a pointed archway to give them plenty of room to pass. She held the carafe of wine she was to deliver to the banquet hall close to her chest.

A *slight* delay in her duties shouldn't be a problem.

She'd seen several groups visit the palace over the years, but never such a strange crew. They must have been from all over the world; they had different skin tones and facial features, and each wore a unique, fanciful costume. The women sported flowing, layered dresses with gossamer strips of fabric spiraling around their chests.

Jewelry dangled from their necks, arms, ears, and noses. The men's outfits were nearly as extravagant, with billowing trousers, colorful sashes, and tasseled headdresses.

She expected the group to put on quite a spectacle, full of dancing and acrobatics, impressive feats of strength, and even magic. Undoubtedly it would be wonderful, but a lowly servant such as herself would never be invited to such an event. However, if she stayed on task this evening, she might finally be promoted and could then enjoy some of the more entertaining activities in the palace.

As the last member of the ensemble exited the hall, Zahra wanted nothing more than to follow them and watch their preparations for the night's production.

Zahra spun around the mosaic archway and immediately bumped into a young woman, who lurched backward, brushing against a pedestal and knocking off a turquoise Nishapur vase. Zahra bent forward hastily and caught the vase with her free hand just before it would have smashed to the floor.

That was close. If it had broken, she would have been flogged for certain.

The woman, who had fair skin and light brown hair, and who wore the loose, colorful silken garb of the other performers, lightly touched Zahra's shoulder. "Quite the reflexes you have there. And you didn't even spill any wine. Maybe you should join our troupe."

"Do you have room for a vase catcher?" Zahra asked.

The woman laughed.

"Forgive me for bumping into you," Zahra said. "I didn't realize there were more of you coming."

"I am the last one, and there is no forgiveness needed. Just show your appreciation for us tonight at the show."

The woman had beautiful bright green eyes, highlighted by ashy makeup, which Zahra thought might be a lovely accent to her own unusual smoke-gray eyes.

"Oh, I ... can't attend. I'm just a servant," Zahra said, replacing the vase atop the pedestal.

"That's a pity. It will be an excellent show, my new friend. A pleasure to have met you."

The woman stepped away as if to leave, then paused. "I wonder if there isn't some task for you in the theater?" She gave Zahra a mischievous wink. "Many of us will practice before the show, in case you should stop by in the course of your duties."

To see them in action? That would be amazing. She never got to see any of the interesting things that happened in the palace; she only heard about them afterward from the higher-ranking servants. But... "I can't. I have to help with the prince's banquet tonight. He has an important visitor."

Curse the prince! She'd spent months preparing for his visitors—potential brides—but how many had he met, to no avail? Would this one catch his fancy any more than the last five had?

Before the woman could respond, the annoyed, authoritative voice of the sultan's vizier, Yaseen, came bellowing from around the corner. "No, no! How many times must I say this? That fraud Ulnar will never set foot within the Palace of Light as long as I'm vizier. I don't care if he's normally a part of their act. Tonight he is not."

The last thing Zahra needed was to get caught loitering by the vizier. "My duties call," she told the woman.

The trouper nodded, crouched, and launched herself backward, flipping and cartwheeling away, her scarves weaving a dazzling pattern of colors. The clink of metal on the stone floor alerted Zahra to something the woman must have dropped as she bounded off. She crouched and retrieved it—a golden hairpin.

"Wait," she called after the woman.

"Zahra!" Vizier Yaseen shouted from behind her.

She shoved the hairpin into her hip satchel.

Yaseen approached, the scent of his overly sweet lilac perfume wafting over Zahra as he moved close enough to loom over her. "Girl, why are you harassing the performers?"

Zahra looked up, unable to avoid staring at the strip of gray hair that traced along his mustache and down his beard. "I was just—"

3

Yaseen's right eye twitched. *"Just* nothing. You've squandered enough time. Get back to it."

She should have known better than to offer an explanation; the vizier only cared about dedication to work.

"My apologies, Vizier Yaseen." Zahra walked toward the banquet hall, heading in the opposite direction of the vizier. She hated the tone he used with her—he rarely spoke to the other servants so harshly.

She hurried away from him, rolling her eyes. It wasn't like the work would not get done, and well within time—she had everything in hand and under control. This wasn't the first feast she'd helped to lay out.

In the enormous dining hall, she placed the wine at the east end of the table, ensuring it was spaced the same distance from the nearest carafe as the others were from each other. *Perfect.*

What wasn't perfect, however, were the fire tulips. The floral arrangements were the responsibility of the new girl, but she was still catching on. The vases were misaligned, and one had an extra bloom. The vizier required everything in the palace to be neat and precise, even the servants' clothes and hair, which had brought punishment upon Zahra more than once. She corrected the girl's mistake and resolved to mention it to her later.

Additional work remained to prepare for the palace dinner, but not much. Her mind wandered to thoughts of the acrobat, the musicians, and the rest of the troupe. Zahra couldn't help but think of the acrobat's hint to stop in and watch the group's practice. Plus, she still needed to return the woman's hairpin. A quick trip to the palace theater's dressing room and she'd be back before anyone noticed she was gone. And if she happened to see any of the troupe practicing, that would just be a lucky happenstance.

She slipped out and rushed through the halls of the palace toward the theater. She wasn't shirking her duties, exactly; they were done for now. Mostly. Besides, she had a responsibility to return the hairpin to the acrobat, and there was plenty of time before the sun set and the feast began.

It took only a few minutes for Zahra to wend her way through the palace and reach the door to the dressing room of the sultan's grand palace theater. At her swift knock, a tall, muscular, wild-haired man greeted her with a broad smile. "You need enter?"

"Yes. I need to return something to one of your associates."

"Ah, and who that is?"

She hadn't gotten the woman's name, but she described her as best she could.

The big man nodded. "Yes, Selene, I think. Last I see, in woman room." He led Zahra inside and pointed toward another door.

In the women's dressing area, an array of colorful outfits lay strewn about the tables and racks. For the first time in her life, her own drab beige clothes caused her to stand out rather than blend in. A woman caught her admiring the outfits and wrapped a few vibrant scarves around her before standing back to admire her handiwork. "Ah, beautiful."

Zahra had never worn anything other than cotton that was dyed the color of sand, and here she was in fabulous flowing silks, every bit as fine and smooth as the vizier's garb. The vizier would have an eye-twitching fit if he saw her wearing them, but she'd be fine for the few minutes it took to find the acrobat and maybe catch a glimpse or two of the acts.

She asked for Selene and the woman directed her toward the theater proper.

It was magnificent, three stories tall and stretched out in an elongated semicircle. A series of horseshoe arches and multicolored tile patterns decorated the walls. The raised stage was bathed in the fading light of the afternoon sun that shone down through a glass-domed ceiling.

There was no sign of Selene among the throng of performers. Perhaps Zahra might get a better vantage point from the balcony above. A better view of the acts would be nice, too.

After ascending to the balcony, she settled her gaze upon a group of dancers below. A thrill rushed through her. Here she was, in the palace theater, watching talented artists from around the world.

She scanned the ensemble, mostly to find the acrobat Selene, but more to watch the troupe practice. She'd seen street performers before, but that was like seeing a sand cat compared to a lion.

Just as a woman on stage blew a blast of fire from her mouth, the door to the opposite balcony opened, and the last person Zahra wanted to see walked in—the vizier.

"Flame!" Zahra cursed under her breath as she ducked, wrapping the scarves around her head and face to conceal her identity. How did the vizier always manage to appear at the most inopportune times?

Zahra peeked over the balcony just as Yaseen looked across from across the theater. He cocked his head, squinting. Zahra spun and exited onto the second floor of the palace.

Maybe the vizier hadn't recognized her. They'd only shared a quick glance. To be safe, she took a circuitous way back to the dining hall. If he caught Zahra here, she could forget about advancement; she'd be mucking out the stables for a month.

She raced around the corner, not waiting to see if the vizier had spotted her. Going this way required her to go up to the third floor and then back down. She wasn't allowed on that floor unattended, so she'd have to be quick.

After a hurried ascent of the stairwell, she headed north along the Conqueror's Corridor, uncomfortably aware of how much she would stand out wrapped in the colorful, flowing scarves. She considered dropping them, but decided that a pile of scarves might raise unwanted attention. Also, she could use them again to hide her face if she needed to.

As she rounded the corner overlooking the Salaam Courtyard, a golden oriole flitted past the window and alighted atop a pomegranate tree. Beyond, someone traversing the hallway on the other side caught her attention. It was the acrobat, Selene. What was she doing? If the area was off-limits to Zahra, it was certainly forbidden for a mere guest to be there on her own. The woman had to be up to something.

Two guards crossed the corridor ahead. Zahra's pulse quickened as she stepped into a small alcove. Should she call the guards and tell them about the woman? She probably wouldn't get into trouble by pointing out someone sneaking around the palace. The guards might not recognize her, but they'd see she was a servant of the palace. She stepped out from the alcove.

"Guar—" she started, but stopped when the vizier's voice called out from the stairwell.

"That had better not be who I think it is," Vizier Yaseen said.

The guards hadn't heard her and were exiting the corridor. She scanned quickly to spot the acrobat, who was about to slip around a corner. Zahra froze. If she went to speak to the guards now, the vizier would see her. She could hide back in the alcove and wait for Yaseen to pass, then return to her duties, but the acrobat might succeed at whatever she was scheming. Or she could tell the vizier directly. Her gut clenched at that thought. No, there was no way she'd escape punishment then.

But ... if she went after the woman herself and caught her, the vizier might overlook her being away from her work. He might even reward her for taking action. This might be a path to finally advancing in rank.

Decision made, she ran down the hall to the northern stairway and hastened in the acrobat's direction. As a common servant, she had no business being up here alone. This was a risky plan, but it was the right thing to do.

Running down another corridor next to the courtyard, she glanced across to look for Selene. The woman had already ascended to another level. Zahra rushed up the nearest stairs to close on her position.

She'd only been to this level—the Floor of Nobility—a few times, at the vizier's specific request, and then only with an escort.

Zahra rounded a corner and stopped. There was Selene ahead, gliding rapidly down the hall. Zahra couldn't risk shouting to her, so she trotted after her as quietly as she could. Selene passed the vizier's quarters and turned right down a narrow hallway adjacent to his room. Where was she going?

A quick check behind her revealed nobody following, so Zahra proceeded full pace and turned down the same hallway Selene had taken. But the acrobat wasn't there.

The way ended at a balcony overlooking the palace grounds, and the city in the distance. Zahra ran to the lookout. A quick movement in the corner of her eye caught her attention: Selene had climbed over to the vizier's balcony and had entered his private chambers. What was this woman doing?

A narrow, decorative ledge along the outer wall connected this balcony to the vizier's, but it clearly was not made for traversal. Zahra was sure she could use it and follow Selene, but decided it would be easier to wait for the woman back out in the main hall.

She didn't have to wait long.

The vizier's door swung open, and out strode the acrobat as if she were there on official business.

Zahra stepped in front of her. "This is not the palace theater. What were you doing in the vizier's chambers?"

The woman paused. "Just taking something dangerous, to put it somewhere safe. Nothing for you to fret about."

She had stolen something from Vizier Yaseen. "Whatever you took, put it back."

"That I cannot do." And Selene bolted down the hall before Zahra could grab her.

Zahra chased after the woman. The time for stealth was over. "Guards!" she shouted as she ran.

As Selene passed the Stairs of Solemn Rain, the guardsmen rounded the corner down the hall. The woman turned back to the stairs, giving Zahra the time she needed to catch up. Zahra reached down as the woman descended the steps and caught hold of her hair.

The acrobat jumped against the spiraling wall and flipped backward to the lower steps, her hair twisting free of Zahra's grip. Zahra stared momentarily at her empty hands. *How did she do that?*

Selene darted down the steps and across the hall, hopping up into a crouch in a window. As Zahra approached, the thief lowered herself outside, hanging from her fingertips high above the ground below.

Zahra again grabbed a handful of Selene's hair, but now the woman returned the favor, taking hold of Zahra's long braid and pushing out from the wall with her feet. They were locked in a stalemate.

"Let go, girl. You know not what you do," Selene said.

"I know I'm stopping a thief."

Selene's eyes briefly darted behind Zahra before locking onto the scarves around her neck. The acrobat took hold of them to use as a line to lower herself down. Zahra's heart nearly stopped as the added weight pulled her against the wall, almost yanking her out the window.

"Hold fast. I've got you," a man's voice said from behind her. A pair of powerful arms wrapped around her waist.

Zahra could barely breathe. She leaned forward against the wall, her head being pulled outside. She grabbed the scarf to ease the tension on her neck.

Selene had reached a window on the floor below. "Goodbye," she said, swinging into the opening and letting go of the scarf.

Released from the weight of the woman, Zahra stumbled backward, slamming into the man behind her and sending them both tumbling to the floor. She gasped, taking a deep breath, flipped over and pushed up and away from him—and peered straight into a pair of piercing amber eyes.

The eyes of Prince Amir.

Her mouth hung agape. Thoughts of catching the thief, of the vizier, of any hope of promotion, vanished from her mind. Her breath caught. She had just flattened the prince.

And he was beautiful.

She'd never seen him up close and hadn't realized he would be so handsome. She'd seen the sultan on many occasions, and he had a ruggedness and charm about him, but nothing like the looks of his son. His intense eyes, and his strong jawline, and the long hair flowing past his broad shoulders... Oh no, she had just landed on the prince and was now staring at him.

"I..." What could she say? "Forgive me, my prince." She rolled off him and stood up quickly.

What had she done? She'd actually touched the prince. She tilted her head down and lowered her eyes. It wasn't required of her, even as a servant, but she was too embarrassed and self-conscious to meet his gaze.

"A thousand pardons. May my eyes be pecked out by hawks for staring at you." She didn't know what else to say, but she'd heard others offer similar apologies, and this was the first thing that came to mind.

She looked at her hands, which had just pushed her off of him. "May my hands be eaten by..."—*Think, Zahra, think. What would eat hands?*—"tigers ... for touching you."

"Tigers?" Prince Amir raised an eyebrow. "I would think tigers would eat more than just your hands."

Why did I say tigers? "I'm sure you're correct, my prince, and I would deserve it. But may I thank you for saving me? May you be blessed with..." Imagination failed her. She desperately wanted to look up at him again and just couldn't think. What should the prince be blessed with that he didn't already have?

"May I be blessed with...?" he prompted, a hint of amusement in his tone.

A mountain of gold? No, he needed no more of that. Gems? A palace? "May you be blessed with ... magic ... and wonder. My prince."

That was terrible. Zahra wanted to die. She wanted to turn around, take a leap, and go flying out the window after the thief. Oh no, the thief! She got to her feet.

"A thief—" she started, trying to think of a way to clearly explain what had just happened.

Prince Amir rose and put his fingers under her chin to lift her head, but before he could reply the vizier charged up to them.

"What is this? You dare come up here and lay your filthy hands upon the prince?"

"No, Vizier Yaseen. I didn't mean to... That is, I was following a thief, and—"

"And you decided to seize the prince on your way, did you?" Yaseen said. "And where is this supposed thief?"

"It's the acrobat from the troupe. She's out there." She pointed toward the window and held up the ribbon of cloth still dangling from her neck, as if that confirmed her story.

The vizier's eyes narrowed. "That's your proof of a thief?"

Angry voices shouted from outside the window and the floor below. "We've got her!"

"Humph. Well, I'll investigate that later," Vizier Yaseen said. "Are you unharmed, my prince?"

"I am. It was an unfortunate incident, Yaseen."

"Fret not, my prince. I will see that this one is dealt with." The vizier gave Zahra a familiar glare.

"Yaseen, I'm not sure that's necessary. She had quite a scare and was trying to help."

"So she says, but I'll get to the truth of it. Just don't you worry about that. It won't change the fact that she laid her hands on you, my prince—I'll have her cleaning the dungeons."

CHAPTER 2

Prince Amir entered the secret passage that only he and his father could access, reflecting on the events of the previous day. The feast had been fine and the show entertaining, though nothing he hadn't seen before. Amir had been itching to see the famed Ulnar the Foreteller, but thanks to Yaseen, the man hadn't been there. The most interesting and exciting thing to happen had been a servant girl trying to catch a thief.

The latest candidate for marriage his father had arranged for him to meet, Princess Kami, was pleasant enough, though not particularly attractive. Playing host to these young women was getting almost tedious. He had no interest in any of them. Amir was afraid his father was eventually going to tire of the whole business and pick someone at random out of frustration. He hoped it wouldn't be Kami.

Amir slipped through the hidden exit. Today he wanted to be free of the palace walls; it felt like they were closing in on him more and more each day. He had no plan at the moment other than to avoid a sham swordplay practice session designed to impress the visiting princess.

He passed the stables and neared the palace wall where he could climb over and slip unnoticed into the city before his conscience—and concerns regarding his father's ire—ate away his resolve. He knew he'd get a verbal lashing for abandoning his princely duties and ignoring the future of Alhad.

And his father would be right. Amir stopped and sighed. Perhaps he could sneak out later, but this wasn't the time. He headed toward the palace entrance.

The voice of Yaseen called out, "Ah, there you are, my prince. Come, come. It's time for your daily practice."

Of course it was—back to the routine. Wonderful.

Amir pretended to be intent on getting out of it anyway, just to annoy the vizier. "I think I'll skip today's session, Yaseen."

"If only that were possible, my prince. Alas, the princess is on a schedule, and besides, your father requires it."

"I don't know why. None of the previous girls have shown much of an interest in swordplay, and as much as I enjoy the practice, it's not like I'll ever have the opportunity to use my scimitar in a real fight."

"You should hope not. In any case, today's session is merely for the sake of a demonstration. You don't have to work up much of a sweat if it's too much for you."

If the vizier had had any skill with a blade, Amir would have been tempted to force the man to grab a weapon and face him for this little show. Perhaps he'd get respect from him then. Instead, he could only bristle with irritation.

Amir dodged to the right to avoid the incoming strike of his sparring partner. Another sweeping attack followed, and Amir dove and then rolled smoothly back to his feet on his opponent's flank. It was a choreographed move designed to look impressive, though it would be impractical and dangerous in an actual fight.

The prince tapped his opponent on the small of the back with his blade, and his partner accepted defeat.

Amir forced a smile before glancing away from the man and across the sandy courtyard toward Princess Kami. She was involved in a conversation with one of her servants, not even looking in Amir's direction.

She's not even paying attention to me? The whole point of this ridiculous show his father made him put on was to impress this girl. As if Amir needed to impress *her*.

Sure, Amir wasn't interested in Kami in any case, but how was she not interested in him? Especially after his dazzling display of swordsmanship.

Frustrating. If he had to spar, at least it could have been an actual practice. Amir shook his head and waved away his sparring partner.

The other man cocked his head. "So we're done?"

"Yes, of course. That's what this,"—Amir waved his hand again—"means. Begone."

A slight hint of a frown crossed the man's brow before he nodded and walked away.

Why is he frowning? I'm the one who has to deal with this girl.

Amir threw back his shoulders and held his head high as he strode toward the princess and her coterie of servants. He scanned the girl's features in the morning light. There was nothing to change his impression of her from the previous night at the feast, unfortunately. Even behind a diaphanous veil, she looked no less homely. She had the gall to ignore *him*? She was a princess of what—some tiny town somewhere to the west that he'd never even heard of?

Vizier Yaseen glided up as Amir neared the girl. "You're getting quite competent, for a seventeen-year-old."

A curse upon your beard, Yaseen. The man could never give a straightforward compliment.

Princess Kami covered her lips to hide a brief smirk at the vizier's words. "Yes, Prince Amir," she said. "You're very skilled with a scimitar."

He *was* skilled, not that the farce of a sparring session had truly shown his abilities, and not that she cared. Still, Amir appreciated that her compliment sounded genuine.

"It's a pleasure to see you again, Princess. I wasn't expecting you so soon, or I would have finished my sparring session earlier." The sultan wouldn't have allowed that. It was a part of the dance, as he called it. "Now that you're here, perhaps we could get to know each other better."

"That would be nice."

"Would you like a tour of the gardens?" Another of his father's suggestions, or rather, his requirements. Amir was ready to be done with her right then, but he knew he had to go through the steps the sultan had prescribed for him.

Princess Kami smiled politely. "That sounds lovely. After you've had time to clean up, of course." She wrinkled her nose slightly.

Of course. He would have suggested that himself; he couldn't very well have walked her around in his sparring clothes, with sweat still dripping from his brow. The princess, on the other hand, appeared to be clean, smelled of fragrant iris, and looked ready to go. She was playing her part in this dance, at least.

"One hour, then, at the Apadana entrance."

"Perfect," she said. "I will see you then."

"I look forward to it." If only he did.

The princess apparently couldn't keep herself from rolling her eyes as she turned to leave, and Amir clenched his jaw to keep from saying anything. How *dare* she! *I'm the Prince of Alhad.* Who was she but the princess of some tiny place no one had even heard of? He would never have shown such disrespect to her. After all, here he was, trying to be welcoming and accommodating.

The worst part was the possibility that his father might choose her to be Amir's wife.

The vizier put on a broad smile as Princess Kami led her entourage away, before swiveling back to face Amir with his grin still plastered on. "She likes you, my prince."

It was this type of behavior from Vizier Yaseen that annoyed Amir. The girl wasn't interested in him at all. Yaseen knew it as well as he did.

Amir let a resentful sigh and shake of his head show his displeasure.

"I think our sultan might choose this girl for you. He seemed to view her favorably at the feast, and even though she's from a small kingdom, she is their princess and only heir."

Amir understood the value of joining with another kingdom—or rather, he understood that his father valued it. Why did it have to come at his expense?

"She's not particularly eye-catching, though, is she?" Amir said.

"Ah yes, it's all about beauty for the young. Certainly a handsome prince such as yourself deserves someone pleasing to behold, but not everyone can be as attractive, engaging, and charming as you are, my prince."

Was this more mockery? Amir stared into the man's eyes and saw no hint of sarcasm, but that didn't mean it wasn't there.

"It's not only that," Amir said. "She's just ... so plain." Or was it boring? He wanted someone bright and attractive, and lively. Someone with maturity; a woman, not these silly girls.

This whole process was frustrating and stressful. One princess after another, and his father barely paid him any heed. Another walk, another dance, another show, another performance.

"I'd just like to make the choice for myself, or have at least some say in it. I didn't even get to select the meal last night. Why couldn't we at least have served a spiced ragout? The food was so bland." In truth it hadn't been so bad, but it was nothing new, and at a special feast he'd expected something more exciting. For the dinner put on for the previous visitor, the aroma alone had had him salivating from the start of the meal.

"The sultan wanted to present a variety of foods that he knew the guests would appreciate, and I think the event went over well. I'm sorry it wasn't up to your exacting standards, my prince." Yaseen sounded defensive.

Maybe the vizier *should* be defensive.

Since Amir's mother had died, the sultan had pulled away from his duties and Yaseen had taken more control, making decisions even when it came to Amir. Including, apparently, the food he would get at his own banquets. His mother would have made sure there was something special for him there.

"In any case," the vizier continued. "About the princess—should I convey your interest to your father?"

Amir frowned. Did he have to spell out his discontent for the man? "I'll do my duty and go with her for a walk as planned, but my feelings won't change. Perhaps you could help convince my father that she's not the right one." It irked him to have to request help from Yaseen to speak with his own father.

"Perhaps." Yaseen stroked his beard, his eyes glazing over for a minute as he thought. "If you are not finding women from the other kingdoms to be of interest, maybe you would prefer someone closer to home. Someone used to the styles, culture, and flavors of our city?"

That was not a bad idea. Did he actually have someone in mind? There were a few girls that had certainly caught Amir's attention, but his father seemed intent on forging an alliance with another kingdom.

"I'll think on it and get back to you," Yaseen said.

Why did it always feel like Yaseen was playing a game with him, or trying to win at a simple conversation? Why couldn't the man just do what he was told, like he did for Amir's father? When Amir was sultan, he wouldn't put up with it—if he even kept Yaseen as his vizier.

"Please do, Yaseen." Amir waved him off.

A hint of a twitch passed through the vizier's eye. "As you wish, my prince."

Amir smiled as the vizier left, taking petty pleasure at having irritated the man. But unfortunately it didn't improve his mood.

He thought briefly about canceling the walk. No, there was no getting out of it; his father would have his head. And though the princess herself might not mind, it would certainly be taken as an insult by her father.

Still, it all was like drudgery, and he felt trapped.

He needed to break out of this routine, to make his own decisions and have some control.

A thought came to him—the one thing that had happened recently that was unexpected, surprising, and amusing—the encounter with that servant girl with the striking gray eyes.

CHAPTER 3

Zahra scrubbed half-heartedly at the floor of the dark, dank prison cell. With the scant flickering light of a single torch on the wall, she could barely see what she was doing, but that was fine with her—she didn't need a good view of the disgusting chamber. Besides, her wandering thoughts weren't focused on the quality of her cleaning.

She had knocked the prince to the ground.

Her mind bounced between two thoughts: she may never advance now, perhaps stuck on cleaning duty for years—and, as horrible as tackling the prince had been, she couldn't help but admit to herself a sense of excitement at recalling the event. Few of the palace servants had even seen the prince up close, and certainly none apart from his personal attendants had ever touched him. But she had. She should feel ashamed at what she'd done, but all she could think of was how he'd lifted her chin to look into her eyes.

Why had she felt the need to behave like such a fool in front of him? What had she wished for him? Magic and wonder? She should have blessed him with a long and happy life with a wonderful wife and family, or that he enjoy the respect of all the kingdoms for his great wisdom, effortless humor, and renowned generosity.

She'd been caught by surprise, that's all, while she was focused on stopping the thief, Selene. That and she had been shocked at discovering just who she'd knocked over. And the fact that he was so ... beautiful.

The girl he married would be the luckiest woman alive. She'd certainly never have to clean out a dungeon, or even wipe scraps from a table. She could go to every show and act and feast in the palace.

Zahra imagined what it would be like to wed the prince. She envisioned her wedding day, switching between seven different dresses, with silks flowing around her and the wisp of a golden veil hanging lightly from a gem-studded circlet, her long, luxurious hair free to flow down her back.

She would have servants do *her* bidding, and her wealth would afford her anything she desired: she could eat the most sumptuous meals, wear the most decadent jewelry, and spend her time leisurely enjoying the palace and its elegant gardens.

Bang! Bang! Bang!

A prison guard, Firuz, was hammering at the cell door. "Hey! Girl! Another cell needs its chamber pot dumped."

That killed all the romantic, fanciful thoughts in her head.

She held her breath as she emptied out the pot. Outside the dungeon, a grating voice greeted her: "Morning blessings upon you, Zahra."

Her 'favorite' fellow servant, Dalal, sauntered up. The girl—though she was four years older than Zahra's sixteen, Zahra refused to think of her as a grown woman—flashed a broad, yet entirely fake, smile.

"And also upon you, Dalal." Zahra didn't return the smile. She couldn't force herself to pretend she was happy to see the other servant.

"It was a wonderful show last night, wasn't it? Oh, that's right, you weren't there." Dalal ran a hand along her flowing, light-green dress while pointedly looking at Zahra's simple beige garb. Ugh, always flaunting her higher rank.

Zahra wished it didn't bother her, but it was unjust. How had Dalal been moved up before her? Yes, the other girl was older, but she was so annoying and fake. Dalal got to go to shows and dances, while Zahra had to work, and it was actual work, not just following some noble around to get him drinks.

"You smell even worse than usual, Zahra."

"And you smell like..."

"Orchids? I know, isn't it lovely?"

"I was going to say 'a camel'."

"I'm not the one covered in filth. And that's because I didn't assault the prince and get assigned to the dungeon."

If Dalal knew about her awkward encounter with Prince Amir, everyone in the palace must have heard about it by now. Why hadn't Maliha come down to see her yet?

Maliha was the vizier's daughter, and the only person Zahra considered a friend. Maliha had latched on to Zahra when they were both young, often pulling her away from her duties to take part in a prank or scheme. The girl had never ceased to get Zahra into trouble, but she'd also kept her from harsh punishments for any mischief they'd been involved in.

Two years ago, when Maliha had turned fifteen, the vizier had handed off much of the management of the general palace servants to her. This, of course, had put her in charge of Zahra. Somehow their friendship remained intact; probably because Maliha still instigated the occasional prank and defended Zahra when necessary. In this case, unfortunately, Vizier Yaseen had assigned Zahra to dungeon duty himself.

"Does Maliha know I'm down here? Could you ask her to come see me?" Her gut clenched at having to ask a favor of Dalal.

"Why do you think I'm here? She sent me to check on you, but don't worry, I'll tell her you're doing just fine."

Ah. Maliha had sent Dalal down here to add to Zahra's punishment and to annoy her. Very funny.

"Please tell Maliha her nose looks like a turtle's beak." Zahra knew Dalal might not pass on that exact message, but it would be enough for her to try to get Zahra into more trouble, which just might get Maliha to come down to the dungeon herself.

Dalal squinted disapprovingly and shook her head. "Always so rude."

Zahra could only take so much of the other girl. "I must return to work."

"Yes, you must," Dalal replied, her obnoxiously huge grin plastered back on her face as she twirled away dramatically in another vain display, waving goodbye with her left hand to show off her copper bracelet.

Yes, Dalal, I know you get to wear jewelry. Congratulations. But you're still required to wear your hair in a braid like the rest of us servants, aren't you?

"Enjoy your time down here in the dark," Dalal said. "I have to get back to my own duties—my master is taking us to wade in the Pond of Serenity." She smirked and strode away like a proud cat. "Have fun with the criminals."

Ha. Ha.

Zahra returned the chamber pot to the cell and looked up at the guard, Firuz, deciding that maybe she could use Dalal's visit to her advantage. "I think that's about it. My time should be up by now; I'm supposed to follow Dalal, the servant who just left."

"My orders say you're here all day."

"That doesn't sound right."

"But it is."

She batted her eyes. "Maybe you could let me go early?"

"Do I want to get flogged? No. No I don't. Now back to it—these cells haven't been cleaned in over a month." Firuz returned to guard the dungeon's entrance.

Why does that never work for me? Dalal made flirting and charming people look so easy. Of course, she was a born manipulator and liar.

The prisoner down in the end cell yelled something to the other guard, Aman.

"...the vizier ... keep telling ... can't trust ... don't ... demon..." It was the voice of the acrobat and thief, Selene.

"Nobody cares about your tall tales!" Aman yelled back. He set a bowl down on the floor a few feet away from the food slot opening at the base of her cell door.

Selene's arm stretched out from the hole, but fell short of the bowl. "A little closer, perhaps?"

The guard stamped his foot down near the bowl and it caught the end of the spoon, sending it flying away and into the open door of another cell. "Now you can eat it with your hands."

Serves her right.

Zahra returned to her odious labor. As she toiled, her mind again wandered; she'd really made a mess of things this time. She'd be wearing these plain, sand-colored clothes for the rest of her life, constrained to wandering the lower level of the palace, sweeping, setting tables, and cleaning up after the guests. That's if the vizier ever took her off dungeon duty.

She finished cleaning the cell she was in and moved down the line to the one at the end, diagonally adjacent to Selene's cell along the back wall. The bowl of food left on the floor for Selene still lay out of the woman's reach. As much as Zahra was mad at the acrobat for getting her into this mess, she didn't deserve to starve.

Zahra pushed the bowl toward Selene's door with her foot.

The woman reached out and pulled it into her cell. "I had heard the Great Sultan of Alhad treated even his prisoners like guests, yet I am treated like a stray dog and worse. Leave it to a lowly cleaning servant to show greater humanity. Blessings on you."

"I have no need of any more of your 'blessings'," Zahra said.

"Oh, it is you. The servant girl with the quick reflexes." Selene sounded surprised.

"It is you—the thief."

"Am I a thief to try to retrieve something already stolen?"

What *had* she stolen? Not that it was any of Zahra's business, and not that it mattered now. The vizier must have retrieved it, or Zahra would have been lashed.

23

She placed a torch in the sconce and found this cell was even grosser than the last. She scrubbed at the grime coating the floor as the thief ate. "I can't believe I'm stuck down here."

"What are you mumbling about?" Selene asked.

"Because of you, I'll never get promoted. I'll be a base servant for another ten years."

"Your mind is so small. You dream of a slightly larger cage, when you could be free like me."

"Free? Locked in a dungeon? Ha!"

Zahra scraped at a stubborn piece of encrusted gunk. Even cleaning out the stables would've been better; at least there'd have been a shovel. And daylight. *And no annoying thief harassing me.*

"You have no idea what you've done, servant," Selene said.

"My name is Zahra."

"Well, Zahra, do you know what trinket I tried to take from your vizier?"

"It's of no concern to me." But that reminded her of something; she still had possession of the woman's hairpin. It had a broad flat section, and the pin protruded from that. Her fingers passed over an engraving on it, but she couldn't make it out.

"Let me ask you, Zahra: have you noticed any noxious smells around your vizier?"

What was the woman talking about? "He usually smells like lilac."

"Just as I feared. He's covering the scent of sulfur. He's summoning a demon—an ifrit."

An ifrit, the darkest of the demons? Zahra knew the vizier to be harsh in his dealings at times, but not foolish or evil.

"Oh, a demon. Why didn't you say so? You want me to tell the sultan about it?"

"Do not mock me, Zahra."

Ignoring her, Zahra rose to her feet and held the hairpin up to the torchlight. Embossed on the flat part was a symbol: it was the outline of an eye, with a short line coming off like a teardrop and another line descending at an angle and ending in a swirl. Simple but pretty. It wasn't the symbol of the performance troupe she'd seen on their banners, but it did look familiar. Where had she seen it before?

"It is known," Selene continued, "that an ifrit appears in a burst of fire and smoke, and smells of sulfur. But the scent of lilac helps obfuscate that odor."

This sounded *less* believable, not more. Zahra had heard many tales of demons—both the jinn and the ifrit—and had never heard anything about lilac covering their scent. Most likely, the thief was tailoring her story to fit whatever Zahra said, to make it sound more plausible.

She rolled the hairpin over in her hand. It appeared to be solid gold. Would an acrobat own such a valuable piece of jewelry to stick in her hair? The only things Zahra possessed were her secret stash of items she'd collected over the years—a torn patch of silk, buttons made from shells, a bent metal spoon, and a handful of other things of value only to her. Among her cache of lost items, this pin would be the one thing that would actually be worth something.

"We need to stop the vizier," Selene said.

"Of course. That makes perfect sense."

Bang! Bang! Bang!

The guard Aman had smacked on a cell door down the corridor. "Come here, girl."

Startled, Zahra dropped the hairpin, and it plopped into a pile of sludge on the floor. Why did these guards always have to slam on things to get someone's attention?

Zahra looked for the hairpin, but in the dim lighting she couldn't spot it. And she had no desire to stick her fingers into whatever mess was on the floor. *Flame! That was the most valuable thing I've ever owned.* Well, technically it was Selene's, but she was a thief and in prison now.

"You must warn someone," Selene said. "We may all be in terrible danger."

"Sure. I'll go talk to my new friend, the prince." Zahra gathered

25

up her brush and bucket of sludgy water.

Bang! Bang! Bang!

"I'm coming." Zahra hurried down to the guard at the dungeon's exit hallway, where she found Maliha waiting. Ha! Her insult ploy had worked.

The vizier's daughter shook her head. "And you wonder why you don't get promoted. Follow me."

As Zahra passed Firuz, she dropped the brush in the bucket and handed it to him. "For you," she said with a friendly smile, as if she were truly offering him a gift.

"Mmmm," Firuz grunted.

Zahra smiled in relief as the entrance to the dungeon closed behind them.

Maliha shook her head. "If you wanted to meet the prince so badly, you could have just asked me."

"It wasn't—I didn't—"

"Why couldn't you have stayed focused on your duties?"

"I only went to return something that woman had dropped, but then I saw her sneaking away. And I helped catch her, didn't I?"

Maliha sighed. "You knocked Prince Amir onto his backside."

"That was an accident."

"We can talk about it all later. First, do you want to get out of dungeon duty?"

Zahra paused uncertainly. "I thought you were already getting me out of here?"

"If you do something for me."

What was this about? Maliha didn't need to beg or bargain with Zahra to have her do something—she could just give her a command.

"Why do I have a bad feeling about this? Is it going to be worse than what got me into this trouble in the first place?"

"No, not at all. I just want you to spy on the prince for me."

CHAPTER 4

"**S**py on the prince?" Zahra said to Maliha. "What are you talking about?"

"Nothing nefarious. There's just one little thing I want you to find out."

One little thing? This is how it often started between them, and it often ended with a reprimand from the vizier. "Wait, isn't your father going to be furious that you pulled me from the dungeons?"

"He won't be able to argue. It's not as if he can override the prince."

"So the prince requested me? This isn't your idea?"

Maliha winced. "He *may* have mentioned something about wanting to see the girl who almost fell from the window."

Zahra's eyes lit up like the full desert moon at midnight.

"Don't get too excited," Maliha said. "Maybe he just wants to punish you himself."

That thought hadn't occurred to her; last evening he hadn't seemed at all upset.

"If you don't want to help, I can always tell him you're feeling unwell and put you back on dungeon-cleaning duty."

"No! I'll help."

This was her chance: if she impressed Prince Amir, maybe he would keep her on as one of his personal attendants. Or it could be that he was summoning her for punishment, or at least admonishment. Zahra's thoughts rapidly shot back and forth. She even considered that he might become so taken with her that he'd choose *her* to be his princess—a ridiculous notion, she knew, but she allowed herself a moment to revel in that fantasy.

"Zahra!" Maliha clapped her hands, bringing Zahra back to reality.

"What do you want me to do?"

"Find out who the prince is planning to marry."

"Why?"

"Because I think it might be me."

Zahra laughed.

"Why is that funny?"

"Oh. You mean you're serious?"

Maliha pushed her along.

"You *are* serious," Zahra said. "That's great. Isn't it?" It would be great for Maliha, anyway. Zahra felt a wave of emotion wash over her. Was it disappointment? She hadn't really believed she had a chance with the prince, though.

Maliha groaned. "Come, we have to clean you up. You can't see the prince looking like this."

A quick wash and a fresh set of bland clothes later, and Maliha pressed Zahra forward.

"You're off to see the prince. Try to find out what he's thinking, but don't make it obvious."

They steadily made their way up through the Palace of Light: each floor was themed according to ideals laid out in an ancient pact forged by the founder of Alhad, from Duty and Service, to Protection, Companionship, Nobility, and Wonder.

Maliha led Zahra finally to the grand, lavish expanse of the royal quarters. Glass ceilings covered the walkway to the prince's chambers, bathing the halls in bright light and offering views of the skies above. Prince Amir was lounging on a luxurious brocade-covered sofa.

Zahra approached, nervous and unsure of what to expect.

"As requested, my prince," Maliha said. "I present the servant Zahra, who ... crossed paths ... with you yesterday. She begs of your generous nature to forgive her insolent behavior. This trouble-maker may be treated like a mongrel, for no task is beneath her."

Thanks, Maliha.

Maliha gave Zahra a teasing smile as she took her leave.

"It is good to see your hands haven't been eaten by tigers since I last saw you."

Zahra cringed. "Yes, my prince."

"Tell me, how did you end up halfway out of a window yesterday?"

Embarrassed, Zahra briefly relayed her story, trying to make it clear that she had the best intentions.

"I think Yaseen was correct—you do deserve to be punished."

Ah, that *was* why he'd summoned her. So much for her fanciful dreams.

"However, you also risked your life to apprehend the thief, and that deserves recognition as well. I think I shall have you perform some duties for me. If you do well, I'll reduce your punishment."

That was something, at least. In the meantime, she'd be helping the prince, and she'd therefore have a chance to find out if he intended to marry Maliha.

"Yes, my prince. If I fail you at all, may I suffer lashes with a reed."

"The tasks may not be so grand that failure requires a beating." Prince Amir took on a pensive look. "Though now that I think about it, I do need something of great value."

"Of course, my prince, whatever I can do."

"Your first task, girl, is to bring me the head of a nasnas. It is said to contain potent magic, to act as a mirror to one's life. Perhaps it will give me insight into a decision I face."

The head of a nasnas? It was purely a creature of fable and myth. Surely he was kidding with her. If they were indeed real, legend said that one touch from the half-bodied human-like creatures would tear the very flesh from a person. She stared at the prince, waiting to see if he was teasing her.

He gave no indication that he was joking.

She raised her head, looked straight into the prince's beautiful eyes, and said with confidence, "My prince, there is no such thing as a nasnas."

Prince Amir's eyebrows shot up. "Are you defying my request?"

"No, my prince. Merely seeking clarification." Was she already ruining her opportunity?

How could she deliver what the prince asked of her? It wasn't possible—or was it? She had an idea. "They are creatures of legend, but if you wish me to bring back the head of a nasnas, then I shall."

The corners of the prince's lips twitched. "Yes, I do so wish."

Zahra nodded and exited the prince's chambers. This had better work; she needed to get the information Maliha desired, and to do so, she had to stay with the prince long enough to discuss his marriage. She didn't know why he would discuss such a topic with her, but she had to try.

"I knew I could count on you," Prince Amir called as she closed the door.

She made a quick trip to the palace library. If the prince wanted to play games, she'd play right back. Zahra found what she was looking for and soon returned to the prince's quarters. She stood at the entrance, waiting for leave to speak.

"Girl, you are back so soon? I thought the task would take you at least a week. Where is my nasnas head?"

"Here it is, my prince, as requested. I cannot speak as to its magical benefit." She handed him a drawing of a nasnas, with the body torn away and just the head remaining.

The prince chuckled. "Yaseen said you might be unruly. You amuse me, girl."

"I'm pleased, my prince. I am here to serve." She could do worse than continue to amuse him, but she also needed to find out what Maliha wanted to know. How was she going to steer the conversation to his choice of bride?

Perhaps the straightforward approach? After all, that was what she did best. "Speaking of amusement, did you enjoy the performance last night? And your guest of honor? Is she to be your bride?"

Prince Amir frowned and ignored the question. "I grow hungry. Fetch me some pheasant. And hurry."

That was a task Zahra was confident of achieving. "As you wish, my prince." She nodded her head and was off. In little time, she returned with both braised pheasant and partridge for him to choose from, along with potatoes seasoned with coriander.

After having eaten, Prince Amir sent her away on numerous assignments, though attendants to the prince remained idle in his chambers. "Girl, take and wash this sash. Girl, bring new pillows for my bed. Girl, take a message to the stables to have my horse prepared for me." She dutifully performed each task. Somehow, being called "girl" didn't seem so demeaning when he said it.

Zahra tried unsuccessfully to steer the conversation back to his choice of bride. It seemed a topic he didn't care to discuss, and he invariably brushed aside her probing.

Finally, he threw his own question at her. "Girl, are you enjoying the tasks I'm giving you?"

"Of course. It's a joy to be trusted with such monumentally important duties."

"Is that sarcasm I detect?"

"Yes, it is," Zahra responded without thinking.

The prince's attendants gasped in shock.

Flirt, Zahra. Be playful. Like Dalal. Why did she always have to be so honest?

Prince Amir's penetrating eyes locked onto her, his face a mask of restraint.

Then he burst out in peals of laughter. "You are … straightforward, aren't you?"

She had told the truth, and the prince had laughed. Her heart soared.

She couldn't imagine why Maliha had seemed opposed to marrying him. Zahra would give anything to do so. Did the prince truly want to marry the vizier's daughter? She was no closer to finding out his intentions—maybe a different approach would help.

"My prince, what do you think of Maliha?"

This seemed to catch his attention. He looked up with a grin. "Maliha? The vizier's daughter?"

Here we go. He was finally talking about something other than doling out tasks for her.

The prince took on a thoughtful look. "She's quite lovely, isn't she? Yaseen tells me you're friends."

She hesitated, not wanting to get Maliha in trouble for favoring a servant. "We're friendly."

"I also hear you get each other into trouble."

Trouble? Of course that's what Vizier Yaseen would tell him.

"The question is," he said, "who is the instigator? I would guess it's you."

"No, it's not me. I mean, we don't..." This conversation had gotten off course, but at least he was communicating with her. "I don't try to get into trouble. It ... finds me sometimes."

Before she could explain further, a servant girl entered the prince's chamber. She hoped it wasn't someone sent to replace her.

It turned out to be worse.

The servant handed a parchment to Prince Amir.

"Girl," Prince Amir said to Zahra, "I have run out of tasks to give you for now, and the vizier has requested your assistance, so I am sending you down to aid him."

The vizier. Of course.

CHAPTER 5

P rince Amir considered the servant girl Zahra after she'd left his chambers. She had the standard look for servants in the palace—her hair in a long braid, and wearing the basic beige garb. But still she stood out with her strange gray eyes and her soft, narrow chin. A surprisingly genuine smile added a hint of charm and made her somewhat attractive, at least for a servant.

He chuckled to himself. There was something about her that engaged him; most of the servants were simple and obsequiously subservient, but she showed a spark of inner fire.

But now he had to face the issue that he'd been delaying—talking to his father about his thoughts on being wed. Amir wasn't sure he was ready to be married. But even if it was to be, none of the girls he'd met so far remotely interested him.

He strode into the sultan's chambers with his back straight and head held high, willing himself to present an aura of authority and confidence in order to hide his anxiety. Ordinarily Amir met with the sultan in the state chamber off the main audience hall, keeping their conversations formal, but today he needed to speak frankly with his father.

The sultan looked up with surprise at his son's entrance and rose to stand at his full height. Broad-shouldered, thick around the chest, and taller than most men in the kingdom, he made for an imposing figure.

"Amir, I don't recall arranging an appointment with you for today. Is there an emergency?"

"No, father. I just wish to speak with you about the plans for my marriage."

He continued quickly without giving the sultan a chance to stop him. "I've been thinking perhaps we should take our time in finding a suitable wife for me. It feels as though we're rushing forward. And ... well, to speak honestly," Amir broke from his formal tone out of sheer exasperation at the thought of marrying one of the girls his father had been considering, "they're all so plain and ... unappealing."

"I see. Unappealing, are they? Three of these girls are princesses and the rest are daughters of highly respected nobles. But they're not good enough for you?" His father's voice was raised, with an air of irritation bordering on anger. "You perhaps wish to marry a queen from Africa? I apologize if my selections are not up to your high standards."

This wasn't going well.

"I meant no offense, father," Amir said, trying to think of an alternative approach.

The sultan's shoulders sagged. "Son, you mustn't set all of your attention on beauty. Still, I have been less than impressed with most of these young women myself. Not in terms of their looks, mind you. They simply do not possess the maturity or intellect we need in a princess of Alhad."

His father shook his head. "Think of your mother: she was educated, but more importantly, gifted of mind. She was always the cleverer of the two of us. Who taught you chess and strategy? It wasn't me."

That was true. Amir's mother had spent hours teaching him, molding him, and supporting him. A sense of sadness washed over him now, followed by a feeling of selfishness in the way he was behaving in this search for a wife.

The sultan's gaze lost focus. "You know I loved her more than I could ever have imagined. True, I found her beautiful, but that's not what leads to a fulfilling marriage. She had an inner strength and often challenged me. We didn't always agree, and that forced me to see the world through different eyes. She was a worthy queen, and her passing was an enormous loss to me and to the kingdom. I intend to find someone near her equal for you."

Was it even possible? And why was it solely the sultan's decision? Could Amir not even have a say in the person he'd marry?

"I trust you, father." Although to be honest, he didn't. If he had, he'd be happy to let the process play out. His father was ignoring Amir's feelings and thoughts on this matter; after all the decisions that had been made for Amir in his life, this one he at least wanted some say in.

His father's words about finding him a partner sounded great. But how would he know ahead of time which girl would have the qualities the sultan valued? How would the sultan himself know? It wasn't as if they were spending weeks with these young women.

The sultan's frustrations mirrored Amir's own. This process was dragging on with not even a decent prospect, in his opinion. It shouldn't be this hard. There had to be an easier way to find a wife—he was the prince, after all.

This seemed like as good a moment as any to address the real reason for his visit.

"Perhaps I might seek some outside guidance to ease my concerns and help me come around to your way of thinking, someone to help focus my thoughts."

"Such as?" the sultan asked, suspicion and doubt creeping into his voice.

"A member of the troupe of traveling entertainers that put on the show last night, the widely heralded Ulnar the Foreteller. I was hoping to visit—"

"Ulnar the Foreteller! You were hoping to visit a speaker of *fortunes?*"

Why was his father so upset? Amir only wanted insight into finding the girl who'd be a perfect match for him.

"I have heard great things about him, amazing stories that he's helped people with their woes and worries, that he has a magical insight into one's future, and I thought—"

"You thought! It seems to me rather like you aren't thinking at all." His father's hands cut the air sharply with each word. "How would it appear to the people for my son, the prince, to be seen consulting a charlatan about matters of importance to the future of the kingdom? Do you think it would add to our renown?" The sultan paced the room, anger clearly written on his face.

"The people respect the man. I've heard nothing but—"

"You've heard? Oh, you've heard, have you? What—nothing but effusive praise? That is what these people do. They pay others to spread word of their amazing deeds and talents, and entice the foolish in. They make money from their gullibility." The sultan fumed.

"Father, I—"

The sultan raised his hand sharply to cut him off. "You say you trust me. Then, in the next breath, your words reveal that to be a lie. Come."

His father led him further into his chambers, toward the Eternal Flame.

"Your mother should have been raising you. She would have instilled more sense in you, boy. She made me promise to watch over you. But it hasn't been easy, has it? This is why I protect you, my son. This is why I keep you so often within the palace, where it is safe and you are protected from hucksters, criminals, and vagabonds."

The sultan shook his head and strode into the Chamber of Light. "You seek a soothsayer, do you, a man of magic? Nonsense, son, this is all the magic our family needs." He pointed at the Flame. "This Eternal Flame has been the magic that holds together our kingdom for centuries."

Amir's father brushed his hand along the elegant, wrought-metal brazier holding the Eternal Flame. Only members of the royal family could gaze directly upon the intensely bright light emanating from the tall pillar of ghostly fire without injuring their eyes. A rotating array of mirrors rose above the Flame, constantly repositioning themselves as if part of a living, breathing organism. They redirected the energy from each flicker of light up into a dome above the ceiling, and then from there out to illuminate the various parts of the city of Alhad.

The room and its magic never failed to impress, but Amir couldn't see how it would help him in this situation.

The sultan spread his arms as if basking in the glory of the flame. "This light serves as a guiding beacon to all who come to our city. Its power suffuses our palace and provides calm in times of turmoil. What need have we for trickery and fraudsters?"

This was going even worse than Amir had expected. He hadn't realized his father had such an aversion to practitioners of lesser magic.

"Ulnar the Foreteller, indeed," the sultan said. "The man and others like him are lucky I even tolerate their presence within my kingdom, let alone my city. And you wish to consult him!"

His father placed his hands over his face and sighed. "I have failed my wife. No, my young naive prince, I will make the decision without involvement from quacks and pretenders."

As usual—decisions made *for* Amir, instead of by him.

"But what if I don't want to be with this girl you find?" He should have kept his mouth shut, but this time he couldn't keep from saying something.

"Then it will be another lesson you must learn. You do not always get what you want in life, not even as a prince. Not even as a sultan, or your mother would still be with us. Ah, how I miss that woman; she had such a good heart, always with insights I struggled to perceive. She would know what to say and do now."

Amir agreed wholeheartedly. He sorely missed his mother as well; she would have had words of encouragement and support for him. She would have told him to listen to his heart.

His heart was telling him that he didn't like any of these girls, that he wasn't interested in them at all. The vizier's daughter, Maliha, was more attractive. Even the servant girl Zahra was.

He was trapped in this palace, and soon to be trapped in a marriage and in a life he did not desire.

He needed guidance that he wasn't getting from his father, and he certainly wasn't getting any from Yaseen.

He was already formulating a plan to sneak out of the palace for a clandestine visit to Ulnar the Foreteller.

CHAPTER 6

Just when Zahra had started to make a connection with Prince Amir, the vizier had had to interrupt. A wave of dread rolled through her; why had he requested her? Was he sending her back down to clean the prison cells?

Maliha was lucky. Even though the vizier was her father, she never had to deal with any of this. She even had the respected position as his assistant, and now she might become the princess. Though Zahra considered Maliha a friend, she couldn't relate to the other girl's status. Maliha could essentially have whatever she wanted. Zahra wasn't allowed even a splash of color on her dull servant's clothes.

She trudged down to the vizier's chamber, the guard at his door announcing her arrival.

A strange sound came from within the room, like the whooshing of flames. Then a small wisp of reddish smoke escaped from beneath the heavy wooden door. A moment passed before the door creaked open and the vizier appeared, ushering her inside.

He seemed flustered and annoyed, but why? It wasn't as if she'd shown up unbidden.

An unusual sensation washed over her as she entered his chamber, as though darkness had suddenly given way to light. A scent of burning wafted upon the air, smelling like ... sulfur.

Hadn't the thief Selene mentioned something about sulfur?

Two jars containing an ocher liquid sat upon a table, a dark vapor slowly dissipating from their mouths. The vizier was obviously creating an alchemical concoction, but he could have covered the jars to reduce the stench a bit.

A brief scowl passed over the vizier's face upon seeing Zahra. "Have you been enjoying your time with the prince, girl?"

When Prince Amir called her *girl*, she didn't mind, but with the vizier, it always came laden with a demeaning tone.

"Yes, Vizier Yaseen."

"Hmm. What did he wish from you?"

That was a good question. What *did* the prince want from her? Sure, he had given her tasks to perform, but anyone could do those. It seemed like he was teasing her. Or maybe he'd just wanted her company. Should she dare hope that he liked her? She wouldn't tell the vizier that.

"He wished to punish me himself, I think."

The vizier looked oddly relieved. "Good. Now I have a task for you, and it will decide your fate. Perform it well and you may remain in the palace."

Remain in the palace? The vizier was threatening to kick her out onto the street? No, he wouldn't, would he? Her throat constricted and her chest felt tight. He couldn't do that. She had no means to survive.

Prince Amir wouldn't allow it, would he? But then again, would he even care? They'd only just met, and to him she was merely a servant. Maliha would try to help her, but in the end she would have no choice but to accede to her father's wishes.

"Yes, Vizier Yaseen." She swallowed hard. "How may I serve?"

"I simply need you to acquire some items from the bazaar. While the task is simple, it is nevertheless of utmost importance to me."

"I understand. What is it you need me to obtain?"

"A jar of frankincense, one of kohl, and a vial of cobra venom."

Zahra thought she must have misunderstood. It sounded like he'd said... "Cobra venom?"

"That's correct. Worry not, you won't have to collect it yourself. You may purchase a vial from the merchant, Jabari. See Maliha and she will give you directions and the money. Do not dally. I expect exactly what I've requested, and quickly. I'll accept no excuses this time."

"I understand, Vizier Yaseen."

"Remember, this is your chance to save yourself. It should not need to be spoken, but I'll say it anyway: keep this to yourself. Speak of it to no one else."

The vizier waved his hand to dismiss her.

When Zahra met with Maliha and explained her father's command, the vizier's daughter furrowed her brow. "He's always asking for strange things. Just yesterday, he wanted me to get him some acid of the darkling beetle."

"Acid of the *what* beetle?" Zahra asked.

"You don't want to know."

Zahra agreed. She didn't want to know anything about a beetle with acid, other than to avoid it.

Maliha shook her head. "I'm sure it's for one of his bizarre concoctions. He's become obsessed with real magic, and mocks everyone else who merely performs tricks. He's always trying to find magical artifacts or craft another weird spell. But forget about that stuff—what did you learn from Prince Amir?"

"Every time I tried to bring up the topic of his desired bride, he just ignored me or changed the subject. Then I asked him about you and he genuinely seemed interested."

"Ah, so my father was right. He does plan to marry me."

"You don't want that?"

"My father wants me to." Maliha's shoulders drooped. "He's mentioned how he himself was meant to wed a princess when he was younger and was cheated out of it, and how I deserve to marry someone of importance. I think he wants me to achieve what he was denied."

"Well ... Prince Amir didn't actually say anything specific. He perked up when I mentioned your name, but maybe he just likes you."

Still, Maliha was probably right. She was so lucky; Zahra's daydreams of wearing her beautiful wedding gowns evaporated like the morning mist beneath a rising sun. They were silly fancies, but it still hurt to know for certain that there was no hope. She had no chance of marrying even a minor noble, let alone the prince, but it had been fun to imagine it for a while.

"We have to stop this," Maliha said.

"What? Why?"

"I have an idea," Maliha said, ignoring Zahra's question. "I'll go with you. While we're out, we can stop for a visit to Ulnar the Foreteller." She grabbed Zahra by the hand and pulled her along.

"I don't have time for any stops," Zahra objected. "Your father made it clear I was to get what he needed and return immediately."

"Don't worry about it."

"I *am* worried. He threatened to banish me from the palace."

Maliha stopped, her mouth hanging open in shock. "He must be *really* upset." She gnawed at her lower lip for a moment. "Even more reason to visit Ulnar." She dragged Zahra from the palace corridors and into the streets of Alhad. "And don't worry—I'll protect you from my father's ire. Even if the worst happens, I'll find you work and a place to stay."

Zahra hoped Maliha could actually do what she claimed, but she'd rather not have to find out.

"Who's this Ulnar person, and why do you want to see him?" Zahra asked.

"He's a magician of sorts."

That caught Zahra's attention.

"I'm told he can see someone's future just by looking into their eyes. More importantly, he's a collector and purveyor of rare and difficult-to-acquire items and knowledge, particularly items of magic." She gave Zahra a wink.

"Why are you winking?"

"Ugh. Catch *up*. Because we need a magical object."

"Specifically...?"

"We, my friend and co-conspirator," Maliha said, "are looking for a very particular magic item, which I overheard my father speaking about when he first learned that Ulnar was coming to town. Apparently, this Ulnar may know the location of the Golden Scarab of Balihar."

"The Golden Scarab ... that's just a story," Zahra said, surprised that the normally level-headed Maliha would believe in such a thing.

"My father is convinced it's real. And if he thinks so, it's probably true."

"Why are you—are we—looking for it? And why would this Ulnar be willing to tell us its location? Wouldn't he just look for it himself?"

"Maybe he has, and maybe we can buy it!" Maliha's eyes lit up as if that possibility hadn't occurred to her.

"How can we buy it—and why—what are we doing?" Zahra had too many questions for her, and they all bubbled up at once. Was Maliha playing at something, or was she completely serious?

"First, let's get those items for Father," Maliha said. "Then we'll go to Ulnar before the day ends."

Before the day ends? Zahra needed to get the frankincense, kohl, and venom and return to the vizier as soon as she possibly could.

But she couldn't help thinking about the Golden Scarab of Balihar. It was said the Scarab contained a powerful jinni, and everyone knew a jinni would grant wishes to those who freed them from confinement, but those were just bedtime tales told to children. Weren't they?

They had entered the city's largest bazaar. Maliha was pulling Zahra through the narrow streets so swiftly that she didn't have time to appreciate any of the wares people were selling. She only caught glimpses of colorful clothing, fine rugs, and glimmering jewelry, not to mention woefully brief whiffs of cumin-spiced ragout and honey-soaked fritters.

Maliha quickly found and purchased the jars of kohl and frankincense and continued on, before stopping short as they turned a corner into a quieter area of the bazaar.

"Jabari—there he is!" Maliha pointed to a wiry, darkened, wrinkled old man facing away from them. Jabari was sitting on a stool, swaying slightly back and forth in time with a soft melody he was playing on a wooden flute, a pungi, his eyes focused on a Caspian cobra rising from a woven wicker basket in front of him.

Maliha rushed over to the old man's side, declaring as she neared him, "Jabari, we need cobra venom."

The poor man flinched at the abrupt intrusion; his melody cut off suddenly as he pulled the flute from his mouth.

The snake froze for a moment, then struck out at the flute. Jabari jerked backward, his stool tilting beneath him, and Maliha hastily reached out a hand to keep him from falling. The cobra swiveled its head toward the vizier's daughter and flared its hood wider.

It was going to strike at Maliha!

The cobra shot forward.

Zahra reacted in an instant, reaching out and grabbing the cobra around its neck.

The snake pulled itself to her, coiling around her arm as Jabari and Maliha looked on in shock, their expressions mirroring her own.

"Zahra!" Maliha exclaimed, her face a mask of wide-eyed concern.

Zahra tensed—what had she just done? Had she eaten or drunk something that had addled her brain? Why would she have grabbed a deadly snake?

She stared, terrified, at the hissing head of the scaly, venomous creature. Her heart pounded as if the snake had actually struck her. She wanted to throw it away, but feared releasing it, so instead she squeezed it tighter.

Fortunately, Jabari regained his wits; he straightened and sat back down upon his stool. "You are a snake charmer, too?" he asked.

"No," Zahra squeaked. "What do I do? Help! Take it away."

"We come from the vizier," Maliha said, "for some of this snake's venom. Are you unharmed, Zahra?"

"It didn't bite me, if that's what you mean."

The tension in Maliha's face drained away. "Then perhaps my friend here can hold the creature while you extract it?" She flashed Zahra one of those annoying smiles of hers.

"Or maybe I should hand it to you," Zahra said, moving her serpent-wrapped arm toward Maliha threateningly.

"Now, now," Jabari interrupted, bringing forth a vial. "Here we go." He brought the vial near the cobra's head. "Hold it very still, and I'll do the rest."

What? Zahra wanted to faint. This couldn't be happening; what was this man doing entrusting his killer reptile to her?

Jabari pushed the vial toward the cobra's mouth and it opened wide and clamped down on it. Then he reached over and placed his hand around its head, motioning for Zahra to release it and back away, which she was overjoyed to do.

The man held the snake carefully so that its fangs injected all its venom into the vial, before finally returning it to its basket and placing the lid over it.

"You have payment, yes?" Jabari said, holding the vial up for inspection.

Maliha handed over the money, while Zahra collected herself and tried to slow her breathing.

"May the rest of your day be much less exciting," Jabari said as they left. "And if you decide you would like me to train you, brave girl, I will be here."

No. Not ever.

"I didn't know you had such a way with animals," Maliha said.

"Just the scaly ones, apparently."

"Joking aside, I owe you a debt for saving me, truly. Let's go see Ulnar and maybe I can repay you."

"He doesn't have any snakes, does he?" Zahra asked.

"I don't know. Maybe!" Maliha sounded far too excited at that prospect.

CHAPTER 7

"I need to get back to the palace," Zahra said. "Your father said not to waste any time, so I should return with this vial of hard-earned cobra juice and the two jars."

"We have another mission, remember—the Golden Scarab of Balihar? Wouldn't you like to have a jinni at your command?"

A jinni that would grant me wishes? Of course I'd like that. "Yes, but—"

"Come on. Father can wait a few minutes for his precious vial. I'll cover for you if he says anything; this affects both of us."

"What do you mean?" Zahra asked.

"What do you think of the prince?"

"He's..." *Gorgeous ... charming ... princely...* "Amazing."

"Wait, have you fallen in love with him?"

"What? No." *It's not like I've thought of what it would be like to marry him or anything.*

"Don't worry. He has that effect on a lot of girls. I don't understand it myself."

"You don't understand? But ... he's the prince. He's handsome, and graceful, and strong. *And* he's the prince."

"I think he's spoiled and obnoxious," Maliha said, "but I can understand why you like him," she added quickly. "He is the prince, after all." There was that mocking smile again.

"My father wants me to marry him," Maliha continued, "and maybe that's what Prince Amir wants too, but not me."

Maliha must be losing her common sense from all the strong smells in the bazaar. How could she not want to become the Princess of Alhad?

"That's why we need the Golden Scarab," Maliha said. "And why we need to talk to Ulnar."

"Why am I involved in all of this? And why don't you want to marry Prince Amir?"

"It's my father's dream to become royalty, not mine. He's upset because he was supposed to marry a princess when he was young and was passed over. Why should I have to marry someone to fulfill his dream? I'm in love with Hani."

Hani, the son of the royal architect—Maliha was obsessed with him. He was attractive enough, but also as clever as a donkey.

"He's smart and handsome and nice," Maliha said. "And he laughs at my jokes."

"You make jokes?"

"I can send you back to work in the dungeon at any moment, you know. And I'm always telling jokes. Hani likes them. I want to marry him, not Amir. But that's where you come in."

"I'm not following."

Maliha looked thoughtful. "Yes ... this can work."

"*What* can work?"

Maliha grabbed her by the shoulders and shook her. "Zahra! Pay attention. The Golden Scarab—first, we get it. Then I repay the debt I owe you by letting you have one wish from the jinni. You make yourself into a noblewoman, you seduce Prince Amir, he falls in love with you, and then I'm free to marry Hani."

Could this work? Could she actually wed the prince? "He would never marry me. I'm just a servant, and he knows that."

"He must like you, or he wouldn't have pulled you off dungeon duty. When you win him over with the aid of magic and enchant him with your charm—oh, wait, I see the issue. Lack of charm."

"Funny."

But maybe Maliha was right; about the magic, not the charm thing. With the aid of a jinni's magic, she could gain the favor of the prince. Forget about rising in the servant ranks; what if she could become the *princess?*

"Yes," Zahra said. "Let's go see Ulnar the Fortune Teller."

"The Foreteller."

"Whatever. As long as he can tell us about the magic scarab and the jinni, count me in, but we have to be quick."

They neared the edges of the bazaar, passing through streets where gossamer cloths of brilliant hues spanned the buildings overhead, where even the awnings and canopies were trimmed with lace, and signs offered wares of absolutely exquisite design and detail at prices it seemed only royalty could afford.

"Do you know where he is?" Zahra asked.

"No, but with his fame I assumed he'd be in the Alraqi section."

They asked a vendor, who waved vaguely in the direction they were already heading. As they neared the end of the row, Zahra saw a booth with a familiar symbol—a sun with red and yellow rays spreading out from it. It was the same thing she'd seen on the banners of the troupe that had performed the previous night. Hadn't the vizier been ranting about Ulnar not being allowed into the palace?

"That's his booth," Zahra said.

Maliha crinkled her brow. "How do you know?"

Zahra pointed to the symbol. "He's part of the troupe that came to the palace yesterday."

"Oh yes, you're right."

"Let's go."

Zahra didn't really think they'd get any valuable information about how to find the Golden Scarab, or be granted wishes by a jinni, but it didn't hurt to try. As long as they were in and out fast.

She ran toward the booth, bumping into a man in plain white

clothes walking in the opposite direction. "A dozen pardons, friend," she said, breathless.

The man wore a kufiyah headdress wrapped around his face so that only his eyes were showing. He lowered his head and met her gaze for just an instant. His eyes widened at the same time as hers. Prince Amir?

Zahra stared after the man as he walked away. Had that really been the prince? What would he be doing here? "That man—I think it was Prince Amir."

"Outside the palace without guards and an entourage of servants? And in such plain clothes? Don't be ridiculous."

Maliha was right—she must have been mistaken. She'd only seen his eyes, after all.

Her friend pulled her onward. Zahra glanced back and caught the man—the prince?—also looking over his shoulder at her and Maliha. But it couldn't be the prince, could it? Maliha tugged at her arm again and led her to Ulnar's booth. A large, heavily muscled man with tattoos all over his body stood guard at the entrance, arms folded across his expansive chest.

He looked down at the two of them, expressionless. "The Foreteller has seen his last visitor for the day. Please return tomorrow."

Zahra opened her mouth but didn't know what to say. Would she have the chance to return tomorrow? Or any other day? It wasn't likely, unless the vizier ejected her from the palace for taking too long, but best not to think about that.

Maliha approached the man confidently. "I am the vizier's daughter, Maliha. I cannot return tomorrow; I wish to see the Foreteller now."

The large man looked her over, as if trying to determine if she was indeed telling the truth. Maliha showed him the ring she wore with the royal insignia on it.

"Hmmm." The man grudgingly stepped aside to allow them in.

When they pushed aside the curtain leading into his booth, Ulnar was sitting on a pile of turquoise pillows next to a chest with an oil lamp shining on top of it, his back straight and eyes closed, chanting. He coughed upon their sudden entrance and quickly stood up in surprise.

The man appeared to be around fifty years old. Despite clearly being Persian, his clothing had the flamboyant style of the others she'd seen in the troupe. There was a bright purple silk cloth twisted around the top of his head, and a strip of deep blue linen wrapped in a tight spiral around his chest, leaving bare a slightly rounded belly. His trousers, a dark green, puffed out around the hips but were cinched tight at his shins, just above red leather boots whose tips extended far beyond the toes and angled up at the ends. Three shining copper rings hung from each ear. A sculpted beard with a dash of gray curled up along each side of his chin like a smile, which stood in sharp contrast to his deep frown at being disturbed.

He looked silly, like a man playing people for fools. Was this a waste of their time?

"How—?" Ulnar began. "I'm afraid I'm settled in for the day, my lovely young ladies, yes quite settled. Perhaps you could return tomorrow, if you would be so kind."

"You are Ulnar?" Maliha asked.

"Yes, that's correct. Just as the sign says out front, that's me. However, I'm afraid my manservant was supposed to intercept and turn away visitors this time of the evening, you see. I'm rather exhausted and I need to refresh, you understand."

"My name is Maliha. I am the daughter of the sultan's vizier, and I haven't the time to tarry about like your more idle customers. I have royal duties to perform, and many of them. So, if it please you, Great Foreteller, might I have a moment of your time?"

"Ah, a daughter of *the* vizier, you say? That would be Vizier Yaseen, I take it?"

Maliha nodded.

"My apologies, then, my darling girl, you seem quite lovely, quite wonderful indeed, but you see I have taken, shall we say, quite a dislike to your father. Yes, I have encountered him on a few occasions, and, no disrespect to you, of course, but I find him rather bothersome. So, unfortunately, that doesn't really help your case here today. And out of respect for my deep abiding … distaste … for the exalted vizier, I must humbly request that you leave forthwith and not return."

CHAPTER 8

Zahra's mouth hung open. She had never seen anyone—other than the vizier himself, of course—refusing Maliha anything.

Maliha stood speechless, appearing flummoxed at the man's dismissal.

Zahra moved forward to touch her friend's shoulder. "Come, Maliha, we should leave."

Then Ulnar's eyes locked onto Zahra and his entire demeanor changed.

"Perhaps I was too hasty, yes, a bit. One full dinar for a reading."

"A full dinar!" Maliha said. "I could almost buy a *camel* for that."

"You're welcome to do so, if that is your pleasure. It is your choice."

Maliha grunted and handed the man a shiny gold dinar. "I don't want a reading—I need information."

"Oh, I'm afraid the offer of a reading wasn't for you, vizier's daughter," Ulnar said, dropping the coin into a satchel.

His eyes shifted to Zahra again. "Ah... But you, my dear ... you are another matter. What unusual eyes. Yes, quite interesting.

Please come closer."

Ulnar had refused Maliha, the vizier's daughter, but was willing to see her, a mere servant? What was happening today?

Zahra stepped toward the Foreteller, ignoring Maliha's tightly pursed lips.

"I sense," Ulnar said, "that you have more at stake than the Great Slippery Eel's daughter. No offense, dear," he added, glancing at Maliha. "Now, what is your name?"

"My name is Zahra."

"And why are you here, Zahra? What do you seek?"

"I seek..." What could she say, other than the truth, which seemed utterly ridiculous now that she was forced to speak it aloud? "The ... Golden Scarab of Balihar?"

"Oh. Is that all?" Ulnar laughed. "You have bold desires. I can see that."

I'm so stupid. What am I doing here? Thinking I have any chance of being a princess because of a mythical magic scarab?

But she was here, so she might as well see it through. "I was told that you might know of its location."

"Were you now? You were told by the sultan's Slimy Toad of a vizier, no doubt. Again, no offense, young one." He winked at Maliha.

Zahra could see Maliha tensing up, doing her best to hold in a retort.

"It is true," Ulnar said. "I know where the Scarab is rumored to be, oh yes. But I fear they are just rumors. I even have a map here."

He searched through various rolls and sheets of parchment, finally retrieving one and laying it on a table at the back of the booth. He looked it over, running his fingers along it. "I searched for it myself, you know. Quite a bit. Yes, quite a bit. The Sands of Fire, they said. But no, I never found anything. If the secret to its location is on this map, I've not discovered it."

"Could we buy the map from you?" Maliha asked.

"No. Not you. I need no ill-gotten money from the Esteemed Oily One. No offense."

"No offense taken," Maliha said, steaming and clearly taking offense.

"But for you…" he said to Zahra. "Come, sit with me a moment."

Ulnar settled back into his pillows, and Zahra sat across from him. With a frustrated sigh, Maliha stomped out of the tent.

Ulnar threw Zahra a mischievous smile. "Her father really is a rather dreadful man, I'm afraid, but perhaps I shouldn't have been so hard on her for the sake of his faults."

Zahra couldn't disagree.

"Now, with your permission, I'll get a glimpse into your future."

She looked at Ulnar's hands folded before him. She'd never touched a man's hand before, not even when she'd accidentally tackled the prince. Her brow began to sweat at the thought of it, but wasn't that why she was here?

She swallowed hard and placed her hand in front of her, palm-up, for him to read.

"No need for that," Ulnar said. "I don't read palms. That is fakery and foolishness."

He lifted a hand toward her. "It merely requires a contact with your forehead, if you're willing."

She nodded.

He touched a few fingers lightly to her head. "My ability is genuine, though less specific than some may like. As a result, I sometimes unfortunately find myself having to embellish things a bit. To satisfy the customer, you understand. But you, I think—"

He took a breath. "Well, there is quite a bit going on here. How my ability works, you see, is not so much that I see into the future, but that I can *feel* into the future. I get a sense of the emotions and sensations to come, and a rough timing of when they'll be."

Ulnar closed his eyes, his eyelids twitching as he sat silently for a few moments. He inhaled, sharp and hearty. A moment passed, and his breath eased out. "You have a complex future. I'm feeling a swirl of emotions: love … surprise … shock … fear … despair, anger, concern…"

He withdrew his hand. "I'm not quite sure what to make of it, to be honest. There is great turmoil. It is strange. I had not felt such a complicated future in a long time, and yet this is twice in one day I've sensed it."

Zahra considered his words. *Shock, fear, despair, anger...* Those didn't sound like good things. What was going to happen to her?

"Ah, but you came for word of the Golden Scarab of Balihar, not to hear a crazy old magician ramble on, isn't that so? Legend says the jinni himself hid the Golden Scarab in a cave near the Sands of Fire."

The Sands of Fire? That didn't sound too welcoming.

"Others say the Scarab was lost in the desert for all time. I can only say that I myself have passed through the Sands more than once, and I have searched every cave, along every cliff, and never seen a glint of gold whatsoever."

"I'll make you a deal," Ulnar said. "I will give you the map, free of charge. I ask only one thing in return." From one of his chests, he pulled a giant talon the length of her arm. "Hold this roc's talon over your heart and swear to me an oath that if you take this map and find the Golden Scarab, you will not use the magic of the jinni to seek wealth or power."

But that was exactly what Zahra wanted from the jinni's magic! Why else would she be seeking the Scarab in the first place?

Zahra felt the heft of the talon in her hand, matching the weight of the oath Ulnar was asking her to make. All she had to do was agree to his request and speak the oath, and the map would be hers. But how could she make that oath, knowing that it was precisely the opposite of what she planned to do? Why would she even seek the Scarab if she couldn't use it to win the prince's favor?

She'd promised her mother she'd always tell the truth, and she tried to keep that promise as much as she could. It was a meaningful connection with her mother that she'd always clung to.

She rippled her fingers over her heart and looked Ulnar in the eyes. She opened her mouth and spoke.

"No. I can't make that promise."

Ulnar raised an eyebrow, but then he smiled, taking back the talon. "Very well. It has been a pleasure meeting you, Zahra. Yes, a great pleasure indeed."

He reached into his satchel. "As I don't feel I've helped you, I am compelled to return the payment."

He dropped the gold dinar Maliha had paid him into Zahra's hand. She stashed the coin safely in her own satchel until she could return it to Maliha.

"I wish you well in the future. And truly, I hope our paths cross again someday. Now, for me, it is time to rest."

Ulnar held open the drapes for her to exit, and she trudged numbly out into the street.

What had she done?

CHAPTER 9

Z ahra walked past Ulnar's watchman and stood in the street, staring into space, wondering what to do now. She could have just agreed to take his oath. Even though it was counter to her intent, maybe she could have thought of another way to use the Scarab to accomplish her goal, something less direct. Maybe Maliha could have helped her figure something out.

Maliha! Where was she?

Zahra spun around and saw her friend slip out from between two booths. She again grabbed Zahra by the arm and led her back the way they'd come.

"I didn't get it," Zahra said.

"Yes, I know," Maliha responded, as if it were obvious.

"He said I could have it—for free. I only had to promise that if I found the Scarab, I wouldn't use it to try to marry the prince."

"That's not what he said." Maliha kept them hurrying through the alleyways, and they rushed back through the main sector of the bazaar.

"That's what it meant to me. Wait, you weren't there—how do you know what he said?"

"I overheard you talking, from the back." She held up a piece of parchment in front of Zahra. "When I took the map off his table."

"You *stole* it?"

"Not exactly; I left him five dinars as payment. Which was more than he deserved, for the way he treated me and spoke about my father."

Once they'd exited the bazaar, Maliha pulled Zahra off into an empty alley. "Let's see what the map shows us."

"You should return it."

"Oh, do you think so?" Maliha pressed the map to Zahra's chest. "Here, go ahead. Take it back to him."

"I will." Zahra took the map and rolled it up.

"Don't you even want to look at it?" Maliha tempted her.

Now that they had it, why *shouldn't* she? They could look it over first, and then she'd take it back. It wasn't like either of them could realistically wander off and search for the mystical treasure, anyway.

"Alright, just a quick look." Zahra unrolled it and checked the alley entrance to make sure nobody was nearby.

The map showed their city of Alhad at one corner, and Kehrad in the other. In between, in the desert nearer to Alhad, was an area marked with a lake and trees—the Hafiz Oasis—and a trail leading from there to the Sands of Fire that Ulnar had mentioned. A boundary bordering the Sands to the north and east was noted as the Grasping Cliffs, with a notation:

The sultans see and the sultans land
In the wondrous cave of the Fiery Sand
At grasping cliffs behold the scar
To find the Scarab of Balihar

"That's it?" Zahra asked. "This isn't anything more than Ulnar has already told me."

"He told where you the Scarab is?"

"It's more like he told me where it isn't. He said he'd searched the cliffs along the Sands of Fire thoroughly and never found anything."

"Maybe the words are a riddle and he couldn't figure it out."

"That could be. Do they mean anything to you?" Zahra asked.

"It sounds like they are saying to look for a cave near a scar in the cliffs."

"I'm sure Ulnar would have realized that. Anyway, it doesn't matter; we can never get there, and we can't send someone to look for us."

Maliha frowned, but wasn't ready to give up yet. She stared at the map, as if she could will the object of their desire to be closer, within their own city perhaps. "I can't think of—wait! You could go."

What was she talking about? Zahra had no means of getting there. "I think your wits have been stolen by a qareen. I have to return all this stuff to your father right away."

"Yes, but after that. You give my father the jars and the vial, then come down to see me. I'll get you a horse from the stables and give you food and money for the journey. You go and search for the cave, and I'll cover for you at the palace."

Zahra laughed. If only it could be that easy. "How many problems with that plan do you want me to point out? Let's start with a simple one: I don't know how to ride a horse."

"Oh, that's easy. You'll learn in a few minutes. This can work."

"It can't. As much as I want this—and I do—it isn't possible. Maybe it seems reasonable to you, but you're not a servant. I can't just leave; if I do, and something goes wrong, I'll be put out on the streets. We need another plan."

"I think you're overreacting, but I'll try to come up with something. We don't have much time, because I think my father is going to speak with the sultan soon. Hold on to the map for now."

Zahra had wanted to return it immediately, but they'd traveled a fair distance from the Foreteller and she felt an urgent need to get back to the vizier to avoid his ire. She'd sneak out and give it back tomorrow.

When they'd returned to the palace, Maliha whispered, "Look over the map and think about what we can do. Please."

Nobody had ever said that word to her before, not even Maliha. *Please.* It felt good to hear and made her want to find a solution, but what could she do? She had no power whatsoever.

After telling Maliha she would try, she left and made haste to the vizier's rooms, concerned that their side trip had taken too long.

She held the jars up to the guard outside his room. "The vizier is expecting me."

The guard knocked, and the door swished open.

"There you are, girl," the vizier said. "Do you have them?"

"Here are your items, Vizier Yaseen. The frankincense, the kohl, and the cobra venom, freshly squeezed." Zahra knew just how true that was.

"Yes, yes, hand it over. Excellent." He turned and halfway closed the door, but then a look of suspicion and worry passed over his features. "You've told no one of this?"

"I've told no one." *Except your daughter, of course.*

"Good. Well, you will keep it that way. You're dismissed." He waved her away and shut the door behind him.

Zahra stepped back. What was Yaseen so concerned about? Why should he be so secretive about a delivery from a servant, even for an item as odd as cobra venom? Unless it could reveal something...

She crept down the hall, to the balcony where Selene had climbed to the vizier's room, reflecting on the acrobat thief's accusation. *Was* the vizier up to something nefarious? She stepped onto the balcony and leaned out toward the vizier's.

She heard a great whooshing sound, as of a flame being suddenly ignited, and a wisp of smoke wafted out from his room. What was he doing over there? A slight breeze carried an odor of sulfur to her nostrils. Was the thief speaking the truth? Was the vizier summoning a demon ifrit?

She had to know.

A small decorative ledge ran along the exterior of the palace wall, just beneath the two balconies. She could cross it as Selene had done, climb onto the vizier's balcony, and peer into his room.

Zahra swung herself over the balcony railing, holding on so

tightly she thought her grip might crack the carved stone.

This is the most foolish thing you've ever done, Zahra scolded herself, even as she slowly reached down with her feet. *And why? Because an imprisoned thief claimed the vizier is hatching an evil plan?*

She couldn't say exactly what had prompted her to take such a risk; something about the way the vizier was acting lately made her take Selene's admonition more seriously. She didn't like the vizier, and wouldn't mind seeing him in trouble, but more importantly she was worried for Maliha, and indeed the entire palace.

But was this *her* responsibility? No, she had to admit, it was not—then again, if the thief was correct, and Zahra was the only one who had an idea what was going on, shouldn't she do something about it?

But even so, this was crazy. If the vizier caught her, she'd be lucky if the only thing he did was kick her out of the palace.

And yet she had to know the truth.

She eased her left foot out along the ledge, then stretched her left arm along the wall, still holding fast with her right hand. She was extended about halfway toward the vizier's balcony. To get there, she'd have to let go and shinny along. She turned her head carefully and looked down.

Mistake. Her breath caught and her heart sunk into her stomach. What was she doing?

A deep voice bellowed out from within the vizier's room, and then a response from Yaseen himself. Someone was in there with him.

Zahra extended her foot along the ledge until she couldn't stretch out any farther. Before she could think any more about her predicament, she released her grip and pressed herself up against the wall. *What am I doing what am I doing what am I doing!*

This traversal had seemed a lot easier from the safety of the balcony.

A slow, full breath, and she slid her right foot closer to her left, and then her left foot farther out and toward the other balcony, shifting her weight as she did so. She could almost reach over now. She stretched again to the left, the fingers of her right hand finding a crack to grab hold of. One more step... She lunged—her left hand caught hold of the balustrade, and she quickly pulled herself along the ledge and clung tightly to it with both hands. She'd made it. She inhaled deeply and released the breath slowly to calm herself.

She climbed over the railing as quietly as she could and landed softly on the floor of the vizier's balcony. Before she could look inside, the deep voice said, "Are you sure?"

"I'll not let that spoiled, arrogant boy control my fate," Vizier Yaseen responded.

Was he talking about Prince Amir?

Sneaking up against the wall, Zahra leaned out and peeked into his room through a translucent silken drapery at the entrance.

And saw it.

Her hand shot up to cover her mouth lest she make any utterance. The thief had been right: the vizier had summoned an ifrit.

Taller than Yaseen by two feet, it had flame-colored skin covered in tattoos of swirling lines and glyphs. Twin spiraled horns protruded from its skull above large, tapered ears. Zahra's heart dropped and her stomach roiled at the sight of it.

Curse you, vizier. Zahra felt a momentary pang of guilt at the thought, but pushed back against her reaction. *No, curse him, for he deserves nothing less for doing this.*

The demon—the ifrit—watched the vizier pour a few drops from the vial Zahra had delivered to him into a clear glass jar half-filled with another foul liquid.

Yaseen stirred the jar, and the concoction hissed and bubbled, a dusky vapor rising from within the glass.

"And one last important ingredient," the vizier said. He lifted a beautiful lily that looked like it had been made of smoky midnight-blue glass and lowered it stem-first into the jar.

Zahra expected another abrupt hiss but instead the lily seemed to be absorbing the liquid, slowly becoming a rich blackish-red, starting from its base and rising up until the whole flower had taken on the stunning hue.

"Is it complete?" Yaseen asked the ifrit.

"It is. Now you may use it to obtain what you wish. Simply have your daughter present the flower to the prince, see that he smells it, and when his gaze meets her face, he will fall instantly in love. Take care to let no other breathe in the flower's scent before the prince does, including your daughter. And remember our bargain, Vizier."

Zahra gasped and quickly covered her mouth again. *By the Eternal Flame.* So *this* was the vizier's plan for his daughter! He was going to bespell the prince and make him fall in love with Maliha.

CHAPTER 10

No. How could the vizier, with all of his wealth, power, and influence, plan to force the prince to marry his daughter using dark magic?

Zahra couldn't let it happen.

She paused—was she recoiling at the thought of Amir marrying Maliha now because she herself had been entertaining the thought of winning him over with the magic of a jinni?

No. Even if that were the case, Amir deserved better than this, and so did Maliha. Zahra had to put a stop to it.

But how?

She had to tell Maliha. But first she had to get back to the other balcony. She wanted to close her eyes and cross over without looking.

Deep breath, deep breath.

There was no time for hesitating—she had to warn her friend.

She vaulted over the balustrade and traversed the gap as fast as she could, replacing her fear with concern for Maliha. Once back inside the palace, she tiptoed into the hall and crept away from the vizier's room. Out of sight of the guard, she raced to the nearest staircase and ran down it, ignoring the surprised looks of people seeing a common servant running through the halls of the palace. She skidded to a breathless halt at Maliha's chambers.

Her friend wasn't there.

Zahra pressed the other servants as to her whereabouts, but no one knew where she'd gone.

Of all the times to disappear, Maliha.

Now what? Where might she be? *Think, Zahra, think.*

She could be anywhere. One place Zahra knew she wasn't was at her father's, but that didn't help her. Maybe she'd gone to get food? Possibly, but Zahra couldn't run around the entire palace looking for her. What else could she do?

The prince!

She could warn Prince Amir. Would he even believe her? He *had* to—they had made a connection. Hadn't they? *Hopefully it wasn't entirely one-sided.*

She would go to the prince and make him believe her. It was her only chance.

She ran back up the steps, up level after level, this time hiding when necessary to avoid being spotted where she shouldn't be. Up past the vizier's, and finally, winded, she arrived at Prince Amir's floor. She paused to catch her breath, frantic, but forced herself to calm down. Wiping the sweat from her forehead, she inhaled slowly to ease her breathing.

She didn't know exactly when the vizier planned to enact his scheme, but she couldn't wait any longer.

Zahra rounded the corner and strode confidently toward the prince's chambers, as if she'd been specially invited. The guards stared at her.

"The prince called for me," Zahra bluffed.

"Prince Amir is not here."

Oh, no.

"I was told I must see him. Do you know where I may find him?"

"The vizier requested his presence in the Fathi Garden."

No. Was she too late?

"Ah, I see," Zahra said, trying to remain calm despite the growing panic rising within her. "May your ... many thanks ... be blessed," she mumbled, not even caring what she said at this point.

She turned and walked away, everything inside screaming at her to run. Which she did, as soon as she passed the corner and reached the staircase.

She took the steps two and three at a time, hoping nobody saw and stopped her. At the ground floor, Dalal crossed the hallway. *No, not now.* Zahra crouched behind a plant and waited.

The girl was deep in conversation with another servant. *Move. Get out of here.* They were headed in the same direction. *Of course.* She couldn't wait; she took the risk and followed behind them at a normal walking pace. She wanted to scream—there was no time for this. At last, the other two turned down another hall.

Zahra continued as quickly as she could through the hallways, head lowered so as not to invite conversation with anyone. She neared the entrance to the courtyard garden, but the doors were closed and two of the vizier's men were guarding the doorway.

They must already be in there.

Time to try the bluff again.

"A dozen apologies for being late," Zahra said as she walked up to the guards. "The vizier will no doubt have me scrubbing the dungeon again for my tardiness."

"If you are late," one of the guards said, "then that is unfortunate for you, and you may indeed be on scrubbing duty, because we've been given a strict, explicit order, and nobody may enter the gardens until the vizier leaves."

So much for that.

Time for another tactic. She lowered her heard and started to sniff. "I..."—sniff sniff—"understand." She dove into her act, and soon the sniffling turned to tears and outright crying, her breath catching as she started to sob.

The guards appeared unmoved. "You may cry elsewhere, girl."

"Y—y—yes..."—sobbing—"I ... under ... stand..."—sniff—"I have to go..." she mumbled, walking away quickly and wiping off her conjured tears.

Now what could she do? She turned the corner and thought hard. There was another entrance from the opposite side of the garden. No, that was certain to be blocked, too.

There were windows with views into the courtyard from above. She quickly ran back upstairs. This time, she only had to ascend one flight. She slowed as she approached the opening and peered into the courtyard below. The vizier stood near the center, with Maliha at his side and two guards behind them.

She breathed a sigh of relief. The prince hadn't arrived yet.

Just as she had that thought, the doors facing the vizier opened. Amir was coming. She had to move.

Positioning herself out of view behind a tree, she lowered herself from the window and dropped to the ground below. She crept through the plants, trying to be as silent as possible.

How am I going to stop this from happening?

As she approached, she knew there was no time to think. The prince had entered and now stood before Maliha.

"Prince Amir, blessings upon you for accepting my invitation," Vizier Yaseen said. "I arranged this meeting because my daughter wishes to present you with a gift."

Yaseen whispered something to Maliha, and brought forth the dark, beautiful lily Zahra had seen him holding earlier.

Maliha, looking uneasy and unsure, held the lily out before her, saying in a flat tone, "Please accept this Soul Lily as a symbol of my feelings for you."

Prince Amir looked surprised at this, accepting her offer and taking the flower from her hand. He raised it toward his face...

"No!" Zahra shouted, rushing to stop him.

But she was too late.

Amir took a long sniff from the lily. As he inhaled the scent, the flower hardened, becoming crystallized like glass. The prince's eyes glazed over. Zahra reached him at that moment and knocked the lily from his hand. Amir looked up and into her eyes.

CHAPTER 11

Z ahra stared into Prince Amir's face, horrified that she'd failed and confused as to why he was looking at her so adoringly.

"No," the vizier gasped.

"Zahra!" Maliha said, obviously shocked as well. "What are you doing?"

Zahra froze. How could she explain her actions without sounding like she was fabricating a story? "I..."

Letting the lily drop from his fingers, Amir reached out to caress Zahra's cheek. Stunned, she didn't even pull away.

"My lovely Zahra," Amir said.

He knew her name? He'd only ever called her "girl." *He knows my name.*

"Your misty gray eyes have enchanted me," he continued. Moving his hand to brush through her hair, he added, "Your locks are like the finest Harappa silk, and your breath is as the scent of sweet honey."

Zahra's mouth dropped open. What? A moment passed before she recalled the words of the ifrit and realized what had just happened.

When his gaze meets her face, he will fall instantly in love.

"Every moment with you is intoxicating, and my mind reels at your beauty and grace. Your smile lights up my day. The sun shines not nearly as bright as you."

Prince Amir had fallen in love with her instead of Maliha!

"Guards!" Vizier Yaseen shouted, his eye twitching. "The girl has attacked the prince. Seize her and take her to the dungeon immediately!"

"No, I didn't—" Zahra said.

"Father, I'm sure she has—" Maliha tried to help.

"She's done no such thing," Prince Amir said. "Can you not see? I am—"

"Guards, now!" Yaseen commanded.

Zahra's options flashed through her mind in an instant. She could try to explain, but it was her word against the vizier's, and why would anyone believe a servant girl over the sultan's trusted advisor?

She could allow herself to be taken by the guards to the dungeon, and hope that Maliha or Prince Amir would get her out, but that still came down to her word over Yaseen's—if she even got the chance to explain what was going on. The vizier would do everything he could to keep her quiet and locked away. Or very possibly have her executed to hide his crime.

Her world closed in around her. There was only one option left. Her mind reeled; for a moment, every sound was muffled as if she were underwater, and everything in her vision became a blur as she realized what she had to do.

She jumped sideways and ran back through the garden the way she'd come, leaving behind so many astonished faces.

"My love, my everything. Have I upset you?" Prince Amir shouted after her as she fled. "See what you've done, Yaseen. You've frightened her."

She didn't wait to hear their conversation, but instead leaped up and clambered back through the window. At the staircase, she saved time by sliding down the marble handrail. The guards at the garden doorway moved to block her escape.

She had to get out of the palace!

There was no chance of making it out the front entrance now, or any entrance for that matter. She dashed down the hall in the opposite direction and headed toward the stables. Maybe she could take a horse and ride away. She didn't know how to ride, but Maliha had said it was easy.

Three of the sultan's administrators passed through an archway ahead, so she ducked down a side corridor. Where to now?

A window!

She dove outside before the guards could spot her. Rolling to her feet, she darted behind a wall out of sight.

The stables were near, and she slowed as she approached. Crouching behind a barrel, she looked from empty stall to empty stall. The last had a horse occupying it, but no saddle. *That's ill luck.*

Even if she'd known how to put one on, she had no time. *I need to leave the city now.*

She raced along the wall separating the palace grounds from the city proper. Vizier Yaseen would soon have every guard after her, the city gates would be locked down, and she'd never escape.

Ahead, she heard a call going out to the guards at the palace gates. No exit that way.

She sprinted up the steps along a section of the palace wall currently unguarded. Pausing only briefly at the top to verify nobody was looking, she scampered over to the edge, hung down, and dropped into the bustling city. She needed to become less conspicuous, and quick.

She hustled through the streets toward the bazaar, thinking to grab new clothes, but when she arrived she realized her mistake. The sun was setting and the vendors had all closed up for the day, packing away their wares.

Where to now?

She had to hope she could get to a city gate before they were all closed. People all along the streets gave her scornful looks or shouted at her to watch herself. She paid them no heed, completely ignoring all civility and courtesy.

Her path took her through a poorer section of the city, where old, worn clothes were hung out to dry. She considered taking them and changing, but decided against it. They'd already closed off access to the palace, so her window to escape Alhad was closing.

She rushed out into the main street leading out of town. A few blocks behind her, guards were marching to the same gate she was headed toward.

What to do now?

A large group of people ahead of her were leaving the city, so she bolted up and joined the throng.

Their pace was infuriatingly slow, but she couldn't risk drawing attention to herself now. The guards steadily advanced on her position, even as she grew closer to the exit. Would she get out before they got close enough to shout ahead and lock it down?

She pushed her way to the front of the line and soon realized why the crowd was moving so slowly. A caravan was leaving the city—a line of horses, wagons, and camels. She wanted nothing more than to run past them all, but knew she'd just draw attention to herself.

How was she going to get out and stay hidden?

The caravan! If she could just sneak into their midst...

She broke away from the people and hurried ahead, almost jogging, passing the camels in order to reach the wagons. The last trailing wagon had nobody next to it. Surreptitiously looking inside, she saw only blankets, rugs, and clothing. No passengers.

Behind her, the lead camel rider was distracted, talking to his companion. This was her chance.

She grabbed the back of the wagon and pulled herself inside, quickly covering herself in the thick, warm cloth.

She held her breath. Had anybody seen her?

The caravan passed slowly through the city gates. Shortly after the last camel had walked through, she heard the guards ordering the gate closed.

She waited, fearing that they would still search the wagons, but minutes went by and the caravan rode on, continuing from the city into the desert scrublands.

She'd escaped.

CHAPTER 12

As dusk passed into night, and the caravan plodded on through the desert, Zahra pondered her fate. What could she do now? By interrupting the vizier's plan, had she really made Prince Amir fall in love with her? As much as she hoped it couldn't be so, she knew in her heart it was true.

And it made her sick to her stomach.

Had she wanted to be chosen as one of his attendants? Had she even entertained wild fantasies of having the prince fall for her? Sure.

But not like this.

She'd thought maybe she could impress him so that he'd fall for her, and if she were to have a little boost from a magical jinni, that wouldn't hurt. But force him to love her with a demon's sorcery? No.

The thief Selene had been right: Yaseen did have a foul plan he was working on. What had he been thinking? Zahra balled her hands into fists. It irritated her that if only she had not pursued the acrobat, this might not have happened.

Now she'd be exiled from the kingdom for sure. Her breath

caught as reality hit her—be exiled? She already was. She couldn't return now. She'd have to move to another land and try to make her way in the world. As little as she'd had for herself in the palace, at least she'd had a home and food, and the hope of something more one day. Now she had nothing.

Her dire situation occupied her mind well into the night, until fatigue and the rocking of the wagon lulled her to sleep.

Chatter between the other travelers in the caravan awakened her. She pushed aside the coarse blanket covering her, nonetheless grateful for its warmth, the dry desert air having cooled considerably during the night. She listened keenly to the talk among the riders, trying to get a sense of where they were headed. Something about an oasis?

She shifted forward to look out the front of the wagon. The horizon glowed with the pink hue of the first light of day, and a short distance ahead, the hard-packed desert transitioned into dunes. As the sun rose, its light revealed them to be beautiful, wavy hills of golden sand, but she saw no signs of life there as far as she could see. They weren't planning to travel into that, were they?

Most of the caravan veered away from the rolling drifts, but a few of the horses and wagons, including hers, continued on toward them. To the east, at the edge of the dunes, a small village sat among a region of trees, bushes, and low cliffs. Amid the continued chatter, a horseman mentioned the Hafiz Oasis. Hadn't that been on the Foreteller's map to the Golden Scarab?

The map she still had in her possession!

She pulled it out, running a finger over the rough parchment as she scanned it. Yes, there it was—the Hafiz Oasis.

A plan formed in her head as she stared at the map: from the Hafiz Oasis, through the Sands of Fire, to the Grasping Cliffs, to a cave that held the Golden Scarab of Balihar...

She rolled up the map, stuffed it back into her waist sash, and waited. The rest of the caravan had continued on into the desert, and her wagon was the last of the group traveling to the oasis. When they crossed into the village-like camp at the edge of the dunes, she slid out from the back of the wagon and walked in from behind.

The morning sun set the tops of the great dunes aglow. It was a new day, and Zahra planned to make use of it.

If she could only find the lost Scarab of Balihar and unlock the jinni within—if either of them actually existed—she had a chance to set things right. She could even expose the vizier's treachery and make him regret all those times he'd belittled and punished her.

The sultan would welcome her as a hero, maybe even see her as worthy of the prince's hand. Dare she hope again?

First she had to get to the Sands of Fire.

The map showed the Sands were northeast of this oasis, which would be through or among the dunes. Where exactly? And how would she get there? And if she did, how would she find the cave—or, indeed, the Scarab?

Panic rose as she considered how unlikely it was for her to succeed. Her plan was absurd; nobody had ever found this Golden Scarab. Not even Ulnar, with a map and clues to its whereabouts. What chance did she have?

Her breath came in gasps and her heart pounded as she mentally grappled with the task ahead of her.

She swallowed and refused to give in to fear.

Her fear wasn't so easily banished. The question repeated itself in her mind: *what chance do I have?*

She knew the answer to that question, but faced it head on.

A more realistic question is, what choice do I have?

What else could she do? In her current state, nothing came to mind. She buried her negative thoughts, or at least tried to. All she could do was move forward.

One thing at a time, Zahra, one thing at a time.

She needed to find someone who could take her to the Sands.

Sparrows chirped overhead and flew off toward the lake in the heart of the oasis. That seemed as good a direction as any. She followed the birds' flight path and soon encountered four disheveled men huddled around a large tent.

"Blessings to you this fine morning, my friends," Zahra said, putting on a broad smile.

All four turned to her, looking upset at being bothered. Perhaps it was the early hour. The largest, dirtiest, and hairiest of the men quickly interrupted her. "Aren't looking for no chatter or no goods. On your way."

Her attempts at charming others were as effective out here as they were in the palace. Great.

"It was ... a pleasure to meet you." The word *pleasure* tasted sour in her mouth.

More people and tents were scattered ahead, with no discernible organization or order to them. She scurried off to the next nearest group.

Surrounding this tent were three young, only slightly less bedraggled, women. They were squinting against the morning sun, beside a man who appeared to be their father.

She tried again with this group. "It's a fine morning to meet such lovely tra—"

"No," the man said, waving dismissively.

Not the friendliest of folk at this oasis. Maybe it was the morning—perhaps they needed time to fully awaken. Bypassing the other tents, she shuffled down to the lakeshore.

Water flowed into the oasis from a horizontal fissure in a cliff at the far edge of the lake. Set in the middle of the clear water was a small island dotted with date palms.

Other people sat near the shore, filling water jugs or scrubbing themselves. After her haphazard escape yesterday, a little clean-up sounded like a good idea. She found a clear spot and stepped into the cool water, crouching down to splash her face.

"A pleasant morning to you," a woman next to her said.

The woman wore plain clothes, like Zahra's, but they were filthy and threadbare. She nodded to Zahra with a warm, friendly expression.

Someone who didn't shoo her away!

"And to you," Zahra responded.

"I'm Amaya," the woman said.

"Zahra."

"Did you arrive with the caravan this morning?"

"No," Zahra said, not wanting to admit she had stowed away. "I mean, yes—I came in with the caravan, but I'm not with their group."

"What brings you to Hafiz?" Amaya dipped a metal ewer into the water to fill it.

How much should she tell this stranger? She looked around. A few tents were nearby, but their occupants were engaged in their own conversations. A young boy was kicking sand near a palm tree, and two other women were scrubbing at clothing farther down the shoreline.

"I'm hoping to find someone traveling northeast, past the Sands of Fire," Zahra said, trying to keep her voice only loud enough for the woman to hear.

"Just you?" Amaya looked surprised. "You are alone?"

Zahra's breath caught. The question hit her like a blow to the gut—alone.

"I ... yes, I'm traveling on my own." That must sound quite unusual. What could she provide as an explanation? Where would she be going? Why would she be alone?

"That can be quite dangerous, especially for a lovely girl like yourself," Amaya said. "What prompts you to take such a risk?"

Oh, not much. I learned that our sultan's vizier was going to place an evil ifrit's love spell upon Alhad's prince, and I interrupted it and now the prince is in love with me, so I'm looking for the magic of a jinni to restore order to my life.

"My ... father ... is ... dying ... and I was told there is medicine that will help him. I need to find a ... plant ... that only grows near the Grasping Cliffs." Zahra cringed inside at her pathetic lie.

Amaya looked at her quizzically. "That ... sounds awful," she said in a sympathetic tone.

"You don't happen to be going anywhere near the Sands of Fire?" Zahra asked.

"I'm afraid not. We're traveling in the other direction."

"I see."

Amaya lifted her jug of water and stepped away from the shore. "If you're going to the Grasping Cliffs, you must be prepared. It will take hours to get there, even if you are riding a strong camel. Take care that you have plenty of water and food, for this oasis is your last chance."

A camel? Food and water? She had none of those things, not even something to carry the food or water in. It would take hours on a camel? On the map it looked so close.

"Blessings on your trip, Zahra," Amaya said. "Be watchful and stay safe, and I hope you're able to help your father."

"May you and your family be blessed, Amaya." Zahra's insides twisted at having made up a story about a dying father.

In truth, she didn't even know who her father was, and her mother had dropped her off to be a servant at the palace when she was only seven. For all she knew, they were both dead. She had nobody in her life, no one to help her out of this situation.

What could she do now? She had no camel, no food, no help, and she wanted to go find a mythical object made of gold that somehow nobody else had ever found? In the middle of a forbidding place called the Sands of Fire? It was impossible.

Despair washed over her as she stared off into the desert sands. The weight of all that had transpired pressed down upon her. How could she proceed? She had nothing, and she was all alone. Tears fell from her cheeks and dripped into the waters of the lake.

CHAPTER 13

"Are you alright?" A voice startled Zahra. It was the little boy she'd seen kicking at the sand.

Zahra splashed water on her face to wash away her tears.

"Yes, I'm ... I'm great," she lied, getting up and walking through the wet sand toward the oasis encampment.

She needed to get food and water, and a camel. Or someone to take her to the Grasping Cliffs, but that seemed increasingly unlikely. She didn't even have any money—*wait, I still have Maliha's dinar that Ulnar the Foreteller gave to me.* Maliha had said she could buy a camel with it.

She looked back at the boy. "Do you know if there is a camel merchant here?"

He nodded and pointed toward the edge of the village. That was where she'd start. She thanked the boy and slogged in that direction.

"Girl! Girl!" the merchant called to her before she even reached him. "My friend, you have the bearing of one who is in need of a camel. You have come to the right place. I am called Hafiz, yes, yes, like the name of the Oasis itself. Perhaps that is why I stay here.

But back to the camels: I have two left, you see." Hafiz held out his arm in a grand gesture as if he were presenting a fine treasure fit for royalty, rather than two beasts of burden.

"Please, please, come see and choose one before they are both gone," he said.

Zahra stepped closer. One looked like a normal, healthy camel and the other looked ... unique. It had an unusual stripe down one side of its neck, small ears, and a truncated tail. And it smelled—bad.

She pointed to the healthy camel. "How much for this one?"

"Ten dinars for a discerning girl like you."

Ten? She had only one. "How much for the other one?"

"Ordinarily I would ask for ten as well, but you strike me as friendly and I like to spread good fortune, so for you I would be willing to part with it for eight dinars."

"Eight?" Zahra said, exaggerating her shock. She pointedly looked over its stubby tail and short ears. "This one isn't worth close to that."

The ugly, smelly camel swiveled its head toward her, and its nostrils flared ominously.

"Perhaps just for you, if you don't tell anyone about this deal, I can sell it for seven," Hafiz said.

With no warning, it spat at her and a glob of disgusting goop splashed against her left arm.

Hafiz grimaced. "Perhaps six," he said.

Zahra tried to shake the nasty sputum from her arm. "Ugh. I'll give you one."

"One!" Hafiz held the back of his hand to her forehead. "Are you feeling well, my friend? One? I cannot possibly sell this animal for less than five dinars."

"All I have is one, so that's all I can pay."

"Ah, that is sad. Return when you have more, and perhaps we can speak again, my friend."

"Where am I going to get more? We're in an oasis in the middle of the desert."

"I see your dilemma, I truly do. But sadly, I cannot help. It is good that you are young and in fine health. I cannot tell you how to get more money, but I leave it to your cleverness to figure that out."

Zahra slunk away, dejected. She couldn't even afford a stinky, disfigured, spitting camel. If she'd only had a couple more dinars, she could probably have convinced Hafiz to sell it to her. Of course, she still had to buy food and a container for water. How was she going to earn any money here?

Maybe people were in a better mood now that the sun had risen. There had to be someone she could help for some coin, or a group that would allow her to ride with them.

It had seemed like a good idea to jump off the caravan and look for the Golden Scarab, but now she was wondering if she wouldn't have been better off staying with the wagons until she reached another city.

She was stuck here now.

She made her way around the camps and indeed people greeted her with more politeness, but still no one could give her work and none were journeying in the direction she wanted to go. The young boy she'd spoken with earlier lingered and appeared to be following her, but whenever she turned toward him, he would disappear behind a tree or a tent.

She'd spoken with most of the people in the oasis when she realized she would have no choice soon but to beg. Even that seemed pointless; who would give her even a single dinar, let alone two or three? Maybe she could convince someone to take her with them, anywhere else, even if they weren't going toward the Sands of Fire.

The sun was already heating up the morning, and she returned to the lagoon for a drink. She arrived alongside a middle-aged man who practically collapsed, moaning, at the water's edge, removed his gray headdress and submerged his entire head into the water.

He lifted his head from the lake and stared at the dunes with a haunted look, water dripping down his neatly trimmed beard and mustache. He must have sensed Zahra's gaze, because he slowly swiveled to face her. "Please forgive my behavior, lovely girl. I must look like a wild man to you indeed."

"No, you don't." He did.

"My name is Josef." He splashed more water on his face.

"Zahra."

"Again, forgive me, Zahra. I am a merchant, and one of some fortune, until a few days ago. I was on my way south with my brother when thieves waylaid us in the desert. We fled, and I was separated from my brother and knocked from my horse. The men chased after me and I was forced to run for my life."

He paused to take another drink of water. "I've walked for two days through the desert with no food or water. Now I am blessed to have found this oasis."

His head drooped. "Alas, I have nothing else. Everything is gone—my horse, my money, my provisions. And I know not if my brother still lives."

Zahra considered the poor man. His state was as sorry as hers, though she had at least eaten last night. "That's horrible. I find myself in a similar predicament; here I am, also trapped and alone in this oasis, with next to nothing to call my own."

But she had something Josef did not—one dinar.

She pulled out the coin. "I have only this. Yet I think you're in more need of it now than I am. I need a camel, but this isn't enough to buy one. You need food more than I do, so take it."

"I could not possibly take your last coin, dear girl."

"Please, take it. I'm not hungry right now, and you've been starving for two days."

She held out the coin, and he graciously accepted it. "Bless you, Zahra, bless you. May you be gifted a dozen camels and more. Trust that I will share what I buy with you. Now, forgive me for being impolite, but I really must get something to eat."

Zahra pointed Josef in the direction of someone who could feed him, and he took his leave.

Now she was alone, with not even a dinar in her possession, and with little thought as to what to do next.

"That was really nice of you," a boy's voice called to her from above.

At the top of a palm tree collecting dates was the little boy who'd followed her earlier. "I'm Rafi."

"I'm Zahra."

"I know. I heard you tell him," Rafi said. "I like your eyes."

Her eyes. A rare, smoky gray, they'd always made her feel like she didn't belong, though they also reminded her of her mother, who shared the same trait. "Thank you, little one."

"Are you a princess?"

As bad as Zahra felt, she still had to laugh at that.

"No, Rafi, I'm only a servant." She shook her head. "Not even that anymore."

"You're beautiful," Rafi added. "And you have nice, clean clothes. You *look* like a princess."

A princess. She'd dared hope for that when Maliha had spoken of the magic she could use to charm the prince. It seemed an increasingly silly dream at this point. The prince loved her, it was true, but it was only a false desire.

"That's very nice of you to say, Rafi. I live—I used to live in the palace. This is the standard robe for a servant."

Rafi looked awed. "Then what does the princess wear?"

"There is no princess in Alhad right now, only a prince."

"So you *could* be the princess." He dropped a few more dates into his satchel.

She laughed again. "If I could make it through the Sands of Fire to the Grasping Cliffs, and find the cave that holds the Golden Scarab of Balihar and bring forth the jinni within, maybe I could be." The absurdity of it hit her again.

"I know where the Grasping Cliffs are. I could show you."

CHAPTER 14

"You know where—" Zahra began.

"There you are!" A plump man wearing fine—if old, worn, and undersized—clothes stomped through the sand toward Rafi's tree. "Why are you taking so long?"

"I have to go," Rafi said to Zahra, climbing nimbly down the tree like a monkey. He took a bite from a date and hopped down onto the sand.

"You don't eat before me," the man shouted.

He slapped Rafi hard across his face, knocking the date from the boy's mouth and causing a trickle of blood to drip down his lower lip. The man grabbed Rafi by the ear and hauled him away, thumping him on the head with his other hand. The boy flinched and dumped half of the dates he'd collected.

"I don't need you eating my food, nor wasting time chatting with other people. Remember who it is that you serve. You listen to what I say, and you do what I say." The man trudged back to his tent. "Now pick up those dates you dropped and add them to the basket," he snapped before disappearing inside.

Rafi scrunched up his face to mock his master behind his back, but quickly scooped up the dates and joined the man in the tent.

That poor boy! How could his master hit him merely for eating a few of the dates he'd collected? Even though Zahra had served at the whim of her masters in the Palace of Light, she'd never been treated so badly. Of course, she was friends with Maliha, who'd assigned and overseen most of her work. Still, she'd never seen any of the other servants smacked about the head, either.

Rafi's portly master returned from inside his tent and scooped out a handful of the dates. "Now stay here and finish readying our supplies for the day's journey," he told the boy, before walking off toward the center of the oasis village.

Rafi made another face at his master's back and kicked sand in his direction, but dutifully went about collecting items and organizing them outside the tent.

She couldn't just stand by and see the boy treated like this.

"Rafi," she called as she walked up to him.

His appearance reflected the care of his master: his black hair was dirty and matted, and choppily cut, sticking out in mud-caked spikes in all directions. He wore linen trousers and a shirt that were loosely ill-fitting and filthy, and he smelled of sweat and rosemary.

"I have to finish before he returns, or Master Mustafa will beat me again."

Zahra gritted her teeth in anger.

"I understand," she said. "I'll help you."

Together, they packed up Mustafa's tent and supplies. When they'd finished, Rafi held out a handful of the dates he'd picked.

Zahra took one and popped it into her mouth. The taste and the sweetness triggered a burst of saliva. She'd only ever eaten dried dates and hadn't known how good a fresh one could be. She took another, and then one more, but stopped there—she didn't want to get the boy into any further trouble.

"He doesn't seem like a kind master," she said carefully. "Is there nowhere else you could go? Someone else you could be with?"

"I could go with you!" Rafi said, his eyes lighting up.

"With me? I have nothing to offer you. I don't even know where

I'm going."

She plopped down on a sack they'd just packed.

"You said you were looking for the Grasping Cliffs," Rafi said.

"Yes, but I have neither any means of getting there nor knowledge of where they are."

"I could guide you." He frowned. "But Master Mustafa is leaving today for Alhad, and he would never let me go. Unless..."

"Unless?"

"You help me escape."

Could she take a servant from his master? She thought only for a moment. Of course she could—Mustafa beat him. Rafi deserved a chance for something better. She didn't know if acting as a guide for her foolish quest through the desert was better, but once free he could decide his own course of action.

"Yes, let's go," Zahra said. She took Rafi by the hand, surprised at how calloused his palm was. "Do you have a camel?"

"No, only Master Mustafa rides a camel. He usually makes me walk. Don't you have one?"

"No."

Could they take Mustafa's mount? Freeing Rafi was one thing, but stealing the man's camel in the middle of the desert was another.

No, they'd just have to travel at night when it was cooler.

"We'll need food and water," Zahra said, but Rafi was already on it. He grabbed a basket and handed it to her, and slung a jug of water by its rope handle over his shoulder.

"But how can we escape?" Rafi asked. "He'll send people after me."

The boy was right. Also, if they went into the dunes, anyone could simply follow their footprints. She stared at the island in the center of the lake. Maybe they could swim there and try to hide behind a tree? No, there wouldn't be enough cover, and everybody would see and hear them swimming out there.

She looked from the island to her right, to where the water flowed out of the cliff. There was a nook there the boy could hide behind, but the oasis wasn't large enough to hide in all day. Mustafa would eventually find him.

Zahra scanned the area and noted that another caravan was departing.

"I have an idea. Look there." She pointed to the nook in the cliff face. "You can hide in that alcove. If you walk along the water's edge, your footprints will be washed away."

"People will see me going there," Rafi rightfully pointed out.

"I'll make a distraction, and you go hide. When your master returns, I'll tell him I saw you leaving on that caravan. He'll go riding after it, and—" she trailed off as Josef, the merchant Zahra had given her coin to, walked up to them.

He held up a sack. "I was able to purchase much food, thanks to your generosity. Plenty to share, and with change left over." He presented her with several silver dirhams and copper fals, and then poured them into Zahra's hands.

"I must confess to having overheard your discussion, dear girl," Josef said, running his fingers through his beard. "I may be able to lend some aid to your plan. I would be pleased to provide the distraction you seek, and I'll lend a second voice to your story as to the boy's disappearance if necessary."

"Why would you want to help us?" Zahra asked.

"Why? Do you have to ask? Because you helped *me*, dear girl. I was on the verge of starvation and now I feel like a new man, with a renewed chance at survival. And from the looks of this scruffy boy, I think he would be better off with someone other than his current master."

"So, then, we have a plan." Zahra faced Rafi. "Josef will provide a distraction, you'll hide, and we'll tell your master that you left." She removed some of the food from Mustafa's basket, stuffed it into a smaller pack, and handed it over to the boy. "Here. Take some extra food and water with you."

Rafi draped the sack over his other shoulder.

"Get ready to go," Josef said, walking to the shore of the lake. He kept going, wading up to his thighs, and then shouted "Aaaaaahaaaaa!" and dove into the water, splashing loudly and swimming toward the island.

"Go," Zahra told Rafi.

The boy left, walking casually through the shallow water at the shoreline.

As Josef continued to splash his way toward the island, everyone in the vicinity turned their attention to him and none of them seemed to pay Rafi any notice. Josef walked onto the island and shouted for the people's attention. He asked them if anyone had seen his older, and slightly less handsome, brother. When nobody responded, he shouted for everyone to come join him for a swim. Meanwhile, Rafi continued along and reached the cliff-side spring.

Josef clapped and danced and made sure he had everyone's attention, while the people of the oasis shook their heads and laughed at his antics. A couple of the children swam out to the island to join him. Rafi disappeared into the nook, and Josef dove back into the water again, swimming and splashing his way loudly back to the shore.

Mustafa returned while Josef was still squeezing the water from his clothes. The boy's master looked all around him, fuming.

"Curse that child," he said. "I'll give him a whipping he'll never forget." He stomped around his tent, looking in all directions.

Zahra leaned against a tree and glanced his way, as if his yelling and stamping about had caught her notice.

"You there, girl. Did you see that lazy boy who was loafing about earlier? I swear I'll take a lash to his hide this time."

"The boy picking dates from that tree earlier?" Zahra asked.

"Yes, yes, of course, that's the one. As useful as a three-legged camel, that boy."

"He left—I assumed he had followed you. He walked off with some supplies and joined that caravan earlier."

"What!" Mustafa's eyes bulged and his face reddened, as if he'd suddenly acquired a bad sunburn. "He left?"

"He was carrying a few sacks and seemed to be in a hurry. I thought he was trying to catch up with you."

"But ... but..." Mustafa stammered, spittle flying from his lips. "That caravan's not even going to Alhad!"

"Oh, forgive my ignorance," Zahra said. "I know nothing about the comings and goings here. I'm just passing through myself."

Josef sauntered nearer, confirming Zahra's claim. "Yes, the boy definitely joined that caravan. He practically knocked me over running past."

"I ... I..." Mustafa gave up looking for words and stopped trying to talk. Clearly, he believed them. He rapidly began collecting his things, and tried to carry it all in his hands, repeatedly dropping various items as he struggled toward his camel and loaded it up. Soon he was off and chasing after the caravan.

It had worked!

"Blessings on you, Josef," she said. "May you find your brother alive and well."

"And may you safely make your way to where the winds take you next."

Zahra thanked him again, backing away and smiling. Now to retrieve Rafi and figure out how to get to the Grasping Cliffs. She turned to run and get him.

And plowed right into Prince Amir.

CHAPTER 15

Surprised at being knocked again onto his back, it took Amir a moment to realize the girl who had landed on top of him was Zahra, his sweet love. He'd found her!

When she'd fled the palace and afterwards the city, he'd feared she might get lost or killed in the harsh desert wilderness. What had possessed her to flee like that? She must have known he wouldn't let the vizier or anyone else imprison or hurt her.

Shock overtook her face as she looked down at him. He grinned broadly and reached up to brush sand from her hair. "Is this how you're always going to greet me?"

"I ... are you here to take me to prison?" She pushed herself off of him and got to her feet.

"No, of course not; I would never imprison the one I love. Why would you think such a thing of me?"

"What are you doing here, then?" She looked utterly adorable when her eyebrows wrinkled like that.

"What do you mean? You belong at my side." Wasn't that obvious?

She stared at him, her mouth moving, but no words came out.

It seemed she was so overjoyed at seeing him again that she was speechless. He could understand that.

"Rafi!" she finally said. "I have to get Rafi."

She ran over toward the cliff, called out, and a boy extricated himself from the rocks and joined them.

Amir looked over the oasis in wonder. "Isn't this place amazing?"

"Yes, it sure is something." Zahra's face scrunched up as if she wasn't quite convinced of her own statement.

"I'm amazed," the boy said.

"Who's your little friend?" Amir asked Zahra.

"This is Rafi. He's going to show me how to get to—wait. If you're not here to take me to prison..." She looked around. "Is the vizier with you? Or his guards?"

"Yaseen? No, it's just me. I came to take you back to the palace."

She looked him over and Amir blushed, embarrassed by his current condition. He'd had to dress in servant's clothes to sneak past Yaseen's guards and escape the palace—why the man was so obsessed with keeping him there, he couldn't say—but he'd still brought a bag of dinars with him. Unfortunately, when he'd reached the oasis and tried to pay someone for information about Zahra's whereabouts, he'd promptly been accosted and robbed. They'd even stolen his horse. If he'd had his scimitar, they'd have been lying bloody in the sand.

Zahra touched his cheek below his eye, rubbing her finger along it. "What happened to you?"

Even the hint of pressure from her light touch hurt—he was obviously bruised there—but he enjoyed her caress. He reached up to hold her hand in his, but she pulled it back.

Her face flushed. "This is not appropriate."

"Yes, it is. I love you."

She smiled at his words, and his heart soared with joy.

"No." Her smile drooped. "You don't, not really. You've been put under a love spell." She lowered her eyes. "That lily was enchanted, and you've been made to fall in love with me."

"The lily? Oh, yes." He grasped both of her hands and held them in his. "Yaseen told me; he said you'd put me under a spell, and he tried to convince me my feelings aren't my own. But they are—I love you."

"Isn't that exactly what someone under a love spell would say?" Zahra asked.

He supposed she was right, but he knew his feelings were true. "I may be under a spell, like you say, but that doesn't mean my feelings aren't real. The spell has just made me realize what was already there. It's opened my eyes to the love I had for you already."

Ever since that moment at the palace window where she'd fallen on him, he'd fallen for her. Couldn't she see that?

"I'm Rafi," the young boy spoke up now, a big smile on his face. "I'm Zahra's servant."

"What?" Zahra looked down at him. "You're not my servant."

Rafi frowned. "Why not? You want me to go back to Mustafa?"

"No, of course not. He's a horrible man."

"Then you are my new master," Rafi said, wrapping his arms around her waist. "Who are you?" he asked Amir.

"I'm Prince Amir of Alhad."

"You don't look like a prince," Rafi said.

What did that mean? Who was this mangy little boy?

"Rafi!" Zahra said. "That's not nice."

No, it is not, Amir thought. "I don't look like a prince? You look like a ... dirty little street urchin." Amir wrinkled his nose in disgust.

"You're *mean*." Rafi kicked sand at Amir's feet. "And you're just as dirty as me."

"Ha!" The impertinence of this little rat. The boy had a point, though—he *was* dirty, and he did look rather like a commoner.

"Stop this," Zahra said. "My prince," she added, lowering her eyes again in that adorable way of hers.

"Please, just call me Amir, my love."

Again Zahra flashed that lovely warm smile of hers, only to lose it a moment later. Was she embarrassed about her feelings?

"We need to hide," she said. "Rafi's former master will probably return soon looking for him, and he'll realize I lied to him."

Amir didn't know the situation he'd walked into, but it didn't matter to him at all. He had no need to hide. "I am the prince. Come with me and we'll return to the palace; you may even bring along your new scruffy servant child."

"I'm not a child." Rafi stood tall. "I'm ten years old."

Zahra stepped in front of the boy. "We can't go back there. Yaseen will do anything to see me thrown in prison."

"No. I will not—" Amir began.

"But wait, you're the prince," she cut him off, eyes lighting up. "You can buy us camels, and Rafi and I can go in search of the Golden Scarab of Balihar. He knows the way."

"The Golden Scarab of Balihar?" Rafi and Amir said simultaneously. What was she talking about?

"It's hidden in a cave at the Grasping Cliffs. Inside the Scarab is a jinni; I can use the jinni's magic to break the love spell that is upon you."

"You don't want me to love you?" His gut clenched at the thought.

"No. I mean, yes—I do. That is, I would, but not like this. Your feelings should be your own, not forced by some spell."

"I've told you. My feelings *are* my own." Why wouldn't she believe him?

"I know. I appreciate that you think so, but don't you want to be sure?"

He *was* sure, but her argument was valid. If they broke the spell, he could prove to her that his feelings were real. If finding a jinni and nullifying a spell was what it took to convince her, he'd cross whatever desert and face whatever cliffs stood in the way. He'd do anything for her.

"You're right; let's get this jinni, and break the spell, and I'll show you I still love you, and then we'll go home and I'll tell my father I've chosen my bride."

And there was her dazzling smile again. "But you can't go," she said. "It's not safe. I'm probably going to die in the desert searching for a treasure that doesn't even exist. You should return to Alhad."

The thought of her dying stunned him. "Nonsense. Where you go, I go. I can't let you take on something so dangerous alone."

"She won't be alone. I'll be with her," Rafi said.

"That's comforting,"—it wasn't, at all—"but I'm still going."

"Great," Rafi said, looking completely unconvinced of that. "Well, let's get some camels and get going before Mas—before Mustafa comes back."

Zahra led them to Hafiz, the camel merchant she'd spoken to earlier.

"He has only two camels," Amir said. "Looks like the slovenly boy will have to remain behind after all."

Zahra cast him a withering look. Why did she like that little scamp so much? "Alright, we'll figure it out somehow."

When Amir tried to use his privilege as the Prince of Alhad, the merchant Hafiz only stared at him, unimpressed.

"I only take dinars, your wonderfulness," Hafiz said, in a highly disrespectful, mocking tone. "Although you look quite ... prince-ly,"—his disgusted look showed otherwise—"I'm afraid I will need more than your word and the word of this lost girl."

One of Hafiz's camels, the ugly one with malformed features and a stripe down its neck, looked over their group as if it wanted nothing to do with them. Its nostrils flared, and it spat at Zahra.

"Again?" she yelled, wiping the sputum from her sleeve. "I hate that thing. I wouldn't ride it if you paid *me*!"

"Control your disgusting beast!" Amir shouted. "May it lose the rest of its tail and ears for befouling my beautiful Zahra."

The merchant huffed. "He doesn't like you," Hafiz said. "I don't like you either. Best fortune in finding mounts elsewhere, oh wonderful prince." He shooed them away.

The audacity of the man—how dare he treat the Prince of Alhad in such a demeaning way.

"Now what?" Rafi said, as they trudged off. "If we have to walk to the Cliffs, it's going to take forever, and the dunes get really hot."

"We should travel at night," Zahra said.

Just as they'd all agreed that it was a good idea, Amir noticed a group of Yaseen's guards arriving at the oasis. Why couldn't the vizier just let him be?

"There." He pointed them out to Zahra. "Yaseen's men are looking for me."

"Or they're here to arrest me," she said. "Or leave me somewhere in the desert to die."

Amir would never allow that to happen. "They wouldn't. While you're with me, you have nothing to fear, my love."

He reached out to caress the lovely curve of her soft cheek. She touched and held his hand there for a moment, before gently lowering it from her face with a sad smile.

"That may be, but we should still avoid them," she said. "With you under this spell, they may not listen to you."

Again, she was right—not only beautiful, but wise.

Rafi led the three of them around to the other side of the oasis, toward the dunes. Wardens of the oasis village patrolled its borders. Apparently, word had already spread of the search for the prince.

Amir was tempted to walk straight by the wardens, daring them to stop him, but due to his current appearance, he knew they wouldn't respect his authority any more than the camel merchant had.

"They probably have our descriptions," Zahra said.

"Still," Amir said, "we'll have a better chance talking our way past those men than Yaseen's guards, who will certainly recognize me. And probably you, too," he added.

They agreed to let Rafi lead them, since the searchers wouldn't know about him and may not think to look for three travelers together. Rafi handed the pack of food to Zahra and led them away from the lake, toward the desolate golden dunes.

An oasis guard looked Zahra over. "Hold there—you look like someone the sultan of Alhad is searching for."

Amir thought about what he'd said earlier. They might indeed be looking for him as well, but his hair was loose and wild, and he looked so dirty and unkempt in his old shoddy clothing that it made sense they wouldn't recognize him. Zahra still looked every bit as lovely as she had in the Palace of Light. Of course they'd have spotted her.

How could they get her out of here now?

Amir improvised. "The sultan is looking for my sister?"

"What does he want with our sister?" Rafi added. The boy was quick; Amir had to give him that.

And then someone else spoke behind them. "Yes, what could the sultan possibly want with my daughter?"

Amir turned around and took a quick look at the man who'd joined them. His clothes were damp—had he gone swimming?—and his hair and beard were a mess, but he was about the same age as the sultan, so he could pass as their father.

"He must be looking for someone else," the newcomer continued. "We're just a poor family and have never met any royalty. Now, we have miles still to travel, and they're not pleasant miles, so we'd like to carry on our journey."

"You're going to walk through the dunes? During the day? In the height of summer?" the guard asked, looking more concerned than suspicious now.

"We've not much choice. We were overtaken by Bedouin bandits, who stole all our horses. We're to meet my sister in Alcuri in but two days, so as I said we've miles to go, and they won't be pleasant."

The guard nodded. "Luck and blessings upon you," he said, waving them on and out into the hot, flowing sands.

CHAPTER 16

Z ahra's heartbeat slowed considerably as soon as they'd crossed over the first dune, leaving sight of the oasis.

"Blessings upon you for your help, Josef," she said.

"Why did you tell him we're going to Alcuri?" Rafi asked him.

"To throw them off your trail," Josef clarified. "Don't want them knowing where you're *actually* headed."

"Oh, that's smart."

"Who *is* this man?" Amir asked Zahra.

"He's Josef," Rafi answered for her, as if that explained everything.

"I am a fellow traveler, in my own sort of trouble," Josef said. "I heard the men from Alhad asking about someone matching Zahra's description, and a young man matching yours." He pointed to Amir. "I don't know what trouble you're in, Zahra, but I know you're a good person."

"Thank you for saying that," she said. "You arrived just in time—oh, and this is Prince Amir of Alhad."

"The prince himself? That explains their interest in you. I'll bet there's an interesting story here."

Zahra briefly explained to him their situation and their mission to find the Golden Scarab. "We're headed through the Sands of Fire."

Josef looked around. Sandy desert surrounded them on all sides. "It appears, then, that I travel with you, dear girl."

She would love to have him along, but she didn't want to drag anyone else into her dangerous quest. "You should return to the oasis and start searching for your brother."

"We weren't traveling to the oasis when we were accosted, and I haven't the means to search. Besides, I don't yet have a plan for reconnecting with him. In the meantime—though I think perhaps your goal is a bit … optimistic—I've learned that such journeys often lead to the most interesting outcomes. If you'll have me, I'll join you and see where your search takes you."

We can use any help we can get.

They agreed he could accompany them, and began their slog through the shifting sands. Climbing the dunes was a struggle, as each footfall slid back downhill. Going down the other side was fun at first: Zahra, Rafi, and Amir took great leaping strides and hopped and skidded their way down, while Josef took a calmer, steadier descent. Then they'd have to go back up another dune, stepping up and sliding back, stepping up and sliding back again.

Soon Zahra was tired, then weary, and finally exhausted. As the sun rose, the heat stole away their energy, until all they could manage was a series of slow, short steps, one after the other, shuffling their way through the seemingly unending sands.

They stopped briefly at midday for a break and some food, as well as much-needed water, before continuing their sweltering march through the desert. Zahra could detect no discernible landmarks, and the trek grew torturous as her legs burned from the effort and the heat beat down upon her. She should have fought against Amir joining them; no prince should be subjected to this suffering. And yet every time she met his gaze, he put on the same brave, yet silly, love-stricken smile.

She wanted to believe him, that his feelings for her were real, that maybe this could all work out and her impossible fantasies could come true.

As they reached the top of another dune, she paused to catch her breath. "Rafi, you were right—the Sands of Fire are scorching hot."

"We haven't reached the Sands of Fire yet."

"*What?*" All this way and they weren't even at the Sands yet? Josef and Amir's faces fell and their shoulders slumped.

"Are you sure we're going the right way?" Zahra asked.

The boy nodded, sweat pouring from his brow. "Do you see the mountain over there?"

She looked where he was pointing. Was there a mountain there? "Yes?"

"We're getting closer."

She hoped he wasn't just seeing what he wanted to.

As the sun descended lower toward the horizon and they crested another dune, he shouted, "There! The Sands of Fire."

He was right: the dunes diminished finally and leveled out into a long valley that gave way to harder earth, edged to the north and east by strange cliffs. Reddish-orange columns of rock jutted up from sands the color of a deep, rich ocher. The rocks looked like they'd been sculpted, with smoothly worn protrusions and twists, like tall static flames rising from the searing desert. The intense shimmering heat radiating off the sands combined with the flaring colors of an impending sunset to amplify the effect.

"Wow," Amir said. "I've never seen anything like this."

Nor had Zahra. She'd had no idea something so unique and wondrous existed. They took in the fiery valley below for a few minutes. It had taken them all day to get here, but they'd made it.

Rafi broke their reverie and ran down the dune and into the Sands of Fire. Zahra herself found a renewed burst of energy and bounded after him. In the valley she paused, marveling at a stone pillar. A swirl of colors along its length—turmeric, saffron, and burnt sienna—truly made it resemble flame. Its surface was worn sandstone, gritty and hard, and it rose twenty feet into the air.

Zahra rubbed her fingers along its rough surface, expecting it to crumble or wear off, but it remained firm.

Rafi clambered up. "Mustafa never stopped to let me climb these."

The boy was a natural climber and scrambled upwards with ease.

Josef pointed into the distance. "Sandstorm. We must find shelter soon."

A dark cloud was approaching from beyond the far cliffs. Zahra called up to the boy: "He's right, Rafi. A sandstorm approaches; please come down from there."

"Awww." Rafi had nearly reached the top, but he obediently worked his way back down and hopped to the ground.

Eyes now on the ominous sky, Zahra hurried onward. Though they'd left the dunes, and the ground was firmer and had mostly leveled out, the sand still limited their pace. The storm's swift approach unsettled her, and the wind picked up, further impeding their progress. They needed to go faster.

"Quickly, run to the cliffs," Josef said.

Zahra didn't think they'd make it, but once the ground transitioned from sand to hard-packed earth their progress increased significantly, to the point where they started jogging. Her whole body ached from the journey, but they couldn't risk getting caught out in the open.

Soon the winds blew in gusts, and then in gales, whipping up the stinging sand and making it hard to see without covering her eyes.

"Line up and hold on to each other," Josef shouted from the rear.

Zahra grabbed onto Rafi's shoulders in front of her. When Amir grasped her about the waist, her abdomen tightened reflexively. A pleasant tingle shot through her, but now was not the time to consider that feeling.

The hot wind blasted their faces, forcing them to continue with their heads down. Zahra squeezed her eyes shut, hoping Rafi could maintain their direction and reach the cliff before the sharp sands shredded them. It felt like needles pricking her skin, over and over.

The boy proved reliable. After only a few minutes, the force and the howl of the wind ebbed as they reached the cliff. Rafi led them along the foot of it until they found a shallow cave to shelter in and wait out the terrible storm. Zahra covered her head as best she could, the sand still whirling around and pelting her even inside their protective recess.

She pulled Rafi close to protect him from the whipping sands as much as possible. The boy wrapped his arms around her and pushed his face against her side, while she pressed against Amir, aware that it was horribly inappropriate for her to be touching the prince like this. Despite having broken the taboo of making close contact with him, she couldn't deny the thrill of feeling his body against hers.

She was glad no one could see the flush on her face. Was he thinking of her right now? Was there any chance that he truly did love her—or even like her enough that love could become a possibility?

Her intrusive thoughts faded as they waited out the storm, everyone remaining silent as the winds howled around them. After an hour spent cowering in their protective recess, they saw the sandstorm had passed, but night had fallen.

When they'd shaken themselves mostly clean of sand, Josef said, "We should settle down here for the night and search in the morning."

Exhausted from the day's journey, they all agreed and nestled down at the base of the cliff.

At dawn, they rose with the sun and ate quickly, eager to start their hunt for the scarab.

Zahra retrieved her map. "According to this, the Golden Scarab lies within a cave near here. The map shows the Sands of Fire and the Grasping Cliffs..."

She looked up and along the rocky wall. She hadn't noticed as she'd squinted through wind and sand upon their approach the day prior, but now the reason for the name of the cliffs was clear:

the rock face was segmented into vertical sections, and the whole cliff curved up and out, reaching over a hundred feet high. It gave the appearance of a long line of ribs, or of stone fingers reaching up from the ground and curling out.

"All I see are small depressions in the rock, like the one we took refuge in," Amir said.

Hours ticked by as they carefully walked along the base of the cliff. Nothing stood out.

"Ulnar said he searched every cave along these cliffs," Zahra said, feeling dejected.

"We'll just have to search even more." Amir leaned close to her.

The prince reached out; her breath caught. Was he going to take hold of her hand? Instead, Amir pressed a finger to the map. "What's this about a scar?"

Zahra shook her head. "A break in the cliff, maybe?"

She scanned along the face and then to the east, where the cliffs turned and veered south. "Is that a crack? There, near the end of the cliffs?"

"Looks like it," Amir said.

Josef turned to face back in the direction from which they'd traveled the day before. "I think we have company."

Amir groaned. "People on camels—must be Yaseen's men. And there's no place to hide here."

Flame! Not now. They'd come all this way, and they were still being pursued by the vizier's men?

"Come on, we have to find the cave," Zahra said.

She ran straight toward the crack in the Grasping Cliffs. It meant passing through a section of the Sands of Fire again, but they didn't have the luxury of following the curve of the escarpment. Amir was right on her heels, with Rafi and Josef catching up.

Yaseen's men spotted them and started their way down into the valley.

They had to find this cave, and fast. Panic rose within her. How would they discover what Ulnar couldn't find, when he'd had all the time he needed?

What if they could win themselves more time?

"Prince Amir, you should go back with the vizier's men. Leave us to find the Scarab, and I will return to free you from the spell."

Amir stopped and placed his hands on her shoulders, holding her in a firm, commanding grip. There was that tingle in her chest again. "My love, I will never leave your side. Our fates are connected. What sort of man would I be if I abandoned you here in the desert? And please, you may call me simply Amir. I am the kingdom's prince, but I am your Amir."

Rafi ran past them. "You're going to get us caught if you don't keep moving."

Zahra checked on the progress of the approaching guards. The lead rider came to an abrupt halt and stopped the others. He reached into his pack and raised a lengthy horn to his lips. Was that Yaseen? She couldn't tell from here.

"What's he *doing*?" Rafi asked.

The man blew a long, deep note, and then a second guard joined him, using a horn of his own. The sound of the notes blended together and seemed to reverberate through the valley. The hair on Zahra's neck lifted.

This couldn't be good.

A wind stirred again amid the stone flames of the Sands, and soon it was swirling in place.

"I don't like this," Rafi said.

Zahra agreed with his sentiment. "Me neither. Go! As fast as you can!"

They redoubled their efforts and pressed on through the thick sand. In the space between them and Yaseen's men, the wind continued to spin faster and faster until it had formed a frenzied whirlwind. A loud, banshee-like scream echoed through the valley. The whirlwind had formed into a dust demon. The thin funnel of whipping sands extended high above the valley, spinning in place. Then another blast from a horn sounded, and the leader of the men pointed to Zahra and her small group.

The dust demon zigzagged its way through the Sands of Fire,

steadily closing on their position.

"Run!" Zahra yelled.

They pushed ahead as fast as they could toward the break in the cliff. Zahra hoped it was the scar mentioned on the map.

The closer they got, the more concerned she became. There was no sign of any cave along the surface of the bluff.

"Does anyone see a cave?" she shouted over the screaming wind of the dust demon.

"I see nothing," Josef yelled back.

"Me neither," Rafi chimed in.

As they came directly in line with the "scar," Zahra felt a strange rippling sensation in the sands beneath her. "What was that?" she asked. "Did anyone else feel it?"

Nobody seemed to have heard her over the howl of the dust demon, which was now almost upon them. Her heart pounded as sand whipped at her flesh again. They had to get out of here—only there was no escape. They wouldn't even make it to the scar-like fissure before the magical whirlwind reached them.

What did the map say? *Along the Cliffs behold the scar...* These are the Cliffs, and there's the scar. What were they supposed to get from that? *The sultans see and the sultans land...* What did that mean?

"There!" Amir yelled, his voice barely pushing past the shriek of the wind. "The cave! It's not in the cliff! It's in the sand." He pointed at the ground dead ahead.

What was he looking at? There was nothing there but the same sand they were standing on, which was being lashed against their skin by the dust demon that would be on them in seconds. "I see nothing."

The earth rippled beneath her once more. Had the vizier's men also summoned an earthquake?

"It's right there!" Amir shouted. "Come here."

Amir grabbed her hand. At his touch, the ground in front of her wavered like a mirage, revealing an opening in the sand that hadn't been there an instant ago. "I see it."

Amir released her and the opening vanished. She must need to be in contact with him to see it. She took hold of him again and grabbed Rafi with her other hand and pulled.

"Grab onto me," she called to Josef.

The older man stepped toward them and reached out, but the dust demon had arrived. Its gale pulled at Josef, sucking him back, his hair and clothes stretching out taut behind him.

Amir pulled Zahra ahead and she in turn dragged Rafi along, and they slid downward, into the sand, as if they were being swallowed.

"*Josef!*" she yelled.

Josef closed his eyes and shouted, "Go!"

Zahra watched in horror as the older man was yanked from his feet and lifted high into the air.

"Josef!" Zahra called again in despair, knowing there was nothing they could do for him.

She slid down the hole and tumbled into a pile of sand in the cave as the entrance closed above them.

CHAPTER 17

D arkness.

Zahra got to her feet and reached around, waiting for her eyes to adjust.

"Where are we?" Rafi asked, confused.

"Under the sands," Amir responded.

This must be the cave they'd been searching for. No wonder Ulnar had never found it; it wasn't in the cliffs at all. What had the writing on the map said? *The wondrous cave of the Fiery Sand.* "Of" the Fiery Sand. The riddle had never said the cave was in the cliffs—they'd just assumed that, as had everyone else who'd searched for the Scarab, no doubt.

Had the cave opened itself for Amir? He had been the first to spot it. She hadn't seen it at all until she was touching him. *The sultans see and the sultans land.* The entrance to the cave must only be visible to a sultan, or to the son of one at least. No wonder Ulnar hadn't found the entrance.

"I see something," Amir said.

He was right—the cave wasn't completely dark. Patches of softly glowing lichen adorned the walls, and vines with globe-like fruits providing a green luminescence grew along the floor. Every so often, the globes dimmed to black before immediately brightening again.

"Where is Josef?" Rafi said, concern in his voice.

Zahra pulled him close. "I couldn't grab him in time. He was pulled away."

"Does that mean...?" Rafi couldn't finish his question, but Zahra knew what he was asking.

She nodded, and Rafi wrapped his arms around her waist.

The boy sniffled. "He helped us."

"I know, I know." Zahra patted him on the back.

Amir clenched his jaw. "He didn't deserve that. I'll have words with Yaseen when we return home."

Zahra tried to offer some hope. "Maybe he got away."

"I hope so," Rafi said. "You won't leave me, will you?"

"No, of course not." She hugged the boy tight. A memory came unbidden into her mind of hugging her mother for the last time, just before the vizier pulled her from her mother's embrace and into the Palace of Light. Zahra's stomach dropped as she relived that moment of loss, the moment of her mother turning and leaving. That feeling of abandonment still ached inside of her.

"No, I won't leave you." She wiped a tear from her eye. She bore the responsibility for the boy, now, and wouldn't let him down.

Amir cleared his throat.

"Yes," Zahra said. "Josef helped us get here, and now we have to do what we came for."

"Find the Scarab?" Rafi asked.

"That's right."

Zahra wiped her face and shook the sand from her hair. The stuff had gotten everywhere—in her clothes, in her ears, even in her mouth. She could feel granules crunching in her teeth and tried to spit them out, with only partial success.

"Check the map," Amir suggested.

She unrolled the parchment, but the soft glow from the plants provided too scant a light to read it. Not that it mattered—she'd memorized everything written and drawn on it, and nothing gave any clue after reaching the cave.

Rafi pointed. "There's new writing there. On the back."

Zahra flipped over the map. The boy was right—there was something visible now.

"Sharp eyes, Rafi," she complimented him.

"Well, I was the one who suggested looking at the map," Amir said.

Was the prince jealous of Rafi? How cute.

The letters on the back of the map were too faint to make out. Maybe if they had more light. She brought the map closer to a glowing fruit, and as she did so, the writing became thicker and sharper until it was easily readable.

Lack of sight, It takes a bite, Nothing can you fight
Uncontrolled, Vines foretold, Now face the stranglehold
The goal will fly, Low becomes high, Before the watchful eye
Nab the gold, Wings unfold, The jinni you'll behold

"What does it all mean?" Amir asked.

Zahra shook her head. "Hopefully it'll make more sense when we continue on."

Their footsteps echoed as they walked, giving Zahra the feeling that they weren't alone. Who else could possibly be in here with them? She stopped the others for a moment to listen, but heard nothing. Still, when they started again, she had a distinct sense they were being watched. She could have sworn the globe fruits shifted like eyes to follow their movements.

The cave meandered before bending sharply to the right. When they turned the corner, the passage narrowed to a corridor leading to another chamber beyond. Stalactites grew down from the ceiling of the hallway, and stalagmites rose from the rock of the floor. Some type of viscous, oozing liquid dripped down each of the protrusions above.

Amir reached up to a stalactite. "What is this goo?"

As soon as his hand touched it, the rock shifted. A loud grating sound crackled through the air. The stalactite grew, extending downward in an instant. It shot all the way to the cave floor, nearly impaling his foot. He lurched backward, bumping into a stalagmite, which likewise shot upward to the ceiling. Yelping in surprise, he rolled away.

Two more sharp sounds rang out as the two spiky rock formations retreated to their original positions.

Rafi, mouth dropped open, turned to Zahra. "We have to go through *there?*"

She swallowed, but tried her best to sound reassuring. "It's not that far. Just ... be careful not to touch anything that sticks out and you should be fine."

Amir stared down the corridor. Ooze dripped from the stalactites and hung down from the roof of the cave. He took a tentative step between the sharp protrusions before moving back again. "I think the boy should go first."

Zahra glared at the prince.

Amir put on an innocent face. "He could go through and then tell us what's on the other side."

Zahra continued to glare. "We all have to get through there, anyway."

"Alright, alright," Amir finally capitulated. "I'll go."

He gingerly navigated his way along the corridor, moving back and forth to stay as far away from the formations as he could.

"Follow my steps," Zahra told Rafi, as she began working her way through.

With the limited light, she was worried about accidentally bumping a rock and getting skewered, especially during those moments when the globes dimmed and left them in near darkness.

And then it got worse. Long strands of slime stretched down from above, like a thick, sticky mucus. She tried her best to avoid the stringy goop, but quickly realized there was no evading it without risking impalement. A thin slimy strand of it dribbled against her face and clung to her, slowly sliding down her cheek like a slug leaving a trail. She tried to wipe it away but only succeeded at catching more of the stuff on her arm.

Gross. She wanted to shriek and run. Instead, she closed her eyes and froze. More of the gooey substance dripped onto her, into her hair, and then down along her left ear.

"Zahra," Amir called from up ahead.

She opened her eyes and saw that he'd made it through. She took a deep breath and was about to take another step forward when a sharp snapping sound came from behind and Rafi bumped into her, screaming.

"Ahhh!" she screamed in turn and took off running, ignoring the slime and dodging the stalagmites. Rafi kept pace, the pointed columns of rock snapping up and down all around them.

She tripped over a small stalagmite near the end of the passage and toppled forward.

Amir caught her mid-fall and pulled her toward him, just as the fang of rock cracked up into the ceiling behind her. Rafi dove to the side, narrowly avoiding it as he skidded to safety beside them.

Amir lifted Zahra to her feet and wiped the slime from her face and hair. "Are you alright, my love?"

My love. She lost herself for a moment in his eyes. He really should stop saying that, but she didn't want him to.

"Don't worry about me. I'm fine," Rafi said, hopping back to his feet.

"Yes, me too." Zahra broke eye contact with Amir and rose. The prince was under a spell—she had to keep reminding herself of that.

Rafi pointed to the nearest stalagmite that had recently settled back to its original size. Impaled atop it, one of his satchels had flopped open and poured out some of their bread and dates. "They're like teeth, trying to bite us."

Lack of sight, it takes a bite. Luckily, none of them had been bitten.

"Let's continue on," Zahra said.

They had to get the Scarab, release the jinni, break the spell on the prince, and then ... what? Then the sultan would hail her as a hero and give her whatever she wanted? Amir would actually be in love with her and they'd get married, and she'd be the princess? Yes, that was it. That was the dream she chose to imagine for now.

As they started down the passageway, the air stirred. It turned to a breeze, and as it brushed past them a voice was carried on the wind.

"...wwwhy are you hhhere, son of the sultannn..."

Zahra spun about, looking for the speaker, but nobody was there. Who had said that? Amir and Rafi looked equally unsettled.

The air shifted to a breeze again. "...wwwhy are you here, son of the sultaaan..." said the voice in the wind, like a drawn-out whisper.

"Who's there? How do you know who I am?" Amir said.

A breeze... "yyyou have the blood of Alhad, passed down through generations... wwwhy are you heeere..."

Zahra felt compelled to answer, because she was the one who'd brought them here. "We seek the Golden Scarab of Balihar."

"...thhhe Scarab is here, but the jinni Nadim wishes to remain undisturbed ... you should leeeave..."

Zahra lifted her head assertively. "We can't turn back now."

"...iiis this your desire as well, Prince of Alhaaad...?"

Amir stepped toward Zahra. "Yes, we will continue."

"...iiit is folly ... the Scarab will not be taken easilyyyy ... you have been waaarned..."

The three of them looked at each other.

"Are we sure about this?" Rafi asked.

Zahra was resolute. Some cave wind voice wasn't going to stop them. "It's just trying to scare us off because we're getting close. Let's go."

Ahead of them the passage narrowed again, and the vines that stretched along the floor, walls, and ceiling of the cavern had thickened and spread across the corridor. Each vine splayed into segments that wove between the others, giving the impression of arms reaching out and interlocking their fingers to block the group's progress. The passageway was completely sealed off.

"I wish I had my sword," Amir said, not for the first time.

"Or some fire," Rafi added.

"Well, let's get to clearing it away," Amir said, walking with Rafi toward the interlaced vines.

Hadn't the map said something about this?

"Wait!" Zahra ran to stop them, but she was too late.

As soon as Amir grabbed hold of the first vine, it snapped out and twisted around his arm, pulling him forward. He braced himself and struggled against its grip, but his feet slid along the cave floor as he was dragged into the other tendrils. Rafi was likewise caught in their grasp, and soon both of them were struggling against a writhing mass that was entangling them.

"Master Zahra, help!" Rafi called.

She ran toward him and extended her arm. "Here, grab hold."

Rafi reached out and clutched her forearm. She braced herself and tugged, pulling him a few inches, but a jerk from the plants yanked him back harder.

"Hold tight," she told the boy, and he did.

That ended up drawing her closer to the mass of creepers. Amir, almost completely wrapped in vines, reached out for help and caught hold of her other arm, and she was hauled into their midst. The vines snaked around her limbs, and she quickly became just as ensnared as the other two were.

Her legs and her torso were pulled into the twisting vegetation, followed by her head and face, and then a tendril wrapped around her neck.

CHAPTER 18

Zahra struggled to breathe. She fought against the tendrils with all her might, but they were just too strong. Amir and Rafi squirmed beside her, their situation as dire as hers.

"Take my hand," Amir called to her.

He must have an idea. She stretched her arm to the side and shifted it around until she found his arm again. He grasped her fingers tightly.

"Now what?" she gasped.

"If I die," Amir groaned, "I just wanted to be holding your hand."

Ugh! Not helpful.

The vine around her throat was cutting off her air supply. She turned her chin toward her shoulder, relieving the pressure on the front of neck. That gave her a chance to take a big breath.

Think, think, think.

The warning in the wind, the map, the riddle...

Uncontrolled... Vines foretold... Now face the stranglehold.

The vines were out of control. Great—that didn't help at all. And they were in a stranglehold, alright. Also not helpful. Zahra gasped for breath and shifted again, turning to her opposite side. The pressure on her throat eased, the vine pressing now into the side of her neck.

Face the stranglehold. What if...

She twisted her body more, wriggling to turn around. The coiling plants pulled her tight, but now more against her side, and then her back, as she rotated to face fully into the mass. Again she could hardly breathe, not from being strangled, but from having her face covered in creepers.

Could this be right? Were they supposed to face directly into the stranglehold?

Her arms were constricted against her chest. She pushed them forward, trying to reach beyond the wall of coiling plant tendrils. She squeezed her hands through an opening here, and a gap there. And then suddenly they broke free.

"Turn around," she tried to tell the other two, though it came out more like "Tmm ar-umm."

She stretched out more, her arms flailing, looking for anything to grab hold of, to latch onto something to pull her out of this nightmare of leaves and bark. Her fingers brushed against something. She lengthened her reach and wrapped her fingers around...

Another vine.

Oh no, not more vines.

But this one was pulling her forward, out past the mass they were stuck in. Another coil grabbed onto her wrist. Soon there was a tug-of-war, the tendrils ahead pulling her forward while the ones wrapped around her fought to keep her in place.

Maybe she could use them against each other.

Zahra tugged hard, yanking the new vines into the clump she was stuck in. She maneuvered her grip and attached the distant vine to one that was holding her. She grabbed another from afar and pulled it near her head, freeing up space and giving her room to breathe. And speak.

"Face into the vines and reach forward," she said, hoping Rafi and Amir could hear her. "Pull the other vines into these."

Zahra yanked more and more of the helpful tendrils toward the strangling ones that were clutching her. With each one, the tension around her body eased. Rafi and Amir were doing the same. Before long, she'd created enough of a battle between the two sets of vines that the ones wrapped around her creaked as they were being pulled back and away, slowly opening and revealing a brighter light from the cavern beyond.

Her strength waned. Her arms were burning, inside and out. She couldn't overpower even a single vine. Next to her, Amir was making steady progress, tearing at one tendril after another until he'd pushed through and lunged free. He turned back and grabbed hold of her. She finally broke free of the last vine at her waist and lurched against the prince, his arms wrapping protectively around her. Gasping, she met his gaze and their eyes locked. He'd saved them.

"Help!" Rafi's muffled squeak came from within the twisted mass behind her.

Ducking to avoid getting herself entangled again, she grasped the boy and quickly helped him escape.

"'Now face the stranglehold'," Amir rasped, rubbing at his neck.

Rafi rested on his hands and knees and inhaled deep breaths. Zahra checked her own skin and then examined her companions. Other than a few scrapes and abrasions, they were unharmed.

They'd been lucky.

"What ... are we ... doing here?" she said, heaving deep breaths. "I'm sorry ... I dragged you two into this."

"Why?" Rafi asked. "This is fun."

The boy had a strange idea of fun. "We almost died, Rafi."

"But we made it. You got us through."

"We may not make it past the next obstacle," Zahra said. "Maybe we should turn back. I'd feel horrible if either of you two got hurt."

Like Josef.

"No, let's go on," Rafi said. "I'll be fine."

"We've come this far," Amir said. "We should see it through."

Zahra was willing to risk her own life, but what about the lives of a young boy and the Prince of Alhad? Still, it was their choice. Or was it? Rafi was only ten years old, and the prince was so beguiled he'd follow her anywhere.

Amir walked ahead. "Forward."

Rafi took Zahra's hand and pulled her after him. "Come on."

She was grateful for their commitment, but was it fair to look past her responsibility here? She'd pulled Rafi away from his previous life. Sure, his master had indeed been cruel, but the boy might easily die on this foolish journey and it would be her fault entirely.

Then again, she couldn't make them go back unless she went with them—and probably not even then. Besides, where could they return? To the cave entrance that was sealed shut? Zahra hoped they'd find an alternate exit ahead.

She followed them into the open space of the next cavern. Her jaw dropped at the sight of the vast chamber they had entered. The cave stretched over a hundred feet across and was more than fifty feet high. The vines had become nearly as thick as her legs and their orb-fruits were the size of her head. The strange plants wound along every surface of the chamber, including the ceiling, their fruits providing an eerie green glow throughout the majestic cavern. Hopefully, these creepers wouldn't attack them like the others had.

The air felt thicker here, more humid, and smelled of rich earth and mustiness.

In the center of the chamber, layers of rock formed a dais, and a spiraling mass of root-like tendrils from overhead draped down to a tapered point just above it. She caught a glint of gold at the tip of the roots hanging over the dais.

"*The Scarab*..." She breathed it more than said it.

"You're right." Amir started forward, Rafi on his heels.

As Zahra followed, something moved in the corner of her vision. Halfway up a section of the cave wall, a thick draping of vines creaked as they peeled apart to reveal a large circular indentation nearly twice her height. There was a quick, wet swishing sound, and the bulbous glowing orbs all dimmed, casting the room into darkness.

Zahra held her breath. What now?

The globes re-illuminated in time with another whoosh, and Zahra saw that the circular area on the cavern wall had become an enormous eye—an actual eye, ten feet high, and set into the rock of the cave.

Zahra stared at the eye. It stared back.

"What is *that*?" Amir asked.

"An eye," Rafi pointed out the obvious.

"Why is there a giant eye in the wall of a cave?"

Rafi shrugged. "Why is there a cave that talks?"

A breeze blew. "...yyyour prize awaaaits..." the cave said. "...iiif you can claim iiit..."

They crept forward, approaching the dais with great caution. There it was—the Golden Scarab of Balihar. It was real. They'd found it!

The Scarab hung from the end of a long, broad vine-root descending from above. On the dais below it there was a marble carving of a black-and-white-striped snake, coiled but extended upward, its jaws opened wide as if about to eat the Scarab.

This has the feeling of another test.

Amir stepped up to the dais, but the Golden Scarab was just out of his reach. The eye on the cave wall moved, its lids opening wider and its thin-slitted pupil expanding. Amir shifted up onto the dais, his left hand about to press down on—

"No, wait!" Zahra reached out.

Amir's hand landed on the snake. The serpent's marbled surface transformed to scales, and the coils writhed beneath his fingers. Its jaws snapped shut and its head rotated to face him.

"Agh!" Amir pushed away just as the snake struck.

The creature's jaws snapped shut an inch from his face, as Amir's foot caught in a vine and he fell hard on his back. The snake coiled back up on the dais, its head swiveling back and forth between Amir, Zahra, and Rafi.

CHAPTER 19

*N*ot another snake.

Zahra recalled her encounter in the bazaar with Jabari and the cobra; it gave her an idea. She walked around to the opposite side of the dais, the snake's attention following her. "You distract it," she said.

"Alright," Amir said. "Rafi, come distract the snake."

"Me?" Rafi whimpered. "I'm not a prince."

Zahra didn't fully understand Rafi's logic, though she appreciated his reluctance. Wasn't Amir supposed to be the adult? How could he ask the boy to put himself in so much danger? "Amir!" she snapped at the prince.

Amir frowned, his eyes lowering. "Yes, my love."

He closed on the dais again, this time kicking at the layers of rock composing its base. The snake whipped around to face him. "Agh!" he shouted again, backing up hastily.

Zahra lashed out and wrapped her fingers around the snake's neck, just as she'd done with Jabari's cobra. The thing hissed at her, and its body pulled up off the dais to coil around her arm.

Amir stared at her, his eyes bulging. "I didn't know you were

119

going to grab it!"

She tried to pull it off her arm with her other hand, but it was wrapped too tightly. "Amir, help me remove it and I'll throw it over there."

He eased his way toward her, obviously nervous about approaching the creature again.

It opened its mouth and hissed sharply as he got close, so Zahra pressed down on the top of its head with her thumb to close its mouth. As soon as she'd done so, it transformed, shrinking and changing into a sort of beaded black and white piece of jewelry that wrapped around her forearm beneath her robe, inert once again.

The pupil of the cave's eye shrank back down to a slit. The eye blinked, making that whooshing sound, and the globes momentarily went dark again, before lighting back up as the eye swished open again.

Amir regarded her new jewelry. "So ... is it safe?"

Zahra looked down at her arm. Even the head of the snake had retreated to rest along her wrist. "I think so."

She didn't like the idea of having a magical snake attached to her body, though. She reached with her other hand again to take it off, but as soon as she brushed its head, the snake transformed once more, regaining its slithery living form, still firmly encircling her arm. She quickly tapped on its head, and it again became merely jewelry. "I'll just let it be for now."

"Good choice," Amir said.

"Wow," Rafi said. "I want to see." The boy reached out to touch Zahra's new accessory.

She pushed away his hand. "No, don't, it's dangerous."

"But it's beautiful. And it comes alive."

"And it's a potentially deadly snake, so let's leave it alone."

Rafi drooped. "Okay." Then he brightened and hopped up to the dais. "Now we can get the Scarab!"

Just as the boy reached up, the cave's enormous eye rotated in its socket.

"Look," Zahra said. The eye's movement made her dizzy, and

she started losing her balance. It continued rotating, and she felt like the world was spinning. She fell to the cave floor, and Amir and Rafi toppled over after her.

The eye turned even more, until the pupil was almost horizontal. Zahra felt herself being pulled toward the cave wall, and she slid along the floor, grasping at the vines to halt her movement. Amir slid along and fell into her, knocking her loose, and Rafi went tumbling past both of them.

When the eye had turned completely to the side, she found herself pressed against the side wall of the cave, and now she could stand and walk along it as if it had become the cave floor. The globes on the vines hung as if the whole world had turned sideways.

The eye kept rotating. She was so disoriented that she sat down to keep from falling. Once again she slid, this time along the wall and toward the top of the cave. By the time the eye stopped, it had flipped upside down, and so had her sense of the world.

She was now standing on the ceiling of the cave, with Rafi and Amir rising to their feet next to her and looking as baffled and unsettled as she felt.

Rafi leaned against her. "I don't feel so good. What happened?"

"It was the cave." Zahra hugged him with her non-snake-covered arm. "It flipped us upside down."

Amir gazed up at the dais that was now above them. "I don't think it wants us to reach the Scarab."

A cool breeze brushed against her. "...the scarab is protecteeed..."

"What do we do now?" Rafi asked.

"It did say taking the Scarab wouldn't be easy," Zahra said.

Amir pointed up. "It's still there."

He was right—the Golden Scarab was attached to the stiff vines, which before had hung down from the ceiling but now rose from the ... new cave floor?

"I can get it." Rafi ran to the trunk-like coil of vines and started climbing.

"Careful," Zahra said. The boy seemed all too eager to get himself into trouble.

Rafi was made for climbing. He scampered up and quickly closed upon the Golden Scarab. As he neared it, the giant eye rotated once more.

Oh, no. "Rafi! Hold on. We're spinning again."

They reversed the process they'd already gone through once—sliding and bumping along the rough, rippled surface of the tendril-covered floor, then into and along the wall, and finally back to where the ceiling of the cave was uppermost again. All the while, Rafi held fast to the massive vines, adjusting and rotating as the world spun around him. Now the Scarab was directly below him.

He reached down to grab it, his fingers closing...

The Golden Scarab hummed.

"It's alive!" Rafi shrieked, and pulled his hand away.

The scarab's rigid elytra lifted, soft flight wings flicking out from underneath them. The beetle flexed once, then released its grip and flew away, landing on an orb-fruit.

"Come down from there, Rafi, in case the cave turns again," Zahra said.

Rafi dropped down and joined them, and together they crept toward the Scarab. When they'd gotten within arm's reach, Amir dove for it. But his hands grasped nothing; the beetle had zipped away once again, this time clinging to the cave wall.

"Curse that thing," Amir said.

"At least the cave didn't spin that time," Zahra said, still recovering from her earlier dizziness.

"I want to try again," Rafi said excitedly, creeping toward the Scarab's new landing spot.

This beetle is just going to keep flying away. We need to sneak up where it can't see us.

Where might that be? The whole cave was open, and they could spend hours chasing the thing around, and who knew if the cave's eye would spin them around again.

What did the map say? 'The goal will fly, Low becomes high, Before the watchful eye...'

If only there was a way they could—"Hold on," she said. "I have an idea."

Zahra whispered her plan to the others, and they decided to try it. They split up, Rafi edging closer to the beetle, while she and Amir walked backward toward the enormous eye on the cave wall.

"Alright, Rafi, try to chase it toward us," she said, her words intended to mislead the cave as to their true plan.

She and Amir pressed up against the wall, directly below the eye. She glanced up and saw that it was fully focused on Rafi. Good. Amir crouched, and she hopped onto his back, then clambered up to crouch on his shoulders. The prince's stance was solid and strong beneath her.

How strange that she felt comfortable enough to recommend a plan in which she would actually climb atop the Prince of Alhad, and be balanced on his shoulders. Though she acknowledged she didn't really know much about the prince outside of the spell he was under, he seemed adaptable to some truly bizarre situations. Maybe if they survived this... She let the thought fade as she focused on the situation at hand.

Leaning against the cavern wall, she shifted her way up until she could stand erect, her head now even with the bottom lid of the giant eye. She hoped this worked, or they may all be in for a rough tumble.

Nothing left but to see what will happen.

She thrust her arm up, balled her hand into a fist, and pressed it directly into the squishy part of the eye. There was a great roar of wind through the cave, the eye's lids snapped shut with a wet thwack, and the chamber was plunged into total darkness.

"Now!" Zahra shouted.

There was a brief scuffle from the boy's direction and then a shout: "I have it!"

Zahra jumped down from Amir's broad shoulders.

A breeze blew. "...thaaat wasn't niiice..."

No, it wasn't, she had to admit. *But what else were we supposed to do?*

The boy held up the Scarab. "Now what?" he asked.

Good question. Zahra took the beetle from him and turned it over in her hands. It was lifeless again, but she clasped it firmly in her fingers just in case. She pressed it on the head like she'd done with the striped snake, but nothing happened.

While she held it tightly, Amir poked and pulled at it, but nothing changed. She rubbed it and prodded it to no effect.

Maybe it has something to do with the wings? She pulled at the golden elytra and they shifted, but were caught on something holding them in place. Perhaps there was a latch to free them? She squeezed the scarab on the sides, and indeed a catch released the forewings. They flicked up in an instant.

The Scarab once again burst into motion. It thrummed and flew from her hand, up into the air in the middle of the cave, sparks and flashes of golden light trailing behind it. A dim glow grew brighter and brighter until it illuminated the whole cave. The shiny insect circled in the air, leaving glimmering metallic dust in its wake.

It flew faster and faster, circling about, gold mist spraying out in an expanding ring. The vibrating hum of its wings pitched higher and higher. A light flared from the beetle and the sound from the Scarab's wings abruptly stopped. Then a burst of smoke filled the cavern, swirling and raining down glittering powder.

Zahra shielded her eyes against the light and smoke, until an object thumped on the ground by her feet. She and her companions coughed and waved at the air, trying to keep the smoke and dust at bay as it slowly dissipated.

Finally the air cleared, revealing a figure standing before them.

CHAPTER 20

A portly man stood before them, who looked to be from India or thereabouts. He was an inch or so shorter than Zahra, who was herself a head shorter than Amir. His ample belly hung over a dusty white wrap covering his loins; other than that, he wore nothing but a pair of sandals and a cream-colored turban. Graying black hair escaped from beneath the turban, and his lengthy beard was separated down the middle and spread out wildly from there.

The short, chubby man considered them, his arms crossed, frowning.

"Oh, wonderful," he said. "What a joy. What a pleasure to be back in the realm of man." His tone clearly belied his words. "And who may I thank for this delightful return?"

Zahra furrowed her brow. Was this the famous jinni?

Her dreams of magic and powerful wishes faded away with the remaining smoke in the room.

"You ... you're just a man," she said. "Wearing very little clothing." She refrained from saying what else she thought of his appearance.

"A man!" the jinni shouted, puffing out his chest (though really this just amounted to pulling in his gut a few inches). "Foolish mortal, this is merely my representative form. I am the jinni Nadim, and I come from a realm you could not comprehend."

He snapped his fingers and golden smoke swirled around until it completely obscured him. The smoke expanded, and from it his body grew larger, forming into a gigantic muscular man with sharp teeth and four arms, each wielding a shining scimitar.

"I have lived for *millennia*," boomed the giant jinni, "and seen more years here among you humans than the three of you shall ever see combined. I wield power beyond your imagination." The jinni's giant face took on a fearsome scowl.

Rafi's eyes went wide. "Wow."

"...iiimpressive..." the voice from the cave said, carried on a stiff breeze.

As the wind of the cave's voice whirled past, it blew apart the four-armed giant, dissipating its form and carrying it away, revealing it as a mere illusion and leaving only the potbellied, disheveled jinni standing as he was before.

Not at all impressive.

The jinni's face reddened. "Ahem. Yes, well, I may be a little rusty. But believe me, I am not to be trifled with."

Amir lowered his brow, looking as indifferent as Zahra was. "Uhhh—" he began.

"I see," Zahra said, cutting Amir off before he said something insulting. "My mistake, oh great jinni." She managed to keep any sarcasm out of her tone. "You are a wonder to behold, and clearly no mortal man."

The jinni—Nadim—seemed mollified. "Perhaps you are not dazzled by my appearance, but I choose to take this form so that I may move freely and without suspicion in your realm. Also, this is the look of the first human I ever ate."

The first human he ate? She'd never heard anything about the jinn eating people. Was he joking? She didn't want to press him to find out.

Rafi had no such qualms. "Why did you eat him?"

"That's really not important right now," Zahra said quickly.

"No, it is not," Nadim agreed. "You summoned me for a reason, I would assume. No doubt one of great importance." Again his tone indicated sarcasm. "Am I right in further assuming that you seek to have your wishes fulfilled?"

"Yes," Zahra said.

"Very well," Nadim said, releasing a great yawn. "Let's have done with this. Make your wishes. You may wish for anything you desire."

That sounded good to Zahra. "Anything I want?"

"Yes. I will grant three wishes."

"Well, if I can wish for anything..." She had her doubts about this jinni's supposed powers, but why not test him? "I wish to be queen of my own kingdom."

Nadim's lip twisted. "Ah, yes, very creative." He rolled his eyes. "But no, I think not."

"What do you mean? That's my wish."

"I understand that, but no. No, I don't care for that one."

What game was he playing? "You just said I could wish for anything."

"Correct," Nadim said. "And you may—you may wish for anything you like. But notice I said I would only *grant* three wishes. I choose not to grant that one. Go ahead, think of another."

What was this? He got to choose which wishes to grant? It wasn't fair.

Now she wanted to push to see what she could get. If she had three, she had a couple to spare for Amir's situation, if necessary. She thought of one that had been brewing in her mind since finding the cave, but she was too afraid to voice it. What if she didn't want to know where that wish led?

Better to go with something more straightforward.

"Alright. Then I wish for a pile of gold."

"You're quite the original one, aren't you?" Nadim said. "No, don't be silly. Try again."

"By the flame! If you won't grant my wishes, what kind of jinni are you?"

"A very powerful one, girl, and you would be wise to be mindful of that. I choose not to wield that power indiscriminately. I'm not like an ifrit; I have scruples, and a discriminating mind regarding the desires of humans. Also, I have a limited number of wishes I may grant before I am stuck in your human realm for ninety-nine years."

The jinni would get stuck among humans?

"I've never heard of such a thing," Amir echoed Zahra's thoughts.

"Your ignorance is of no concern to me," Nadim replied.

"How many wishes until you reach ninety-nine?" Rafi asked.

Nadim heaved a great sigh. "Three, you nosy little boy."

"So my three wishes will be your last before you must live among us for ninety-nine years?" Zahra asked.

"Now you see why I am particular about the wishes I choose to grant."

"Oh." Zahra tried to think of new things to ask for.

"Ahem." Amir nudged her in the ribs.

Of course—why was she avoiding the main reason they'd come in search of the jinni in the first place? Was she afraid to find out the truth of Amir's feelings, or lack thereof? Was she afraid of how she would feel about him? At the same time, she wondered if Nadim would even grant the wish. Or *if* he could.

"Yes, the reason we came here..." She briefly explained their predicament to Nadim.

"And so," she finished, "I wish for the spell cast upon Prince Amir to be removed."

"Then she'll see that I really love her." Amir beamed a dashing smile.

Nadim's brows rose. "Ahhh... Now that's an interesting wish. That gets my attention. It's a noble request I can get behind. Yes, I will accept the challenge."

The eye of the cave blinked—was it surprised?

Nadim approached Zahra, inspecting her eyes and face. "You

have been touched by my realm, I think."

What did that mean? Before she could ask, the jinni switched his focus to Amir.

"And you," Nadim's nostrils twitched, "have the stink of an ifrit upon you."

Amir frowned and sniffed at his hands, then his underarms. "I don't smell anything."

The jinni ignored him. "I'm afraid that for this wish, I cannot simply snap my fingers and grant your desire. I will have to confront the ifrit and send it back to its realm."

If that's what it would take, Zahra was fine with it. "Alright, let's do it."

"Do you know where this ifrit is?" Nadim asked.

"Not precisely, but it's likely to be in the Palace of Light."

The jinni pursed his lips. "Well, then. Let's consider this wish to be 'in-progress.' One in the works, two to go."

"We need to get back to my palace and talk to Yaseen," Amir said.

Nadim faced Zahra. "Do you wish me to take the three of you to the Palace of Light?"

"Yes," Amir said.

"No," Zahra spoke up quickly. "We only have three wishes. We shouldn't spend one on something we can do ourselves."

"Oh, right. That's a good thought," Amir agreed. "We should start our way back to Alhad, then."

Nadim held up a finger, then pointed to the ground at Zahra's feet. "You might want to bring that with you."

The Golden Scarab. She bent down to retrieve it—

"Eh—" Nadim said, interrupting her, "would you mind grabbing it with your left hand?"

An odd request, but this jinni was full of oddities and seemed to take offense easily, so she obliged and took hold of the Scarab with her left hand and placed it in her satchel.

"Do we have to go back out the way we came?" Rafi asked, his face scrunched up with worry.

Zahra scanned the chamber. No other exits were visible.

"There is only the one way in and out," Nadim confirmed.

As they left, the cave shifted beneath them. Zahra feared they would be sent tumbling around the walls again, but the movement never amounted to more than a bumpy shaking.

"I don't think Balihar is pleased with you," Nadim said as they struggled to maintain their balance.

"Who's Balihar?" Rafi asked.

"This is Balihar." Nadim waved his arms to indicate the surrounding cave.

"We're inside of...?" Zahra's question petered out.

"It is a long and fascinating story," Nadim said. "I call it the Tale of Two Realms. Many years ago, ages before the sultanates, at the dawn of humanity, when people were only beginning to learn—"

"I'd love to hear this story, but perhaps another time," Zahra said.

"Of course," Nadim said. "After we clear the spell from your lover."

"No, he's not my lover ... I mean, he's in love with me, but not ... I don't ... it's not like..." Flustered, she gave up. How could she explain her situation? And why should she have to?

"It's fine, my love." Amir reached out to hold her hand.

She let his fingers wrap around her palm, and wanted him to keep them there, but she knew it wasn't right. She pulled away, sad to see his frown in response.

The vine barrier was still being held open, so they had little trouble squeezing back through. By the time they neared the tooth-like stalagmites, the rumbling of the cave had increased. It was going to be difficult to make it back through them with the ground shifting beneath their feet.

They stopped before the stalagmite Zahra had tripped over on the way in, the one that had impaled Rafi's pack. "Who wants to go first?" she asked.

"Him," Rafi said, pointing to Amir.

"I went first last time."

"But you're the *prince*," Rafi responded, as if that settled it.

Amir sighed. "Fine."

The ground shifted as he stepped in, and he almost fell over, but Zahra pulled him back to safety.

"Cave?" Amir said. "Balihar? Could you be steady for a few minutes?"

A breeze... "...quuuiet ... I am busyyy..."

What did that mean? How could a cave be busy?

"Nadim, any suggestions?" Zahra asked.

"Don't fall."

"Thanks," Amir said. He wasted no time and sprinted through the stalagmites like Zahra had last time. The cave jolted again, and he bumped into a couple of the protrusions and fell. He dove forward and the jagged spires of rock shot up around him.

No! Zahra's heart was in her throat. "Amir!"

The prince rolled away as a stalactite shot down from overhead, grazing his leg, but he sprang to safety.

Zahra swallowed and took a deep breath. She wanted to hold Rafi's hand as she led him through, but that would only make their situation more perilous. The shaking of the cave calmed, and it was as good a time to go as any they might get.

She ran, Rafi on her heels.

Luck was on her side, for the cave remained steady during their charge. They sprinted safely through, only having to deal with some of the slime.

The cave shuddered hard, knocking them onto their backsides. Zahra was about to tell Nadim to wait to come through, but he dissolved into smoke and reappeared next to them.

"That's cheating," Rafi said.

Nadim smiled. "Shall we continue?"

They returned to the entrance of the cave, where they'd fallen in from the Sands of Fire. It was still closed when they approached.

"Now what do we do?" Rafi asked.

The ground heaved and rose up beneath them, pushing them higher and higher toward the cave ceiling, which split apart again, giving them an exit, revealing the outside world...

And a giant scorpion blocking their way.

CHAPTER 21

It took a moment for Amir to register what he was seeing—it was nighttime outside right now, but there was no mistaking the outline of a huge scorpion in the light of the moon. Where had it come from? They hadn't seen any signs of living things in the Sands of Fire, certainly not a creature this size.

He stood frozen, unsure of what to do. The scorpion likewise remained motionless, directly facing the opening of the cave with its claws held out before it and its stinger raised. The thing's body was the size of a horse, with its tail easily as long.

Rafi tilted his head. "Is it real?"

The beast snapped a claw in response.

Amir jerked backward. "I think it's definitely real," he said, retreating and shoving the others back into the cave, despite the cavern itself doing its best to push them out.

As they retreated, the scorpion advanced, its claws clacking at them. Rafi ran further into the cave, screaming in fear, Zahra right behind him. Nadim evaporated and then reappeared behind the scorpion. He ran his fingers along its tail and it spun around, thrusting its stinger at him. He smoked away again and reformed near Zahra and Rafi, chuckling. "Interesting creature."

Interesting? More like terrifying.

It stalked into the cave, barely fitting through the opening, and skittered up along the wall and to the ceiling, its tail hanging all the way to the floor. How could something that huge cling to the ceiling?

Amir looked at the others. "What do we do?"

"You're the prince!" Rafi shouted.

Why did the boy keep bringing that up? It wasn't as if being a prince meant he had all the answers and could somehow protect them from every danger they encountered.

"As prince, I suggest we sacrifice the youngest as a distraction and run past it."

"No, that's not fair," Rafi shrieked.

The look of horror on the boy's face was entirely worth it.

"Amir, that's not funny," Zahra said.

Amir thought it was funny. Still, it was charming that Zahra was so protective of the boy. She was amazing. He was so happy to have met her, and now she would be his wife.

Another snap from the scorpion's claws reminded him they were still in a life-or-death situation. It crawled along the ceiling, and they backed further into the cavern.

"Go around the corner, quickly," Amir suggested.

The scorpion followed them, still crawling along the roof of the cave. It halted when they did, its stinger out of range. Maybe they could go beneath.

"Let's run for it," he said.

He burst forward, Rafi on his heels.

Zahra shouted, "Watch out!"

The scorpion dropped down from above and flipped over in the air just after Amir and the boy had passed under it. They were now separated from Zahra and Nadim.

His love was backed up against the cave wall, the huge chitinous beast closing in on her and the jinni. He came up with a brilliant idea. "Remember what we did with the snake?" he asked. "I'll distract the scorpion and you grab its tail."

"*What?*" Zahra ducked as a claw snapped shut inches above her head. "Are you daft?"

Amir didn't understand her complaint—it was a fine plan. Few people could have snatched that snake as easily as she had, and with her amazing reflexes and dexterity she'd have no problem grabbing onto the scorpion's tail. "Just keep its stinger from lashing out at us."

"I'm *not* grabbing its tail," Zahra said.

He took hold of a glowing vine-fruit and tugged. When it snapped off the vine, the cave went dark for a moment and shuddered, and the scorpion retreated a few steps.

Amir took advantage of its confusion and hurled the fruit at it. The orb bounced off the beast's head and the monstrous thing turned to face him. It approached again, claws extended, snapping at both him and Rafi. They each dove aside and rolled in opposite directions, out of the monster's path.

The scorpion shifted to face Rafi, and its tail lifted into the air for a strike.

"I can't believe I'm doing this!" Zahra yelled as she leaped and wrapped her arms and legs around the scorpion's tail, her weight pulling it toward the ground.

"You're amazing, my love," Amir encouraged her. "Hold on tight."

"I'm holding as tightly as possible! Now what?"

The scorpion skittered about, trying to raise its tail and shake her loose.

"Help!" she shouted frantically.

Amir ran at the scorpion from one side and jumped onto its back, Rafi following his example from the other. "We're going to ride it out of the cave."

The creature spun, then climbed up the wall, forcing them both to jump off. That hadn't worked.

"That was your plan?" Zahra said.

The jinni was leaning casually against the cave wall. He popped a date into his mouth. "This is entertaining."

"Jinni, what are you doing? We could use some help," Amir said.

"You can handle this." The jinni tossed another date into his mouth. "I have confidence in you—you're the prince."

Not him, too! Amir was getting tired of this.

"Besides," Nadim added, "these situations strengthen one's character."

The scorpion was again clinging to the ceiling. Zahra hung from the beast's tail, its stinger dangerously close to impaling her chest. "Help," she squealed.

His love was in terrible danger. He had to save her. If only he had his scimitar ... he looked around. They needed a weapon, something better than vines and soft fruits. Something big and hard and sharp. "I have an idea!"

"I hope it's ... better than ... the last one," Zahra said as the scorpion kept trying to fling her off.

"You'll love it."

"What I'd really ... love ... is to let go of this thing."

Amir grabbed another of the fruits, and the cave rocked again, the globes going dark for a moment. He heaved the orb at the monster and it dropped to the ground, with Zahra somehow maintaining her hold on its tail. The beast tried to shake her loose once more before chasing after him and Rafi.

"Follow me," he yelled to the boy.

Rafi ran right by his side, back to the slimy, stalagmite-filled corridor.

"What ... are you ... doing?" Zahra called worriedly, bouncing around as the scorpion bore down on them.

Amir hoped this would work, because he didn't have any other ideas. "Let go now!"

He and Rafi reached the stalagmites and bounded among them. The monster slashed out with a claw aimed straight at Rafi's neck. Amir threw his hands up to catch the pincer. He deflected the strike sufficiently to save Rafi, but the momentum of the attack knocked him to the ground and pushed his hand against a stalactite. The stalactite shot down, smacking against the scorpion's claw. The pincer snapped shut and lopped off Amir's pinkie finger. Pain seared through his hand. "Aagghh!" He yanked away his arm and turned onto his side.

The beast kept moving, walking straight over Amir and going after the boy. Rafi deftly zigzagged through the passage, but the scorpion had no such ability. Amir rolled out from beneath the huge creature to avoid what was coming. The scorpion's wide body brushed against several of the cave protrusions.

Crack!—Snap!—Squish!—Snick!—Splash! Spike after spike slammed up and down and into and through the carapace of the scorpion. Amir squeezed his eyes shut and huddled in place as blood and gore from the monster splattered onto him. The spikes continued to gnash up and down, and he didn't move, hoping that Rafi and his beloved Zahra were safe.

This may not have been the best plan.

Snap!—Snip!—Crack!—Squish! Over and over it went until finally the cave settled down. Amir covered the bleeding spot where his severed finger used to be, moaning at the pain. He squinted his eyes open and looked around.

Rafi was crouched into a ball further down the passageway, hands over his ears, his eyes open in horrified shock.

Zahra! Amir spun and saw her flat against the ground near the tip of the dead beast's tail.

"Zahra?"

She raised a hand. "Mmm awight," she mumbled into the cave floor.

He and Rafi carefully worked their way back out, trying as best as they could to avoid the crushed remains of the giant scorpion.

Zahra had regained her feet. He wrapped her in a hug, which she fell into for a few seconds before pushing back from him. Why wouldn't she believe his feelings? They *had* to get rid of this spell so he could prove that he loved her.

"Rafi, are you alright?" she asked.

"I'm fine, I think." The boy checked himself for injuries, but appeared unharmed.

"You almost got us killed," Zahra said, pointing angrily at Amir. That hurt; her rebuke stung right to his core. He'd only been trying to save her from the beast. If anything had happened to her... "I admit the plan lacked finesse. But it worked. And ... I couldn't think of anything else to do. You were in danger, and I had to do something."

Her face softened. "Well... It *was* brave. And it did work."

She'd said he was brave—the compliment invigorated him like the cool waters of Fatima Falls.

"Well done," Nadim said, picking date pulp out of his teeth. "I knew you could do it."

CHAPTER 22

Zahra had had enough of the cave. She led the group back to the entrance and demanded, "Let us out."

The ground again rose beneath them and lurched forward, disgorging them into the cooling air of the desert night. A blast from the cave shot sand and rocks high into the air, and when it had cleared, any sign of an entrance had vanished.

She stood and brushed sand from her hair and clothes. "Is everyone alright?"

"Not entirely," Amir groaned. He clutched at his hand, blood dripping along the length of his arm.

She hurried to him. "What happened?"

Amir moaned. "That scorpion chopped off my finger."

He'd lost a finger? Zahra grabbed a jug of water from Rafi, pouring it over the prince's finger, eliciting a howl of pain. "Hold still," she told him as she used more of the water to clean away any bits of the monster that still stuck to him.

She tore off a strip of cloth from her robe and placed it over his wound, wrapping it around his hand to hold it fast and help stop the bleeding. She couldn't imagine how it must hurt. *Oh, my prince, what have I gotten you into?*

"I'm surprised you had so much trouble with that thing," Nadim said, yawning. "It was just a bug."

"Just a bug?" Amir said. "It was bigger than a camel. And it cut off my finger." He held up his bandaged hand, pointing to the place his missing digit should be.

"It's only a finger," Nadim said. "You can regrow those quite easily."

"No," Zahra said. "No, we can't."

"I seem to remember that you can. Look, it's easy." Nadim held up a hand, manifested a sharp knife, and sliced off his own pinkie finger. Blood spurted out and started pouring down his hand.

"Argh!" Rafi screeched, burying his head in Zahra's back.

"Not to worry, little one," Nadim said. "See, you just regrow it." His finger formed new bone and flesh and was whole again. "Easy."

"Easy for you," Amir said. "We can't do that."

"No? But you're of the royal bloodline."

"Still, no," Amir said.

"Ah. That explains why you were screaming like a baby crying for its mother. I forgot how frail you humans are." He faced Zahra. "Well, even with one of your wishes taken up by undoing this charming spell he's under, you still have two more. You can wish for his finger back—I'd allow that."

"Why must you be so rude?" Zahra asked. "You know what I wish? I wish—"

Rafi clamped his hands over Zahra's mouth before she could finish her thought. "Master Zahra, we might need those two wishes for something more important than a finger, or whatever you were thinking."

"Easy for the ten-fingered little boy to say," Amir said.

Zahra peeled Rafi's hand away. "You're right, Rafi. Let's—"

Something made a snapping sound a short distance away. It was another scorpion, this one much smaller than the other—only about the size of a dog—but still large enough. Behind it, five others were working their way through the sand toward them.

Rafi shrieked and jumped onto her back.

"Let's get out of here!" Zahra said.

Rafi hopped down, and they plodded quickly through the sand until they encountered a dune and ran up it, continuing on until they'd left the scorpions far behind.

"I really *hate* those things," Amir said.

"They're fun, aren't they?" Nadim said blithely.

Rafi whispered to Zahra, "I think there's something wrong with the jinni."

Nadim said, "You know what's not wrong with the jinni? His hearing."

Zahra wondered if Rafi might be right about Nadim, but there was another issue she was more concerned with at the moment: the light of the nearly full moon illuminated their surroundings perfectly, and they hadn't exited the cave in the Sands of Fire. No flame-like rocks protruded from the earth, and no grasping cliffs reached up from the earth.

"Where are we?" she asked.

"This isn't the Sands of Fire," Amir said. "Did ... did the cave move?"

"I think you annoyed it," Nadim said.

Nothing around them looked familiar. They were lost. "How can we get back to the palace if we don't even know where we are?" Zahra asked.

"He can lead us back," Rafi said, pointing at Amir.

"Why do you think I can do that?" Amir asked.

"You're the prince."

"Would you stop saying that!"

Despite their situation, Zahra giggled.

"Not you, too," Amir said.

She laughed harder. "It's ... funny ... because ... you're the prince." She doubled over, snorting with laughter.

Amir sulked as she and Rafi enjoyed their mirth. She didn't know why it was funny, but it didn't matter. She'd been so tense ever since learning of Vizier Yaseen's dark plan that having a moment of peace to let that go was a welcome release.

Nadim glanced at the prince. "I don't get it, either," the jinni said.

That made it even funnier to Zahra, and she and Rafi howled and rolled on the sand, completely unable to contain themselves.

"You do realize we're lost?" Amir said.

That was true. They might not be safe yet and their situation could still be serious. She forced a few deep breaths to calm herself. "You're right."

Getting back to her feet, she scanned the sky and the horizon. "The night's clear, with no clouds, and I see no sign of the Palace of Light, or any civilization. Any thoughts?"

The jinni pointed. "It is that way."

"How do you know that?" Amir asked.

"We have recently left the Dunes of Qarab, home of the giant scorpions. Since Alhad lies to the south of these dunes, and there is the star marking north, that means this way is south. Really, should you not know your own world better than I?"

"Ah," Amir said, "the Dunes of Qarab. Yes, I'd forgotten."

"I don't think you forgot," Rafi said. "I think you didn't know."

"I am your prince, little boy. When we return home, I have it in mind to make you a slave."

Rafi scrunched up his face and looked at Zahra. "You're really not a princess? And he's really the prince?"

"Yes, that's correct."

"I don't get it. Life seems backwards."

Nadim gave a snort.

Zahra had to admit that sometimes things did indeed feel backwards from how they should be, but that didn't change their current circumstances. "We have a long way still to travel. It's late, and I'm tired. I say we sleep here for a bit, and then start back before the sun rises."

They settled down for the night, the verbal barbs between Rafi and Amir dying off as they nestled onto the sands.

Apparently Nadim couldn't handle the silence. "Would you like to hear a nighttime tale?"

Before Zahra could respond, Rafi replied with an enthusiastic, "Yes!"

"Your encounter with the scorpion today reminds me of the Tale of the Fisherman, the Carpenter, and the Thief."

"Ooh, what's that about?" Rafi asked.

"A fisherman had left some pieces of fish out near an open window as he was preparing dinner. When he returned, the fish was gone, and he noticed a cat on the street eating the last piece. It was a beautiful striped cat, healthy and with glossy fur. He decided to adopt it and so left food out for it regularly. But then a week went by and he didn't see the cat the whole time."

"Aw. What happened to it?" Rafi asked.

"The fisherman searched for the cat, and found a plate with scraps of food at the door of a neighbor's house, a carpenter.

"He knocked upon the carpenter's door and, pointing to the plate, accused the carpenter of trying to steal his wonderful cat. The carpenter admitted to feeding the cat, but said that he himself hadn't seen the cat in a few days. Together they searched further along the street, and again discovered a plate sitting out. They knocked upon the door of this neighbor and, pointing to his plate, accused him of trying to steal the lovely cat."

Zahra yawned. How long was this story going to be?

Nadim continued: "This man stated that he'd seen the cat roaming the streets, and so he set out cuts of chicken for it. But he also had not seen the animal for a few days, and he joined the other two in their search.

"When they reached the public square, they heard a loud mewling and looked up, to find that nobody had taken their beloved cat. It had climbed so high into a tree that it found itself stuck on a small branch overhead."

Zahra waited for the jinni to continue, but Nadim merely looked at them with a satisfied smile.

"That's it?" asked Rafi, obviously disappointed in the tale.

"I don't understand," Zahra said. "What does that story have to do with our fight with a giant scorpion?"

"What do you mean?" Nadim asked. "They were humans, like you. And there were three of them. Like you. And a strange animal."

"Strange animal? It was just a cat," Amir said.

"But it climbed up a tree," the jinni said, "like the scorpion climbed up inside the cave."

Rafi crossed his arms and shook his head. "You said it was the Tale of the Fisherman, the Carpenter, and the Thief. There wasn't even a thief in the story."

"The cat was the thief," Nadim said, as if that should have been obvious. "It stole their food."

Zahra shook her head. *This* was the jinni she'd pinned all her hopes on? "I think it's time to get some sleep."

"One of us needs to stay awake," Amir said. "What if more of those scorpions show up? Or something else?"

"Fear not, I will watch over you, my human companions," Nadim said grandly.

"Uhhh..." Amir muttered, obviously not sure if he was willing to trust the jinni.

Zahra wasn't sure herself, but she was achingly tired. She couldn't walk any further, and she definitely couldn't keep her eyes open, so the jinni would have to do as a watchman. She formed a mound of sand to support her head, lay back, and was asleep in moments.

CHAPTER 23

When Zahra awoke, it was still nighttime, the moon having drifted lower toward the horizon. Amir was on his side next to her, his arm draped over her, and Rafi's head was on her thigh. Nadim—was nowhere to be found.

So much for watching over them.

"Nadim!" she shouted, startling her two companions awake. "Nadim."

Poof. There was a burst of golden smoke in front of her, which dissipated to reveal the jinni.

"At your service," Nadim said.

"Where were you? You were supposed to be keeping guard over us."

"Yes, that is true."

"And?"

"I got bored."

"Ugh!" Zahra stamped her foot. "Come on, let's get moving while it's still cool."

They trudged through the Dunes of Qarab—how many dunes were there?—until the stars disappeared with the rising of the sun.

Nadim yawned. "This is tiresome, and it's getting hot. My realm is much more comfortable. And there are no,"—he pinched his nose as if warding off a pungent smell—"humans there. If you need me, give the Scarab a little squeeze."

"Wait," Zahra said. "You're the only one who knows where we're going."

"Just keep going in that direction. You'll be fine."—*poof*.

In the increasing heat of the rising sun, Zahra strongly considered using a wish to have the jinni take them straight to the palace. Hours passed, and sweat drenched her clothes, and she finally brought it up to the others.

"We've come this far, and we still have water," Amir said. "We may as well keep walking. How much farther can it be?"

Soon the dunes flattened; the ground mercifully turned back to the hard cracked earth that made progress easier and quicker, and there were scattered scrub trees in various gulches. They paused beneath one around midday to escape the direct sun, before pressing on again.

"I just wish we had a camel," Zahra said.

Poof.

There was a swirl of golden smoke that cleared to reveal Nadim, standing next to a camel. A familiar, ugly camel with a stubby tail, short ears, and a stripe down its neck.

"Wish granted," Nadim said, a huge smile splayed across his stupid face.

The camel spat at Zahra, but this time she dodged it.

"Two wishes down, one remains," the jinni said.

"No!" Zahra shouted. Was Nadim kidding them? "That's not what I wanted. I didn't mean to wish for that."

"Nevertheless, the wish was spoken and heard. It was a respectable wish, a worthy one, and it has been granted. Fret not, one wish remains."

"You are the worst jinni I could have ever imagined."

"That's not fair. I watched over you while you slept, and that didn't even cost a wish."

That insulting statement, combined with the wasted wish and the heat of the day, flared Zahra's temper. "You *watched*? You didn't—I didn't even wish—and then—argh! I'm so mad right now."

"Calm down, my love," Amir said, taking one of her hands in his.

"And you! Stop that!" She pulled away and squeezed her hands into fists in frustration. She looked at the ugly, stinky camel. *Since I wasted a wish on it, I might as well ride it.*

She had never ridden a camel before, but how hard could it be? She stomped over to it, grabbed hold of its fur, and pulled herself up. "Let's go."

The camel didn't move.

"I think you have to kick it a little," Rafi said.

She tapped it with her foot and it started moving. It was nice to be moving without walking, but the thing reeked. She rode it for five minutes before giving up. The smell was overwhelming. "You can ride it, Rafi."

Rafi neared it and took a whiff of its odor. "Blessings upon you, Master Zahra, but I think the prince should be the one to ride."

"I'll not ride while my precious Zahra walks."

Rafi looked at Nadim. "Jinni?"

Indeed, Nadim hopped onto the back of the camel with such a big smile on his face that Zahra wanted to punch him.

The three of them walked while the jinni rode next to them.

"Have you ever seen the Giant Sea Serpent of Bahamut?" Nadim asked as they plodded through the desert.

"No," Zahra said. "Until yesterday, I'd never been out of Alhad."

"And you, prince?"

"No, and I'm not sure I want to. Losing a finger to a giant scorpion is enough for me." He accidentally bumped his injured hand as he held it up. "Ow!"

"Oh, it's a wonder to behold, a truly majestic creature. A thousand feet long, and with shiny scales of silver."

"Wow," Rafi said. "What made you think of that?"

"Well, there's not a lot of water around here, and so naturally I thought of the sea, and that thought led to the serpent. Maybe you'd like to have your next journey be on the sea, instead of in the desert."

Maybe. Anything would be better than trudging through scorching sand with no end in sight. They could skip the sea serpent, though.

The jinni must have seen a lot of strange and amazing things, like the Cave of Balihar. A thought about that occurred to her. "Nadim, we followed a map to get to the cave, and it described the obstacles we'd face. Only someone who knew everything about the cave could have made that map. It was you, wasn't it?"

"Of course. Did you like it?"

Her lips tilted downward. "It could have been clearer. Why all the riddles?"

"I didn't want just anyone to find my Scarab. I was only interested in returning for someone in a position of consequence, where I might provide assistance on a large scale. So, a sultan—or prince—who'd be compelled to push through until the end. Plus, I like riddles."

"So, why a golden scarab?" Zahra continued.

"Ah, it was an heirloom belonging to one I had a bond with in this realm, as I'm now bonded to you, Zahra. He had a strong emotional connection with it, and that powerful resonance is necessary to form a portal to my realm. The portal is linked to it now. I like it—it's unique, and I can make it fly."

There was a whole world of things Zahra knew nothing about. Faraway places and jinn and magic and portals. "So once you remove the spell from Amir, there will only be one wish left before you remain here for ninety-nine years?"

"Ah, yes. It had better be an amazing wish."

Zahra was sure she'd think of something. "Where did all these rules come from?"

"My father established the rules ages ago as a compact between our realm and your people. The agreement was made, in fact, with the founder of Alhad. Your home is special; no jinni or ifrit may perform magic at all within the Palace of Light without express permission granted by the sultan or a member of his family."

It was a good thing they had Amir on their side.

"But then, how did Yaseen make the love spell? He was in the Palace of Light with the ifrit."

"*He* made the spell himself, did he not? As far as I know, humans have no restriction on the use and practice of magic within the palace. It is probable the ifrit explained to him how to do it, but had no direct hand in it."

"Ah. That fits with what I saw."

As they traveled on, Nadim asked them if they'd seen this thing or been to that place, knowing of course that they hadn't, but keeping them entertained with one tale after another.

Zahra wondered how many of the things he spoke of were true, but at this moment, it didn't matter. Thoughts of exotic lands and peoples and beasts distracted her from their dreary march through the desert.

Finally, they encountered a sign of civilization—a bridge across a river.

"Good news, friends." Nadim announced from atop his smelly camel. "We're halfway there."

"We're only *halfway*?" Amir, Zahra, and Rafi said in unison.

How had they traveled so far and only gotten halfway there? That stupid cave must have taken them even further away from Alhad than the Sands of Fire were.

"Let's get some more water," she said, clambering down the short bank to the river.

The water felt wonderful and she waded in, keeping near the shore to avoid the faster moving waters further out. Amir followed her, but screamed in pain when he submerged his hand.

"Ow, ow, ow, ow," he moaned. As he undid Zahra's makeshift bandage, he gave a final loud yelp.

"Alright, alright," Nadim said. "I can't take another moment of your whining. Here's your finger back."

There was a golden *poof* around Amir's hand. "Yes!" the prince yelled, holding it up, showing off his new finger.

"Wait," Zahra shouted. "I didn't wish for that."

"Hey." Amir looked hurt. He splashed water at her with his freshly healed hand.

Nadim waved dismissively. "Consider that one a gift. Don't worry, my lovely girl, I am in no hurry to roam your realm for nearly a hundred years once again—you still have one wish left."

"Oh," Zahra said. "Good."

Not that she wasn't relieved that Amir was whole again; she had no desire to see him suffer. But he deserved to be splashed back. "Take that." She laughed as the water hit his face.

Amir dove under the water and grabbed her, pulling her down. She panicked momentarily and pushed him away, springing back to the surface. "I can't swim," she gasped.

"Oh, then I'll have to teach you."

"I can teach her better," Rafi said. "Just do this." He swam around, belly down, arms shooting forward and then pushing out and back. Amir dunked him under.

"Hey!" Rafi complained after he'd bounced back up.

Zahra splashed both of them again.

Amir swam over and had Zahra lie flat in the water, face down, while he supported her around her waist. He held her afloat and taught her how to paddle properly, leading her along through the shallow riverbank.

Was this how it would be if she were wed to him? Would they spend their days floating in the Pond of Serenity or splashing under Fatima Falls? What *did* the prince do all day? What was he like outside of this spell?

She lowered her legs to stand on the river bottom, wading away from Nadim and Rafi to get some privacy. "Who are you?" she asked.

He looked perplexed. "I'm ... the Prince of Alhad."

She rubbed at the body of her snake bracelet, careful not to touch its head, thinking of magic and the trouble it had caused them.

"I know that, but what are you like normally, without the spell? What do you do all day? What kind of things do you actually want?"

He reached out to caress her cheek. "I want you, of course. You'll be my wife. We'll do whatever you wish, go wherever you wish."

Wishes. Spells. Magic. But what was real? What was the truth? "What do *you* wish for? Why haven't you wed one of the women who've visited the palace?"

"They weren't..." Confusion wrinkled Amir's face, as if he couldn't determine a reason. Or maybe he was battling the effects of the spell he was under. "They were ... simple."

Simple? Like me. It doesn't get any simpler than a servant in a beige robe.

Amir frowned. "They were silly. Or childish. Or plain. Not beautiful, and amazing, and clever, like you."

The words sent a warmth through her. She'd never before been referred to in any of those terms, and she'd just had them spoken by the Prince of Alhad. But again, spells and magic—could she trust what he said in his current state? "You have to know those thoughts will go away when we remove the spell. You said those girls were simple, but look at me. I'm a servant; I'm as plain as can be."

Amir smiled. "Hardly. You're honest, not obsequious like some of them were. You're smart. And you *are* beautiful."

"I think so, too." Rafi sloshed his way over to them.

Nadim shrugged. "I've seen worse human females."

Warmth spread through her again, this time flushing her cheeks. She didn't know what to say or to think, so she just splashed at them again. She wanted to spend the rest of the day here, learning to swim, frolicking, and learning more about Amir if possible, but they still had a long walk ahead of them to get back to Alhad. Reluctantly, she waded out of the refreshing water. "We should get going."

They tramped up from the river and started back onto the road.

Halfway across the bridge, two men on horses galloped toward them, coming to a halt behind them above the water.

Zahra recognized their uniforms. "Oh, no."

From around the corner ahead, two more men trotted up and stopped in front of them on the bridge.

"Out for a walk, my prince?" said Vizier Yaseen.

CHAPTER 24

N ot *Yaseen*, Amir thought. He really didn't want to deal with
the man right now.

Still, he might as well make the best of the situation.

*No more walking through the desert. We can ride back to Alhad
and sort all this out.*

"Yaseen," he said. "It's good that you're here."

"Indeed, my prince. You and your new ... friends ... didn't make
it easy. If you'll just come with me, we'll return you to the palace
in short order. Your father is quite worried about you."

Amir felt bad about that. He hadn't expected to be gone so long,
but now he could return with news of his choice of bride. He
would explain that he was in love with Zahra. His father wanted
him to marry the daughter of a sultan, or a noblewoman, but he
was sure once he saw how wonderful Zahra was, he'd be happy to
have her as the princess.

Zahra nudged him in the side. "You can't trust him, Amir."

She had a point. If she was right and the vizier had tried to
manipulate his feelings, he couldn't trust the man. Yaseen had told
him that Zahra had cast a spell upon him, but Zahra said the magic

had come from the lily that Maliha had given him. Had the vizier tried to enchant him? Or was it Maliha? Or indeed Zahra?

He couldn't remember what had happened exactly—it was all still foggy in his mind. But maybe that was an effect of the spell? All the more reason to undo the enchantment and set things back to normal again.

Yaseen shook his head calmly. "I'm very disappointed in you, girl. I took you in as a kindness, as a favor to your mother. I provided for you and raised you. Is this treachery your repayment?"

Zahra's mouth hung open. "You're disappointed in—"

"No, my prince," Yaseen cut her off, turning to speak with Amir. "It is this sad, desperate servant girl who is unworthy of your trust. As I tried to tell you before, she placed a spell on you for her own gain. Think about it. Who is more believable here? Me, your ally and adviser, and chief vizier to the sultan, or the wild, pathetic, sopping wet tramp next to you?"

How dare Yaseen talk about his Zahra in such words and with such a tone. "She is my love, Yaseen. You will show her respect. Spell or not, I will have her as my wife when we return. I'll tolerate no insults toward her."

Amir had little admiration for his father's vizier, and this affront to his beloved was uncalled for. However, Yaseen's words made him think. Something was muddling his thoughts, and he could only guess the source to be the spell. As much as Amir disliked Yaseen, his father had entrusted him with running the palace for decades. On the other hand, Zahra had proved herself honorable and loyal. It made little sense for her to be the one to use magic on him. *Was* it the vizier?

Yaseen called to the guards behind Amir's group. "Enough of this. The prince has been bespelled and is not thinking clearly. Take him onto your horse and let's be off."

"Run!" Zahra yelled.

She and Rafi turned to flee back across the bridge, but Yaseen's men had dismounted and easily caught them.

"Stop this. Release them," Amir commanded. But for the first time in his life, the palace guards disobeyed him. Shocked, he waited for them to realize he had given them an order.

"Did you not hear me? I said release them—at once."

The guard next to Yaseen dismounted and grabbed Amir himself, hauling him backward toward his horse. "I apologize, my prince, but you are not yourself."

"What are you doing?" Amir shouted into the hand over his mouth. What was happening? How dare this man lay hands on him! He'd have him flogged and beaten for this betrayal.

Nadim hopped off his stinky camel and approached the guards who held Zahra and Rafi. "Ah, it's quite the situation we have here. This reminds me of the Tale of the—" He sniffed at the air. "What is that smell? It's familiar ..."

The eyes of the guard holding Zahra widened, then focused on her satchel. He yanked it open and pulled out the Golden Scarab. "Nadim, my old *friend*," the guard said. "I didn't recognize you."

One of Yaseen's guards knew the jinni? How could that be?

The guard retrieved something from his own satchel—a ball of a yellowish-brown, waxy substance.

"Ghazi." Nadim looked stunned. "You dung-rolling fool. Get your hands off my—"

Ghazi slapped the wax onto the Scarab, covering it entirely.

"No!" Nadim lunged toward the guard.

Ghazi transferred the Scarab to his other hand and held it up, away from the jinni. The waxy coating quickly hardened into a shell.

Nadim grabbed for it again, launching himself at the man. The jinni pushed Ghazi against the railing of the bridge and worked to pry his scarab free from the guard's grip. He prized open the man's fingers, but Ghazi jerked his hand away, releasing the Golden Scarab. It was launched through the air, off the bridge, and into the river below.

Ghazi sneered at Nadim. "Now you're cut off from your powers. You'll be no further hindrance to us, *jinni*."

No. We need the scarab and the jinni to cancel the spell. Amir

155

struggled against his captor, but was held tight, with a hand still clamped over his mouth.

He watched in shock as the Scarab was swept away by the river's current.

Ghazi mounted his horse. "What about these three?"

"Take their camel and supplies, and leave them to the desert," Yaseen said.

Leave them to the desert? How could his father's vizier be so callous and cruel? Especially to Zahra. Even if she had placed the spell on him, as Yaseen claimed, Amir still loved her.

Amir strained with all his might to break free, but as strong as he was, the guard was massive and overpowered him easily.

"I'll take the prince," Ghazi said, hauling Amir onto the horse with him.

"Yaseen, stop this," Amir said as soon as his mouth was uncovered. "We can't leave them. Nadim is a jinni who can help break the spell placed upon me." As annoying as the vizier was, he was a reasonable man. He must understand.

"Vizier, you know not what you're doing here," Nadim said. "I have lived for thousands of years and I *do* know. That ... thing ... on the horse there is a wretched ifrit. I have tangled with him before. If he's involved with this, know that he'll stop at nothing to tear your kingdom to pieces."

Amir's heart dropped. *This guard is an ifrit?*

Amir tried to yell at Yaseen, but Ghazi was already working a cloth into his mouth.

For the briefest moment, the vizier paused.

"I suggest ignoring the sore loser, oh wise one," Ghazi said to Yaseen.

The vizier's face again hardened with resolve. "My prince, fear not—I have learned what is needed to nullify the foul servant girl's enchantment. We will have you back to the Palace of Light and free in no time, your mind clear, and happy to be reunited with your father. Then we will all discuss whom you shall marry. Do you not remember your feelings for my beautiful daughter, Maliha? She is eagerly awaiting your return."

Maliha. Oh, yes, the vizier's daughter. She *was* a fetching girl. But... "I wnnnt to mmrryy Zzhhhraaa..."

"Back to Alhad!" Yaseen shouted, kicking his horse into motion as the other guards did likewise.

Amir felt the hot, fetid breath of Ghazi as the guard (or was it the ifrit?) whispered into his ear: "The jinni is correct. Once my bargain with your fool of a vizier is complete, I'm going to raze your kingdom to rubble."

It couldn't be. What was Yaseen doing, working with this monster?

Ghazi flicked a powder into Amir's face and he couldn't avoid breathing it in. "Forget," the guard said.

What was that? Amir was confused. He had to remember what Ghazi had just said. *Kingdom to rubble. Kingdom to rubble. Kingdom to...* What was it? Something about the kingdom?

Amir tried to remember, but it was like a dream upon waking. And then it was gone. It was probably not important, anyway, unlike Zahra being stranded here.

Amir struggled and looked back over his shoulder, trying to shout to Zahra that he would fight his way free and return for her. As they rounded the corner, he caught his last glimpse of her staring after him, her face a pained expression of shock and concern.

CHAPTER 25

Z ahra could hardly believe what had just happened. She looked
back and forth between the river and the road, gripped
by indecision. Should they go after the Scarab or Prince Amir?
They needed to retrieve the Scarab so they could regain access to
Nadim's power, but on the other hand, Amir might be in danger—or at least be forced to marry Maliha against his will.

Rafi decided for her. "Go rescue Amir. I'll get the Scarab." He
climbed onto the bridge's railing, dove headfirst into the river, and
started swimming downstream.

Blessings upon that boy.

How were they going to catch up to the vizier? Yaseen had even
taken their horrible camel. As much as she despised that thing, she
would have swallowed her disdain in order to save the prince.

"We need to go." She started after the vizier and his guards.

Nadim stared at her, nonplussed. "But they took the camel."

"Come on. We'll chase after them."

"You want me to walk? In this heat?"

"Nadim! Amir's in trouble."

The jinni sighed. "That is true." He frowned a moment before giving in and following behind her. "In fact, your prince is in more danger than we knew. The one called Ghazi, who sealed off my magical connection to the scarab, is the ifrit responsible for the spell placed on your lover."

"He's not my lov—never mind that. That guard is not the ifrit. I saw the demon who's working with Yaseen; it was huge, with fiery skin and tattoos and horns."

"That's his more natural form, but he can change his shape with ease."

"Oh." *I should have realized that.*

"I know this Ghazi—he harbors great ill will against the royal line of Alhad. If he has had a hand in making the prince fall in love, it is for nefarious purposes. Those of royal blood are blessed with an ancient magic, and if he gains access to that, I fear for the future of Alhad."

"Amir wouldn't help the ifrit."

"He may be coerced. Or the one he marries will be."

"Maliha? She's my friend, and she would never help him, either. Besides, she's not of royal blood."

"Ah, but once she weds the prince, the magic will apply to her as well."

This was too much for Zahra to contemplate. Right now, they had to free the prince from the clutches of Yaseen and his ifrit. Maybe Amir would cause trouble and force the vizier to slow down or even stop.

At least she had Nadim and wasn't all alone, like Rafi. She hoped the boy would be safe, whether or not he found the Scarab. She'd rather see him alive and well, even if he failed to reacquire the treasured object.

Determined to help Amir and then get back to Rafi, she started running down the trail.

"Hold, girl. You'll be out of energy in minutes."

Come on, Nadim. "We have to hurry." She balled her frustration into her fists. The jinni was right, curse him. She wasn't used to running and would be exhausted in no time.

As the afternoon wore on, the dust rising from Yaseen's mounts faded from view. *How far away is Amir now? And Rafi?*

"I can't believe Yaseen is doing this," she grumbled. "He only wants the prince to marry Maliha so he can have the prestige of being part of the sultan's family."

"Hmm..." Nadim looked at her wryly.

"What? What is that look?"

The jinni stopped walking to stand in the shade of a nearby cliff. "Isn't that much the same reason you sought access to my power? To become royalty?"

"No! I—I wanted to help Amir."

"Yet the first thing you wished for was to be queen of your own land."

"That was just—I was surprised that I could actually wish for anything. I wanted to test it out."

"Ah, of course."

"That's not fair. Look at me: I'm not royalty or nobility. I have no trade, or craft, or anything like that. I'm just a servant."

"And you thought, maybe with my power, you could become something more? Something with a title, with prestige?"

"No." On uttering that word, her gut tightened. Her mother's admonition against lying came back to her. "Maybe."

Nadim said nothing.

"Fine. Yes, of course that's what I wanted. Before the spell was even placed on Amir, I hoped I could use the Golden Scarab to improve my standing. And maybe win Amir over, and become a princess. I never wanted to force it on him, though, unlike Yaseen. It's just that—"

How could she explain to a jinni how she felt? What she'd been through? How could a being with such power understand someone so powerless?

"I've toiled loyally for the vizier for nearly a decade, and he has never advanced me. He says I'm not focused, or I cause trouble, or I don't work hard enough. *I'm* not working hard enough? He's the one who wants easy advancement. He's going to strip away Amir's will in order to become part of the royal family. Plus, he is risking everyone's lives by working with an ifrit."

Nadim's expression softened. "I understand your frustration. And I can't disagree with your assessment."

"Yaseen already has everything—wealth, and power, and the run of the palace and the city."

She kicked a rock down the path. The situation made her so mad. It wasn't fair. Now the vizier was going to force Amir into a marriage, working with a demon who had a vendetta against the kingdom. And she was stuck in the middle of the desert, without even little Rafi at her side. Tears rolled down her cheeks. Once again, she was left with nothing. "I used to collect lost buttons and threads just so I could have something of my own."

The jinni patted her on the back.

"I just," —she sniffled—"wanted to have something. To experience something. To be a part of something. To belong somewhere."

She wiped her tears. "Besides, why can't I help Amir *and* help myself? I still have two wishes left."

"One."

"Oh, that's right—the horrible camel. Don't remind me." That had sure been a great wish.

Nadim grimaced. "I have to say, I feel bad about that in retrospect."

"I don't even have that disgusting beast now. The vizier has Amir. And Rafi is..."

Please be safe, Rafi. Curse Yaseen!

Nadim softly touched her shoulder again and gave it a gentle squeeze. Some of the tension eased from her neck muscles. "We shall work this all out."

She couldn't see how. "Let's go and get Amir back."

She marched on in silence, long angry steps matching her mood. How could she be in this position? Against all odds and reason, they'd found the Golden Scarab of Balihar, yet now they couldn't even use the fabled power of the jinni.

As they plodded along the trail, Nadim occasionally opened his mouth as if he were about to speak, and then closed it again. Until finally he could contain himself no longer.

"This whole situation with you, the prince, and the ifrit reminds me of the Tale of the Demon and the Sultan's Wife."

"Why? Because we're humans and there's a demon involved?"

Nadim laughed. "I do love sarcasm. But please pay attention; there's a point to my stories."

There is?

"Centuries ago, a sultan chose the most beautiful woman in the kingdom to be his wife. As the years passed, the queen feared growing old and sought to live forever with her youthful beauty. She found and seduced a demon ifrit to gain access to its magic. The queen's seduction was powerful, and the demon wished to have her for himself, and thus planned to kill the sultan and steal his kingdom and his wife."

Maybe this story *did* have similarities to their current circumstances. "What happened?"

"Oh, now you're interested, are you? Well, the sultan was not without power of his own—he was friends with the Father of Jinn. When the treacherous ifrit tried to enact his scheme, magical wards placed on the palace by the Father of Jinn saved the sultan from certain death. The ifrit was defeated and forced by our Father to forever serve the whims of the nation he'd attempted to usurp. He was stripped of his freedom, and much of his magical power. That ifrit was Ghazi."

So this tale *was* relevant to their situation.

"What became of the queen?"

"The marriage was annulled, she was stripped of her royal position, and she was also made to serve the kingdom, in her own way. It's a tale of—"

Nadim stopped himself at the sound of horses approaching from behind. Zahra turned and saw—

It can't be. Her heart leaped, and tears came again to her eyes, but this time tears of joy.

"Josef!"

CHAPTER 26

J osef and another man pulled up next to them along the trail. "Zahra!" Josef jumped from his horse and enfolded her in a massive hug. "You're alive."

"And you." She hugged him back just as hard. "I'm so happy to see you again. How did you survive that dust demon?"

"With a fair bit of luck, I'll tell you. It sucked me into the air, and I squeezed my eyes shut, covered my ears, and waited for death. I was flung far away, and with great fortune I tumbled into soft sand. When I looked up, you were all gone, and the dust demon had blown apart."

"What about the guards?"

"They were intently interested in you and Prince Amir, but I told them I didn't know you and had only agreed to travel with you because I'd lost everything and had nowhere else to go. They were frustrated, but accepted my story and even gave me a ride back to the oasis. And then who should show up but my dear brother." He motioned to the other man still sitting on his horse. "Alive and well and with a pouch of dinars. We bought another horse and set forth to continue our journey south, and here we are. I am overjoyed to find you alive and well. Where are Amir and Rafi? And who is your new friend?"

"Ah, allow me to recount the tale," Nadim said. "I was in the Cave of—"

"Maybe I should tell this one," Zahra interrupted him. She relayed their story, much more succinctly than the jinni would have. "And now we're tracking down the vizier to free Prince Amir."

"You've had quite the adventure. If anyone else were to tell me such a story, I'd likely not believe it. And, truly, this man from India is the jinni?" Skepticism furrowed Josef's brow as he looked over Nadim's less than impressive physique and garb.

Nadim sighed. "Yes, this is the human form I choose to present. I am quite fearsome and frightening in my natural state. Would you like me to show you?"

Josef opened his mouth to speak, but Zahra cut him off. "No, no, Nadim. Josef believes you. And we need to get after Amir."

Josef nodded and hopped back onto his stallion. "Of course—we'll rescue the prince and then go back for little Rafi." He extended a hand down to Zahra. "Come, you'll not get far on foot. Yurem, make room for Nadim. I owe a great debt to Zahra, and I intend to repay it."

A debt? "You owe me nothing, Josef."

"Then I do no more than what I know you would do for me. Come. Up, up." He pulled her onto his horse.

What fortune. Josef was alive, healthy, and had reunited with his brother, and now they had a chance to rescue Amir before the vizier reached the palace.

It took less than an hour to close in on Yaseen's position. Apparently, the vizier wasn't at all worried about being followed, had set a leisurely pace, and was now resting just off the path. The vizier's horses were ahead, near a crescent-shaped cliff and a small copse of trees that provided shade.

Josef motioned to his brother to slow, and they veered off the road to circle around and approach the vizier and his men from the side.

The horses shuffled around at the edge of Yaseen's group. Zahra almost laughed when she noticed that they no longer had the camel with them; only Nadim could stand that thing.

We'll have to take their horses so they can't chase us when we rescue Amir.

She came up with a plan, which she whispered to the others, and then she and Nadim dismounted. Josef and Yurem returned the way they'd come and veered back onto the road.

Nadim stealthily worked his way toward the horses, hiding behind rocks and trees, while Zahra crept her way to the top of the small cliff, peeking over the edge. Yaseen and the guards were drinking water, while Amir sat awkwardly with hands tied behind his back and his mouth gagged.

Josef and Yurem galloped down the road, shouting and heading straight for the guards, who bolted upright in surprise. Josef didn't slow, but instead charged at the men, sending them dodging to the side to avoid being trampled underfoot.

"What's the meaning of this?" Yaseen flattened himself against the cliff to avoid the fracas.

Taking advantage of the utter chaos, Nadim gathered the reins of the vizier's horses and led them away. Josef and his brother were doing a fantastic job of creating mayhem, charging and kicking at Yaseen's men, keeping them from even being able to retrieve their scimitars. Only the ifrit Ghazi, still in his guise as guardsman, had managed to reach his weapon. He drew the blade and moved toward the brothers.

They were all distracted—it was time to free Amir. Zahra dropped from her perch on the cliff, intending to land next to Amir, but her robe got caught. She swung down, flailing, getting her arms in front of her just before she hit the side of the rock face. The cloth tore, and she plopped in a heap at the vizier's feet.

Yaseen glared down at her. "You! Foolish, meddlesome girl." He stepped on her back to hold her in place, his weight pressing her hard into the earth. She tried to push herself away or roll over, but any movement caused pain.

Yaseen kneeled atop her. "You give me no choice now but to deal with you in a more precise and permanent manner."

From the corner of her eye, she saw him draw forth a curved dagger. He was going to kill her! She thrashed, trying to escape from under his weight or knock him off of her.

"Nadim," she tried to yell, barely able to force the breath out.

It was the prince who came to her rescue. He barreled into Yaseen, sending the man flying into the dirt.

Zahra regained her feet and yanked out the prince's gag.

"Yaseen, that's enough," Amir said.

The vizier was not done. He pointed the dagger at Zahra. "This girl is a liar, an enchantress, and a danger to everyone she encounters."

"You have this wrong—" Amir started.

This wasn't the time for a discussion. Zahra grabbed Amir by the arm and pulled him along. "Let's go."

Josef and his brother kept the guards dancing around and distracted long enough for her and Amir to reach Nadim and mount the horses.

Behind them, Yaseen sang out a chant. Zahra risked a glance back and saw the vizier wave his hands and throw something to the ground. Three swirling, acrid clouds of smoke formed. Beneath them, mounds of sand rose from the earth. The sands formed into columns and then into the shape of men. In their hands, jagged bits of rock took the form of curved blades.

Yaseen commanded the sand warriors, "Bring the prince back alive and unharmed. Kill the others."

"Josef," Zahra called, "time to go."

Zahra heeled her horse's flanks, and she and her friends galloped off, the sand warriors striding eerily along the ground after them. With a few glances back as they rode, it became clear to them that the magical warriors were limited in their movement and soon would be left behind.

When they'd traveled far enough to be well out of sight of Yaseen's otherworldly fighters, they paused to consider their next move. Zahra untied Amir's hands, freeing the prince to clasp Josef's arm with a vigorous shake of gratitude.

"It is good to find you well," Amir said. "Blessings upon you for helping us yet again."

"Anytime, Prince. Now there is the matter of retrieving Rafi. Do you wish us to accompany you?"

"We have only to follow the river," Zahra said. "Now that we have horses, I think we can manage on our own in this."

Josef spun his horse around. "In that case, it seems this is where we part ways."

"If you ever find yourself in Alhad," Amir said, "I will make sure my father rewards you richly."

"Who knows where the future will take us? South for now." Josef waved as he and his brother rode off, and he shouted behind him, "May your paths be blessed, Zahra and Prince Amir of Alhad."

CHAPTER 27

"Where's Rafi?" Amir asked while they were watching Josef and his brother ride away.

Zahra smiled. "Worried about him, are you?"

"No," Amir said. "That is to say, I don't wish ill upon him—not until I make him my slave, that is. Then I'll have to punish him for his insolence."

"How thoughtful of you," Zahra said. "But remember, he's *my* servant." She laughed, though she felt guilty for even having said that. Rafi was not her servant; the boy was free to do as he chose, as far as she was concerned. She was just happy he chose to stay with them.

"Where is he?" Amir looked around, as if he were expecting the boy to jump out from behind a rock.

"He went swimming after the Scarab," she told Amir. "We're going to find him now."

Amir looked at Nadim. "Can't you just..."—he made a bursting gesture with his hand—"*poof* to the Scarab and get it?"

"Ordinarily, yes, I would be able to do just that. But alas, Ghazi has sealed it away in a special ambergris, which severed the link to my realm and, therefore, my access to its magic. I have less power here than you do until we retrieve the Scarab and remove the ambergris, which will not be easy."

"Why does the ambergris cut off your power?" Amir asked.

"That's a long story, but the simple version is that it comes from the Great Sea Serpent I mentioned before, and we jinn have a weakness to the bile of serpents. And that one in particular."

"How do we remove the coating from the Scarab?" Zahra asked.

"Our closest and best option lies back at your palace—the Eternal Flame. I believe that it should be able to burn it off."

"That's easy enough," Amir said.

"If we do not cleanse it of that coating," Nadim said, "I will slowly be pulled back into my realm."

"We'll get there," Zahra said. "But first we need to find Rafi."

They retraced their path back to the bridge where the boy had jumped into the river.

Amir gazed down the canyon at the rapidly flowing water. "Rafi swam down that river? The boy is crazy," he said.

"Or really brave," Zahra said. "And remember, he did it for you."

"More likely for you."

"He did it for all of us," Nadim stated.

"I hope he's alright," Zahra said.

Amir waved his hand in the air. "He'll be fine. We're back together now, my love, and we'll find him."

"Yes, we're back together." Zahra reached out and took hold of his hand, relieved to have saved him from the vizier's clutches, for the moment at least.

Amir squeezed her fingers. "You do love me." He leaned out from his saddle toward her. "Kiss me, my love."

Maybe when this was all done, she could see how Amir really felt about her, but it wasn't appropriate now. She held her hand to his chest and gently pushed him back upright. "It's your love that is the whole problem."

"Don't be so stubborn—you know I love you. How many times must I tell you so?"

"How many times must I tell you that your feelings are not your own? You saw the vizier's true intentions. Now let's focus on finding Rafi and the Scarab."

Though riding a horse was a new challenge for Zahra, it felt natural and she took to it quickly. It also had an enormous impact on her morale. She was weary from all their walking, yet now they were covering so much ground with ease.

They trotted beside the river, going up and down with the canyon, veering away from the water only when they were forced to. Nadim trailed them, leading the extra horse along for Rafi. They crossed a final rise before the canyon flattened out and the ground lowered to nearly the same level as the river. As they wound their way through a series of knolls, voices called out from up ahead.

"Give it here, boy."

"Throw it over."

Zahra motioned for her companions to dismount, and they moved forward with caution, crouching low behind desert scrub. Three scruffy men were standing against a cliff at the side of the river, which flowed past and dropped off into a waterfall beyond. At the top of the falls, on a small island of rock, Rafi was holding fast to a tree with one hand and clutching the Golden Scarab in the other. He'd found it. Just in time, by the look of things.

But now he was trapped. He wouldn't be able to swim to either shore quickly enough before getting carried over the falls. And judging from the roar, they landed far enough below to ensure certain death.

"Come on, boy. Toss us that bit of gold you've got there, and we'll find a way to haul you in."

Common bandits. How could they endanger the poor boy's life just for some gold? What awful people.

How was she going to get Rafi safely to shore?

"Those jackals," Amir whispered, standing up with an intent look in his eyes.

Zahra grabbed him and pulled him back down behind the bush.

"Quiet. Look, they have scimitars and we have nothing. We can't fight them."

"The boy needs our help."

"I can see that. But we need a plan."

"I'll send them scurrying. These men wouldn't harm the prince of Alhad."

"Oh, I think they very much would."

Amir puffed out his chest. "I know how to fight with a sword."

"You don't *have* a sword. And there are three of them."

Amir furrowed his brow. "You make very good points. Then let's sneak up behind them and push them into the river."

While Zahra agreed with the sentiment, she didn't think they'd make it halfway before being spotted.

Nadim shook his head. "We need to come up with a better plan."

"Well, I don't hear any better ideas coming from you, demon," Amir whispered.

"We jinn dislike being referred to by that word, mortal boy."

"It appears I'm not the only one who's mortal now," Amir said.

"Not amusing," Nadim said. "Alas, I'm already starting to be pulled back to my realm." He held up his hands and one of his fingers was partially transparent.

"Ha! Now who's missing a finger?"

Enough of this squabbling. "This isn't getting us any closer to a plan," Zahra said, "and Rafi needs our—"

Zahra turned upon noticing an odd rustling sound that had slowly been getting louder from behind them. At first she only saw a column of dust rising, as if horses were being ridden along the dirt path, but then she saw shapes. The sand warriors that had been summoned by the vizier! The magical fighters had followed them all this way.

She pointed. "Look."

Amir's eyes widened.

A sense of panic washed over Zahra, but it was followed by relief. "At least they all came after us."

"Why is that good?"

"It means they didn't hunt down Josef and his brother. Those two have endured enough misfortune."

Nadim turned his head toward her slightly and nodded in agreement.

Amir crouched down. "The misfortune is ours now, and we'd better come up with something fast. We can't deal with the bandits and those things at the same time—or even individually."

Think, think, think. What if... Zahra had an idea, which she quickly relayed to her companions.

"I like it," Amir said, standing up and running straight toward the bandits. "Agh!" He screamed as he ran, pretending to be frightened.

He could have waited for us.

"That boy is going to get us all killed," Nadim said, but he followed Amir anyway, doing his own horrible impression at being terrified.

Zahra joined them. "Run for your lives! Magic sand demons!"

The bandits had turned to face them, confusion on their faces. At Zahra's exclamation, their bewilderment deepened until they noticed the sand men sliding along the ground toward them.

"Help us," Zahra pleaded in her best defenseless-girl voice. "Please, brave fighters, protect us." It made her sick even to pretend to appeal to them for protection, but this was the best she could come up with.

She ran to their side, all the way to the cliff, pulling Amir and Nadim with her. "We have no weapons," she said.

"And he's the prince," Nadim said. "He can reward you handsomely."

No! Why had he said that? You don't tell a group of bandits you have an unarmed, unprotected prince in their midst. Zahra cast the jinni a withering look and shook her head.

Nadim smiled back innocently.

Fortunately, the bandits seemed so shocked at the approach of the sand men that they had paid little attention to his words.

"Kill the warriors," Nadim prompted. "Your scimitars should

make short work of them. They're only made of sand."

Now that's not a bad tactic. "Yes, you men should be able to easily kill those beasts. We felled one with our bare hands, but it took the three of us together. With your weapons, they should be no match for you."

It worked. The bandits put on cocky grins and stalked out to meet the supernatural fighters. Zahra didn't know how this was going to play out, but she was already thinking about how they were going to rescue Rafi. None of them could swim to him, or they'd be in the same predicament. They needed a rope. They'd also have to deal with the survivors of the coming clash between the sand warriors and the brigands.

The earthen men shifted and slid forward, their movement unnervingly disconnected from the motion of their legs. The bandits yelled and charged.

The first bandit swung his blade at a sand warrior's chest. The fighter didn't bother to block, but absorbed the impact full force, and the thief's blade sunk into its body. Then it slid harmlessly out its side. The creature swung its own weapon at the bandit's waist, sending him sprawling to the earth.

Uh-oh. This is going to be a quick fight, and it won't be good for any of us.

The brigands yelled again and slashed and hacked at the sand warriors, managing to chop off arms and legs and even a couple of heads, but the warriors absorbed sand from beneath them and regrew their body parts. Their progress having been impeded by the bandits, the sand warriors fought back. The battle was quick; in a short time, three dead brigands lay sprawled in the dirt.

And three surviving, fully reformed sand warriors stalked toward Zahra and her companions.

CHAPTER 28

A mir shouted for them to run in different directions.

He soon realized the warriors were only chasing Zahra and Nadim, and leaving him alone—for now. He recalled Yaseen's words: "Bring the prince back alive and unharmed." So then, these unnatural creations shouldn't hurt him. Hopefully.

"Get behind me," he called to the others, moving between Zahra and an approaching sand fighter. He held out his hands in front of him. "Halt," he commanded the unnatural monster.

The sand warrior plodded forward, ignoring his order. Amir stood his ground, gritting his teeth and squinting as it approached. It was nearly upon him and hadn't moved its sword arm at all, so that at least was a good sign. But it also didn't slow as it met him.

Its chest pressed up against his outstretched hands. It paused for a moment, then pushed forward. Amir's hands sank into the thing's torso as it continued on. Sand wrapped around his wrists until his arms had penetrated through its chest and out its back. It advanced further, unfazed by Amir's arms embedded in its body. It wrapped its own arms around the prince and pulled him even closer, apparently content to take him captive. Amir swallowed hard and stared, horrified, at the monster's soulless eyes made entirely of sand, no expression on its face.

What had the vizier unleashed upon them?

With an angry yell, Amir hurled himself against the beast. He created just enough momentum to tackle it to the ground. An outer layer of the creature's sand scattered to the earth and its grip loosened enough for Amir to pull his arms free. The monstrosity oozed back into a standing position without having moved to get up, its fallen sands reabsorbed into the man-shaped figure. Amir rolled and scampered away. The thing shuffled on toward his beloved Zahra, and she ran once again.

Amir had done little but delay its progress, though he had confirmed his hunch that the things wouldn't attack him. How could he use that against them? He hopped back to his feet. "I have an idea."

He chased down the warrior that he'd tackled and grabbed it by the wrist that held the sword. It pulled against him and the sand passed around his hands. Amir jerked hard, squeezing his hands straight through its arm. Its hand disintegrated, the sand falling to the ground, along with its sword. As it reached down to regrow its hand and grab the sword, Amir kicked hard at the weapon, scattering it back into its component shards of rock.

He ran to the next creature and squeezed its hand off as well, again kicking its sword away, and repeated the process with the third.

With the weaponless monsters slowly pursuing Nadim and Zahra, Amir retrieved the scimitars from the fallen bandits.

"Ha. Now what can they do to us?" Immensely pleased with himself, he handed a sword to each of the others.

"Choke us? Suffocate us?" Zahra suggested.

"Crush us?" the jinni added.

Zahra swiped her sword at her stalker, barely grazing it. Her hand shook even while holding the weapon. "I don't know how to use this." Her voice quavered.

"Swing hard, like this." Amir hacked into the thing's chest. As the bandits had discovered, it merely cut into it with little effect. Some sand spattered onto the ground, but coalesced back into the beast a moment later.

The warrior's arms extended and pulled Zahra to its body. Sand flowed along its form and began surrounding her. She was right—it was trying to suffocate her.

Amir grabbed her by one arm, yanking her from the thing's grasp. "You were right. We need a new plan."

"The water!" shouted Rafi, still standing on the tiny rocky island at the edge of the waterfall.

"He's right," Zahra said. "Maybe they'll dissolve in the river. Nadim, can you swim?"

"Silly girl, I have lived for thousands of your years, and traveled kingdoms and realms you've—"

"I'll take that as a yes," she said. "Can you take me to the other side of the river?"

Thankfully, the sand men, though relentless, moved slowly. This gave Amir's precious Zahra time to run around and craft a plan. Amir hacked off sand limbs again and again, forcing the creatures to slow even more as they reabsorbed the granules. Despite the danger of their situation, Amir felt invigorated at finally using his skill with a sword, even if it was against nearly mindless adversaries.

Zahra ran upriver along the bank as far as she could and waded in, the jinni following her.

Nadim let her grab hold of his waist. "Hold on tight." He began to swim to the opposite bank.

"Take care with her, jinni." It was a plea as much as a command. Amir knew Zahra had not yet mastered even the most basic swimming techniques, and despite Nadim's boasts, the jinni didn't look particularly strong or able-bodied.

Soon, they saw their plan was working. The sand warriors followed them into the river and trudged after them. Amir was relieved when Nadim made it across with Zahra and they stepped onto the shore. Unfortunately, the sand creatures, even though they struggled, continued on and also made it to the other side. They were smaller, having lost much of their mass to the river, but they still lived. As they stood in place, they grew larger as they pulled in sand from the shoreline.

"It didn't work," Zahra said, looking concerned.

It almost had, but the warriors hadn't been in the water long enough. Unfortunately, what with the flow of the river, Amir couldn't expect them to swim around and keep the things immersed, especially considering Zahra's inability to swim. But maybe...

"Swim to the rock with Rafi. I'll fashion a rope and throw it to you, and hopefully we can get them to fully dissolve."

"What? You want us to get stuck on that rock, too?"

"Trust me."

Amir started tearing clothes from the corpses of the bandits and tying them together. He worked as quickly as he could, looking up to see that Nadim had indeed reentered the water, Zahra in tow. This had better work. If he lost her over those falls... Well, he didn't want to think about that.

Zahra splashed against the current. "This is madness."

Nadim continued, steering them directly toward Rafi's refuge.

Amir yanked off another piece of clothing from a dead bandit. Just a little more and he should have enough length. The jinni pulled Zahra onto the rock and up to the solitary tree to which Rafi clung. "It's alright, Rafi," Zahra said, panting. "Amir has a plan."

Her statement didn't remove the mask of fear and worry from the boy's face. "He'd better hurry," Rafi said.

Amir glanced up again. The sand warriors had reached the rock. His makeshift rope would have to do.

"Catch." He tossed one end of it to them, but it didn't have enough weight and fell far short.

"Hold on!" Amir shouted.

Zahra screamed. The sand warriors rose to their feet. "Hurry!"

He needed more time. How could he slow the beasts? Maybe the boy?

"Rafi," Amir shouted as he wrapped a rock inside the last segment of his lifeline to give it more heft. "Stand in front of them. The warriors won't attack you if you don't threaten them."

The boy stood frozen with fear.

Amir tied the other end of his rope around an outcrop of rock and hurled the weighted end toward them. It floated out in a perfect arc and landed...

A few feet short. *No!* "Hold on, hold on."

"Stop saying that!" Zahra shouted.

Amir ran to the corpses and grabbed two more shirts, fastening them to his line and repositioning the rock he was using as a weight.

Nadim faced off with the sand warriors and wrapped his arms around all three of the beasts to hold them back. The sand mostly enveloped his body and started to encase Zahra.

Amir swung the newly lengthened rope. It flew out and up...

Zahra reached out from the mass of sand and caught it.

"Quick, all of you grab on and climb to shore," Amir shouted to them.

Zahra seized the Golden Scarab from Rafi and stowed it safely away. The boy slipped, but managed to grab the end of the improvised lifeline. His movement caused her to slide as well, but she maintained her footing long enough for Nadim to take hold of the line in front of her.

The sand warriors had now fully covered the jinni, and almost entirely encased Zahra. They were running out of time. Zahra struggled against the sand and tried to break free. Her hands slid along the rope until they caught on a knot in the clothes. The abrupt stop jarred her.

This time she did lose her footing and slipped, her fall yanking the line and sending all of them toppling over the edge of the waterfall.

CHAPTER 29

Zahra held her breath and closed her eyes as she fell off their rocky perch and over the lip of the falls. One thing she did not do was let go of the tether Amir had thrown them.

She bounced along the top of the falls, rolling across as the force of the water pushed them against the side of the canyon. Nadim bumped against her face and chest, and Rafi shouted from below. But at least they were still with her.

She pushed away from the cliff with her legs, opening her eyes and taking a deep breath. The sand from her enchanted attacker had completely washed off her head and was slowly being dissolved away from her body. Looking up through the splashes from the torrent of water coming over the ridge, she saw Nadim was mostly free of the sand warriors, as well.

"Rafi!" she called. "Are you alright?"

"I ... think ... so ... but there's too much ... water."

They'd survived thus far. Now they only had to get back up over the falls. She again pushed with her legs, straightening them in order to get out of the direct flow of the water. Above her, Nadim did the same, and she saw that Rafi had finally managed to do so as well. As hard as she tried, she couldn't walk up over the edge—the rush of the water was simply too strong. Even Nadim made little progress, his feet slipping out from under him whenever he tried to step up.

She barely heard over the roar of the falls a shout from Amir to hold on.

She really wished he would stop saying that. It wasn't like they were going to let go, now, was it? She looked down. Her stomach clenched. It was a long, long drop. No, she was definitely going to hold on as long as she could. She desperately hoped Rafi could hold out.

"How are you, Rafi?"

"Scared. My arms hurt."

"I know, we'll—"

Their tether moved, sliding up and over the top of the falls. Nadim walked his feet along with the movement, and he made it over. She tried and succeeded for a bit before her legs were swept out from under her and she plunged back into the violent cascade of water.

She held her breath again as the makeshift rope pulled her upward. Zahra managed to regain her footing, but she would not go over that edge without Rafi.

"Rafi, climb up."

The boy maneuvered himself onto her back, then climbed up and over her. The rope tugged again from above, and Rafi made it over the lip.

Soon she, too, crossed the edge and saw Rafi crawling onto the shore. She relaxed. The tension she'd been feeling since she'd first seen him trapped by the bandits oozed away. He was finally safe.

She held her head above the water as she was pulled to the riverbank. Amir had tied the line of clothes to one of their horses and it had hauled them to safety.

At the shore, Nadim and Rafi helped her onto dry land. Rafi wrapped his arms around her waist. "You didn't leave me."

"I'll never leave you." She returned his powerful hug. She meant it; the boy was alone in the world, just like her, and she would never leave him to fend for himself.

Amir rushed up, relief plastered all over his face.

"That was quick thinking, my prince," she complimented him.

"I couldn't let anything happen to you, my love." Amir pulled her into a kiss.

What was he—

She lost herself in his firm embrace and in the feel of his lips on hers. She had imagined this more than once, ever since he'd saved her from falling out that window in the palace. For a long moment, she forgot he was under a spell. She seized hold of him and kissed him back, having never experienced these feelings before. The world faded from her thoughts and she clutched him tightly, not wanting their embrace to end.

Rafi mumbled something, but his words failed to fully penetrate her consciousness.

Would it be so bad if they failed in their mission? She could go back to the palace and become Amir's princess. Isn't that what they both wanted? She immediately felt guilty and ashamed for thinking that and broke off the kiss, gently pushing him away from her.

"I'm fine, too, Prince," Rafi said. "In case you were wondering."

Amir patted the boy's head. "Well, you did retrieve the Golden Scarab, so it seems you're not completely useless. Maybe you'll make a fine slave after all."

"I don't think—" Rafi began.

"He's teasing you, Rafi," Zahra said. "And you did great. Both of you."

The boy and the prince both puffed up, grins widening across their faces.

"Yes, well done, everyone," Nadim said. "Congratulations all around." The jinni didn't even sound sarcastic this time.

Zahra's mind grudgingly started to return to reality after that kiss. "We've survived this, but we have a new problem: we have the Scarab back, and we're all together again, which is great, but

Nadim doesn't have access to his magic anymore. And look, he's still fading."

More of the jinni's features had turned ghostly; she could see through part of his hands now, and his ears.

Rafi's eyes grew wide and concerned. "He's disappearing? How will we get his magic back?"

"We think we can clear the ambergris from his Scarab, which will return his power, but we'll need access to the Eternal Flame."

"The Flame is in my father's personal chambers," Amir said. "Ordinarily I could easily take us there, but now we'll have to sneak past Yaseen and his men. They'll be all over the palace, and, knowing the vizier, stationed throughout the city as well."

"Even when we've restored my powers," Nadim added, "I will have to defeat Ghazi, which will be no easy feat."

Amir cast the jinni a dubious look. "Are you sure you will even be able to do that?"

Zahra wondered the same thing, not for the first time. This scruffy, paunchy little man against the huge, fiery demon she'd seen in the vizier's chambers?

"Hey," Rafi countered, "he's a powerful jinni who's lived for thousands of years."

Amir didn't look convinced. "Don't get me wrong, I appreciate having had my finger restored, but other than that and the awful camel, we've mostly just seen smoke."

Again, Amir mirrored Zahra's concern.

The jinni seemed not to have taken offense. "I have revealed but a tiny portion of my power. Still, as I've said, defeating the ifrit will not be easy. What is worse, I believe I know the spell used on you, my prince. Because it was not a direct use of the ifrit's magic, even if I banished him back to our realm, that in itself likely wouldn't nullify the spell."

"So what do we do?" Amir asked.

"I propose we craft our own spell to undo it."

"Great," Zahra said. "Let's do that."

"I think it is our best chance, but it will also be difficult," Nadim said. "The spell requires a number of components, such as kohl, frankincense, darkling beetle acid—"

"Cobra venom?" Zahra interjected.

"Yes. You know this spell?"

"I know that component." She recalled her brush with the snake in the bazaar.

Nadim continued: "It also requires opium poppy seeds, a Midnight Lily, and a—"

"What's a Midnight Lily?" Rafi asked.

The flower Vizier Yaseen had used. This is *the same spell.*

"A beautiful translucent lily, extremely rare, with a potent scent," Nadim said.

"Like the one Maliha presented to you," Zahra said to Amir. She had called it a Soul Lily, but it must be the same as this Midnight Lily.

Amir nodded. "With those ingredients, we can make a counter-spell?"

"With those ... and one other ingredient." Nadim frowned. "A drop of the ifrit's blood."

"What?" Amir said. "How on earth are we going to get that?"

Rafi shrugged. "I'm not worried. You'll figure it out. You're the prince." The boy smiled up at Amir.

Amir shook his head, stammering but unable to find words this time.

"So," Zahra said, "if we get all those things—"

"And mix them together properly," Nadim interjected.

"—we can undo the spell?"

"Yes. Hopefully."

"Hopefully? You don't even know if it will work?" Zahra asked.

"I've never made the spell myself," the jinni admitted, "but it should work. We mix the components, add the lily, and have the prince sniff the flower. This time, instead of looking at you or anyone else after smelling it, he will look in a mirror. Seeing himself rather than another should neutralize the effect and leave his mind free and clear."

"*Should?*"

Amir squeezed her shoulder. "Whether it works or not, I'll still be in love with you, so it's fine either way."

Zahra desperately wanted to believe his feelings toward her would remain once they'd broken the spell. "At least we have a plan now." *Assuming Nadim is as powerful as he says he is, and can defeat Ghazi.*

They buried the bodies of the three thieves, gathered the horses, and told an overjoyed Rafi that Josef had survived and had helped them once again. With the sunset soon upon them, they opted to spend the night by the river, choosing a spot away from the battleground.

Zahra ascended a dusty hill to watch the shimmering orange sun sink below the horizon.

Footsteps alerted her to Amir's approach. He sat silently for a few moments as the dusk grew.

"When you went over the falls, I thought I'd lost you," he said in barely more than a whisper.

"And I thought we'd lost you when Yaseen took you away."

She was horrified at the thought of the vizier getting what he wanted. Regardless of how Amir felt about Zahra once the spell was canceled, at least his thoughts and feelings would be true. If he felt nothing for her, she would be hurt but would understand—she hoped.

What must the sultan be thinking about all this? "Your father must be so worried about you."

The corner of Amir's lips turned down. "I don't know. I love him, but I feel like he wants to control my whole life. For once, I wanted to do something myself—choose my own bride." He sighed. "But now that I've found the girl I want to marry, I think maybe she's not interested in me."

"I'm interested, but I don't even really know you," Zahra said.

"What do you mean? We spent a great day together before any of this even started."

"A day? You think you can know someone in a day?"

"I know that I love you."

"And we both know that you're under a love spell."

Amir opened his mouth as if to argue his point again, but stopped himself. "Tell me more about you: what of your father, your mother?" he asked.

"My mother was poor, and became sick, and could no longer take care of me. I haven't seen or heard from her since the day she consigned me to the palace."

The memory of that moment crashed down upon her. It was one she'd tried hard to forget. Standing at the palace entrance, being handed off to Yaseen. Her mother explaining that this was for the best, telling Zahra not to worry about her, that she'd find the help she needed from magic healers. Zahra reaching for her, her hand clasping onto the medallion on her mother's necklace. Her mother forcing a smile, sniffing and blinking away tears as she peeled Zahra's fingers off of it. Seeing her mother for the last time as she turned and walked away.

Feeling terrified and alone. Abandoned.

She still carried anger at her mother for leaving her. She knew it wasn't fair, but the pain had never left her.

Zahra wiped at her eyes. "She handed me over so that I could have a chance at a better life."

Despite the hurt, Zahra had missed her mother so much she'd thought more than once about running away to find her. She might have, if she'd had any idea where to look. "I thought of using my first wish to take me to her, but I don't even know if she's still alive."

If she was alive, why hadn't she come back to take Zahra from the palace? "And my father died before I was even born."

Amir put his arm around her shoulder and pulled her close.

"My mother died when I was young," Amir said quietly. "She was always so good to me. My father said she doted on me too much, but she truly cared for me. And she wasn't ... demanding or controlling. I miss her." A tear trickled down his cheek.

Prior to fleeing the palace, Zahra hadn't thought about her

mother much recently. Her gut clenched as immense guilt rose up in her. "I don't..." Her breath caught. "I don't even remember my mother's face." She started to cry and barely noticed Rafi approaching.

"I don't remember my mother, either," the boy said, settling down next to her. "When she died, my father hated me, and sold me to Master Mustafa. I was alone, too. But now I have you, Master Zahra."

Zahra squeezed tears out of her eyes. "You're not my servant, Rafi."

"Please don't sell me. I don't want to be alone again."

She hugged him as the last arc of the sun disappeared beneath the distant sands. "Don't worry, I will not leave you."

CHAPTER 30

Zahra awoke first in the morning and roused the others. Exhaustion still weighed on her—from all the traveling, from nearly dying, and from her sad and dark thoughts the evening before—but she managed to get them on the road well before dawn.

Hours later, a bright light shone on the base of the clouds ahead—it could only be coming from the Eternal Flame atop the Palace of Light. They were almost home.

They crested the final hill and saw the city below, bathed in resplendent beauty. The light from the Eternal Flame shone brightly from within a glass dome at the peak of the Palace. Its intense beam split at the top, deflecting to five other similar domes around the city. These absorbed and diffused the light, highlighting a blanket of fog that floated among the buildings, creating an ethereal aquamarine glow.

Zahra had never seen Alhad from the outside; she paused and quietly took in the view with the others. As the sun breached the horizon, it rose into a striking pink and orange sky, casting a magical, warm radiance upon the city and the Palace of Light.

She had mixed feelings about returning. Alhad truly was a magnificent place, and it felt good to be coming home, but doubts and fears about the massive task ahead seeped into her, like the darkness had seeped into the core of the palace.

They needed to be vigilant, to avoid the countless guards and spies the vizier would have watching for them. At Nadim's suggestion, they removed any tack with royal insignia from their horses. Then they waited for other travelers along the road, hoping to slip in unnoticed among a larger group.

When a small caravan approached, they traded two of their horses for new clothing and enough dinars to purchase the items they needed for their spell. With only two horses remaining, Zahra rode behind Amir, and Nadim shared his mount with Rafi.

Wrapping themselves up from head to toe, they rode at the tail end of the caravan, trying to look inconspicuous. As they approached the gate, the caravan slowed, and Zahra leaned out to see why. The guards were carefully inspecting every wagon and forcing everyone to reveal their faces.

She exchanged a worried look with Amir. Her heart sank. This wasn't going to work. While Nadim and Rafi could easily pass through, she and the prince would certainly be recognized.

"What are we going to do?" she whispered to the others.

Amir sat tall on his horse. "I shall declare myself to be the prince and march straight to the palace to set things right."

Was he daft? Zahra glared at him.

"Never mind," he said.

"This reminds me of the Tale of Barad and the Seamstress," Nadim said.

Could the jinni ever get straight to the point? They were getting closer to the gate by the minute.

Rafi perked up. "Ooh, what's the Tale of Barad and—?"

"*Skip* the tale," Zahra said. "Tell us your idea."

"You see, Barad was a strong and handsome blacksmith who was married to a—"

Zahra's patience grew short. "Nadim! Do you have a plan?"

The jinni heaved a great sigh. "You humans are always so impatient. Very well. The idea is this..."

He revealed his plan, which was surprisingly simple and clever.

They agreed it was the best chance they had. She and Amir dismounted from their horse, Rafi taking control of the reins. They then purchased blankets from a fellow traveler in the caravan and draped them over the front and sides of the two horses. After running a few straps over the horses' backs and down under their bellies, she and Amir each clung to the straps from the undersides of the animals, where they were hidden from casual view. Amir at first complained about how unfitting this was for a prince, but ultimately he accepted the indignation.

Zahra strained with the effort of holding on and wrapped her hands around the straps to make it easier. Still, by the time they reached the gate the exertion was nearly too much. They approached the guards.

"Show us your faces," a guard said.

Hurry up, hurry up. The strain was getting to her. And then her nose started to itch.

A sneeze? Not now!

The tickle in her nose wouldn't go away. She pulled in a sharp breath and knew it was too late. She shoved her face against the belly of the horse and the sneeze burst out, muffled by the animal's chest. Had the guards heard her? She could feel another sneeze coming on, and again pressed her face into the horse to let it out, and then suffered a final sneeze after that.

"Many pardons," Nadim said from atop her mount. "This animal is rather flatulent today."

Good one, Nadim.

"Move on," the guards said, waving them past.

As soon as they were in the clear, Nadim dismounted and helped her out from under the horse. "That was exciting," he said.

"Like the Tale of Barad and the Seamstress?" Zahra asked.

Nadim laughed. "Now you're getting into the spirit of the adventure. I'll have a new set of tales to tell soon, about the journey of Zahra and the Prince."

"Hey!" Rafi said. "What about me?"

"You'll be in there. Let me think ... the Tale of the Boy, the Scarab, and the Waterfall..."

Rafi shone with pride, but Amir shook his head and brought them back to the present. "We have to assume Yaseen will have people watching within the city as well."

He was right; they agreed they would attract less attention individually, so they split up to acquire the necessary components of the spell. Zahra assigned the task of getting the cobra venom to Amir because she didn't want to risk being recognized by the snake charmer, Jabari. Rafi went to buy the more mundane ingredients.

She and the jinni headed to the exotic part of the bazaar, where rare and expensive items were sold, hoping to find someone offering Midnight Lilies for sale. Luck was with her: on a stand behind one of the merchants, amid other strange items, was a smoky, dark blue lily. The merchant's sign read "Zain's Wonderful and Magical Curiosities."

She approached, eyes locked on the Midnight Lily. Before she could address the merchant, Nadim stepped in front of her.

"A fine day to you, my friend," Nadim said. "I see you are a purveyor of truly exquisite and unique specimens. I thought perhaps of all the people in this bazaar, you might have the one thing I'm looking for."

The merchant looked Nadim over as if wondering what a pauper like him was doing in this section of the bazaar. Still, the man greeted the jinni cheerfully enough. "Ah, indeed, my friend, and a wonderful day to you. If it's a rare and exotic item you seek, none other here shall likely have it, and you've come to the right place. What are you looking for, friend?"

"I seek a golden orchid, a strange flower from the forests of China, purported to have an enchanting effect on any who inhale its intoxicating sweet scent. I know not how well they travel, but it occurred to me that if anybody would know how to keep such a thing alive during a journey, it would be one well-versed in rarities, such as yourself."

What is he talking about? We don't need an orchid, we need that lily sitting right there.

Nadim obviously knew that very well—he was the one who'd told her the components they needed, after all—so she let him continue without interruption, assuming he had a plan.

"Ah," Zain the Merchant said. "The golden orchid. Yes, yes, rare indeed. I must admit I've not seen its like in years, nor do I have the exact specimen you seek, but—"

"Oh, how dreadfully unfortunate, my good man," Nadim interrupted. "I had my hopes high, but it seems I must search elsewhere."

"No, no." The merchant halted him. "I have not that particular flower, but I have something which may be its equal. No—its superior." Zain slid forward the flower they sought. "I present to you the Midnight Lily: a flower unequaled in beauty, in scent, or in its magical and enchanting potency. Surely this will meet your desires, beyond that even of the golden orchid you mention."

Zain lifted the glass covering and presented the flower to Nadim, who took a slight whiff of the lily. "Hmm... It does have a certain delicate charm to it, and yet I am dubious as to its suitability for my needs. What do you ask for this?"

"For you, my friend—a scant two hundred dinars for this rare, exquisite beauty."

Two hundred? They barely had twenty-five. Zahra had had no idea it would cost so much. Now what were they going to do?

Nadim shook his head. "Ah, far too much for something that may not even match my needs, I'm afraid. I appreciate your time and—"

"No, no, I assure you, it is a wonder. The sultan's vizier himself purchased its twin only yesterday. This is a singular flower, found only in the Garden of the Moon, and no easy feat to acquire. I understand that it's not precisely what you seek, my friend, and for that special consideration and knowing you are obviously one of distinguished tastes..." He lowered his voice, shooting a look at their surroundings before saying, "I can offer this amazing flower to you for one hundred fifty dinars."

Nadim took another sniff, but again shook his head. "I'm afraid the price is far too high to take a chance that it will suffice. A fine day to you, my friend."

Zahra had to admit he was excellent at feigning indifference. Now she understood Nadim's approach; had they arrived and asked for it straight out, as she had planned to do, they would have never convinced him to haggle to such an extent. Not that it was likely to matter, given how far off they were on the price. She would have happily paid one hundred fifty dinars for it, or even two hundred, if she'd had that much.

"Friend, friend, do not be so hasty," Zain the Merchant said, calling Nadim back to his table, and also waving over a young girl who was standing nearby.

The merchant took a long look at Zahra before speaking to the girl he'd called over. "Can't you see? I'm busy here. Now go and find your mother." He winked at the girl and she scurried off.

The merchant leaned forward and again cast a long glance down the aisle of booths before returning his attention to Nadim. "This is the last of these that I currently possess, and I am reluctant to part with it. However, its true value is not often known, and so I am in the unfortunate position of being willing to let it go for what is truly a bargain price. For you—and may it meet your needs—I will be willing to sell it for seventy-five dinars."

That was a huge drop in price, but still thrice what they could afford. Nadim seemed to realize this as well and merely offered the merchant a frown this time as he walked away.

"What will you pay?" Zain called after him, again casting a look down the aisle of the bazaar. "Fifty dinars? Forty?"

Nadim paused, and Zahra began to wonder if they actually could get him down to twenty-five. She saw the jinni's gaze locked onto something behind her. "The merchant is not negotiating, but stalling," Nadim said. She turned. The young girl Zain had sent off was returning with two guards. The vizier must have told him about them.

"Guards!" Zain called out, pointing at Zahra.

Nadim ducked between two booths, pulling Zahra along with him. A shout from a guard behind them prompted them to forget stealth and run. They turned a corner and ran straight into another guard. The man swiftly grabbed Zahra around the waist and called out to his companions. Zahra shot her elbow into the guard's gut, but he held her tight.

"Let ... go!" She struggled in his grip.

As the guard squeezed her arms together, her left hand pushed against the head of the petrified serpent wrapped around her right forearm. The snake came to life once more, growing rapidly in size. Still coiled around her arm, it hissed and snapped at the guard.

I'll have to remember that trick.

The man jolted back in shock, releasing Zahra from his grip, and Nadim slammed his body into the man and sent him sprawling to the ground. Zahra quickly pressed down on the serpent's head again, and it snapped back, returning to its jewelry form spiraled around her arm.

Nadim grabbed her and dove into an alley, ran under an archway into another street, and bolted into a crowd before sidestepping into a different alley. Crouching behind a fruit stand, Zahra huffed and puffed as she caught her breath.

She considered their situation: if she'd been with Maliha, her friend probably would have stolen the flower while the merchant was distracted. If only Amir could be ... the prince ... they could have bought it without a second thought.

"I'm glad to see you made use of my little serpent trap," Nadim said, pointing to the snake wrapped around her arm. "Well done."

"It was an accident. Anyway—what do we do now?"

"Now we'll have to get a Midnight Lily ourselves," Nadim said.

"How?"

"From the Garden of the Moon."

CHAPTER 31

A mir was disappointed to learn that Zahra had failed to acquire a Midnight Lily, but glad she'd escaped capture. "Did the guards hurt you?"

"No. One grabbed me, but I used this to scare him off." She pointed to the snake bracelet around her forearm.

He'd make sure that guard was kicked out onto the streets when this was over, but when that would be he didn't know. He and Rafi had acquired the other ingredients necessary for the spell, but that still left two that they didn't have. The drop of the ifrit's blood seemed impossible at the moment, but how would they even obtain the lily?

Nadim told them his plan, explaining that the nearest place the Midnight Lilies grew was in the fabled Garden of the Moon.

Rafi turned to face Amir. "How do we get to the Garden of the Moon?"

"Why do you assume I would know?" Amir wanted to smack himself as soon as he asked that question, because he knew the answer would be—

"You're the prince."

"Yes, yes, very funny. I do know the Garden of the Moon, in fact; I've never visited it, but I know its general direction from the city. It rests within the Unbreachable Cliffs of Ka'Run."

"First we have to sneak back out of the city," Zahra said.

"I doubt the guards will investigate the people exiting," Amir said.

Nadim nodded in agreement. "Nevertheless, we should avoid speaking to anyone or bringing any attention to ourselves."

They sent Rafi to purchase some supplies, ate a quick lunch, and rode to the city exit, this time with Zahra and Amir riding together atop one of the horses instead of hanging from underneath. Amir breathed a huge sigh of relief as they made their way out of the city with no interest from the guards.

He was excited to see the Garden of the Moon—it was said to be wondrous. He pointed in the direction he thought the Cliffs of Ka'Run ought to be. Nadim took hold of his arm and adjusted it about 45 degrees to the right.

Rafi shook his head at the correction.

That boy had some nerve. As if *he* had any idea where they were going, either.

At least I was generally in the right direction. Not bad for having never been there, or even outside the city walls, before I tracked down Zahra.

Amir nudged his horse and led them in the direction the jinni had indicated. Other than a few adjustments to their heading, courtesy of surreptitious glances at Nadim, he took them on a straight path through yet more desert. Shortly after midday, they approached the towering ring of the Unbreachable Cliffs.

"We've arrived!" Amir proclaimed. He knew he'd get them there with no issues.

Zahra's eyes scanned the cliffs. "Where is the entrance to the Garden?"

That was an excellent question. "My father told me nobody can remember precisely how to enter, but he guessed it had to do with the phases of the moon."

"What does that even mean?" Rafi asked.

Amir gnawed on his lower lip. "I don't know."

Rafi frowned. "But you're the—"

"I know, I know," Amir cut him off. "I've learned much from my father's mathematicians and astrologers, but I can't see how that would apply here."

"You don't know how to get in?" Zahra asked.

"Well, I... No."

"And you?" she asked Nadim.

"I've never been to the Garden myself," the jinni said, "but I'm told the entrance has something to do with the phases of the moon."

Amir's brow furrowed. "I just said that."

"Maybe that's where I heard it, then."

They spent the next hour circling around the massive wall of stone, before they reached an area they decided must be the entryway. A large circular region of the otherwise rough cliff face was indented and smooth, and on the ground before it a flat stone slab extended out. A dozen evenly spaced columns rose up from the stone, forming what clearly looked like a path to an entrance.

Amir approached the smooth, rounded area of the wall. To each side, two glass sculptures of plants protruded up from depressions in the stone base, as if they were growing up from planters. He ran his hands along the wall, tracing a continuous groove around the circular region. Could this be a door?

"This might be the entrance." He pushed firmly against it, but it felt every bit as solid as a mountain.

Around the circular door were a series of engravings, showing the different phases of the moon. He tried pressing each of them, but they were no more than they appeared—just etchings in the rock.

"Maybe we have to do something with these columns," Zahra said.

They examined the pillars, which turned out to be more like tall pedestals. Atop each sat a crystalline lens, set in a device that allowed the lens to rotate and redirect the sun's light. Nadim adjusted a lens such that the light played along the wall near the Garden's entrance door.

"What if we have to line up the light from these lenses to those engravings around the door?" Zahra suggested.

She moved a lens to overlap with a phase of the moon engraved on the cliff face around the entryway. The projected light was in a different shape than the phase she had selected, so she moved it to the proper phase and rotated it to line up.

Amir and Nadim joined her, and they matched a number of the lenses to phases on the wall, but there were more engravings than lenses.

"Hold on," Amir said. "We're not getting anywhere. What is it that we're trying to do?"

They discussed the current phase of the moon, which was nearly full, and saw multiple carvings of a full moon on the wall. Which one did they have to light up? All of them? They tried every combination they could think of, still with no result.

Zahra stomped her foot. "We're making no progress. Aren't people supposed to be able to get in here?"

Her words echoed his thoughts. How hard could this truly be?

"My father said the Garden of the Moon was created centuries ago by a great magician, but sealed so that only those who were worthy would have access to it. It was a gift to Alhad, but a gift not to be taken for granted."

"Maybe we're just not worthy," Zahra said.

How could she say that? "There's nothing you're not worthy of, my love."

Amir moved to the shade to take a break and have a drink of water, tying the horses to the nearest pedestal. Hours had passed, and yet they'd accomplished nothing.

This was annoying. How could the Prince of Alhad be denied access to the garden made for his kingdom?

Zahra looked as frustrated as he felt, but Nadim was amused. "This is wonderful," the jinni said. "Truly something unexpected and intriguing."

Well, at least the jinni was enjoying himself. That made it all worthwhile.

"Although," Nadim said, "we should probably figure this out soon." He held up his left arm, revealing a hand that was nearly invisible.

Rafi, meanwhile, had wandered back toward the door, his water jug in hand. He went to one of the glass plant sculptures and tilted his water at its base. What was he thinking? Why was he pouring water on the ground?

"Rafi, what are you doing?" Zahra shouted.

"I was just giving it some water. Its leaves are drooping."

"It's made of glass," she said.

"Look, the door's opening," Rafi said.

The door hadn't moved—was the boy seeing things? Rafi poured more water into the depression holding the glass plant.

Was he mad? He was going to pour out all of his water, just when the sun was reaching its peak.

"Rafi, stop!" Zahra shouted, getting up to keep him from pouring more of their water away.

But he didn't stop. He trickled more onto the plant before she reached him. "See? The door's open now."

The door hadn't budged. "Rafi, it's still closed," Amir said.

"No, look." The boy walked up to it and pointed. "See, there's an opening."

Amir joined Zahra. There was no split in the rock. Had the heat gotten to the boy? Was he suffering from dehydration?

Rafi walked up to the door ... and continued on right through it, disappearing.

Nadim joined Amir and Zahra as they stared at the entryway. "Where did he go?" Zahra asked. "Rafi!"

There was no response. It looked like Rafi had just walked right through the door. Amir went to it and pressed his hand forward, but he was met with solid rock, just as he had been before. Zahra also patted at the rock.

"Marvelous," Nadim said.

How had Rafi managed to get in? By pouring out his water? But how did that even make sense? They had to pour out their precious water just to be able to go inside? They were in the middle of a desert—they couldn't just throw away their water.

The words of his father came back to Amir: *Only those worthy can get in... It was a gift not to be taken for granted...* Maybe they had to be willing to sacrifice something for the garden. What did a garden need most?

"I think the boy has stumbled onto the solution," Amir said. "A garden needs water. To prove ourselves worthy, we must sacrifice some of ours to gain entrance."

Amir followed Rafi's lead, dripping water onto the glass plant. As he did so, it took on color and its leaves stood taller and grew larger. A grating sound came from the door and it shifted slightly. A tiny opening had formed along its right edge. "It's working."

Zahra and Nadim moved to the opposite plant to try it themselves.

As Amir's water seeped into the ground, the round door shifted further, rolling to the left, increasing the size of the opening. At the same time, the plant became straighter and more colorful. He continued, and the plant sprouted new leaves, and then flower buds, and finally the buds burst into bright shining flowers. The door opened wide, providing a crescent-shaped aperture large enough to walk through.

So it had absolutely nothing to do with the phases of the moon. He'd have to remember to tell his father that when he returned.

Shuffling past the door, Amir immediately found himself inside the circular grounds of the Unbreachable Cliffs. How could that be? He hadn't passed through any tunnel or walkway or rock at all. He had simply gone from outside to inside, as if the Cliffs themselves had no substance.

Zahra bumped into him from behind, and he stepped further into the open grounds, Nadim joining them a moment later.

"Amazing," the jinni said, before adding to Rafi, "Well done, boy. Sometimes it takes the simplest mind to come up with the simplest solution."

Rafi looked first at the jinni, and then to Zahra. "I don't think that was a compliment."

Amir laughed, but Zahra was staring off with a confused look.

"Am I the only one," she said, "who doesn't see a garden of any kind here?"

CHAPTER 32

Zahra's hope of finding the Midnight Lily dimmed.

The area within the cliffs must have stretched for a few miles. Over that entire space, the ground was a dark, rich soil that looked tilled, with rows here and a pattern of divots there. But in the whole of the supposed garden, there was not a single plant.

"I don't see anything, either," Amir said.

Rafi kicked at the soil. "It's just dirt."

It looked like every plant had been dug up and removed. "What could have done this?" Zahra wondered aloud.

"Or who?" Amir said.

"Look here," Nadim called.

He'd found engravings on the cliff walls. In fact, there were inscriptions and carvings all the way around the Garden, as far as they could see. Most depicted various types of plants and seeds, as well as insects and other animals, along with pictographic information about them. What could have happened to everything?

High above the engravings, small holes were set into the rock. *What are those for?*

"Perhaps we must progress deeper and search the grounds,"

Nadim suggested.

"Or maybe we'll find something among these inscriptions," Amir countered.

Both options seemed reasonable. "Let's split up," Zahra said. "Rafi, you go along the cliffs to the right. Amir, you take the left. Nadim and I will walk the middle."

Amir jumped to her side. "I'll go with you, and Nadim can check the wall."

"Fine, but we must hurry. The sun will set very soon."

"And I'm feeling lighter by the hour," Nadim said, showing that his arms were now translucent. "My time in your realm grows short, unless we get back to your palace and free my Scarab."

If they lost Nadim, what chance did they have to stop the vizier and his ifrit? He'd already told them how to combine the components of the spell, but how were they going to get a drop of the demon's blood? Even if they somehow did so and removed Amir's enchantment, they couldn't deal with Ghazi without Nadim. They needed to get this flower and free the jinni's scarab from its containment before he disappeared entirely.

Maybe they should return to the palace straight away and try to release the scarab first. But they'd have to come all the way back here to search the Garden again, and they were here already. Of course, they could use a wish to return immediately, but that was assuming that everything went to plan. What if they left now and didn't even make it back before Nadim faded away? They'd just have to return straight away to the garden and try again. No, better to just search for the lily while they were here.

Zahra and Amir headed right toward the center of the Garden. As she looked for any sign of plant-life, Amir asked her, "Would it be so bad if we're unable to break the spell?"

"Yes," she said without hesitation.

Still, her face flushed and guilt forced her to swallow. She couldn't deny to herself that the thought had crossed her mind. A little voice agreed, *Would it be so bad?*

Yes, it would. "You don't even remember everything clearly,

because that spell has clouded your mind. The kingdom needs you to be sharp, Amir. You need your wits back. That ifrit, Ghazi, is planning something terrible."

Amir nodded, but kicked at a loose chunk of dirt. He didn't look entirely convinced.

"Even if he weren't," Zahra continued, "I couldn't live with myself knowing my actions had taken your will from you. And I couldn't be with you, knowing your feelings were the result of magic."

"Nadim said you originally wanted to find him so you could marry me."

"Why did he tell you—?" Ugh, she would have a talk with the jinni later. "That's different. I was trying to ... I don't know, raise myself more to your level ... so I would impress you. To..."

"Make me fall in love with you?" he said.

"No." Heat rose to her cheeks. Her eyes roamed the empty garden, as if seeking a place to hide from this conversation. "I didn't want to *make* you do anything. I wanted you to have the chance to see me as I saw you."

"As you *saw* me—you don't see me like that anymore?"

"I don't know; it's different now. After the spell, and what we've been through." How could she explain it to him? She had a hard time understanding her feelings herself. Anyway, it wasn't the best time to have this distracting conversation. "Let's just find out how to get this lily and work on the counter-spell. If we still can."

Were Nadim or Rafi having any better luck? The boy was heading back to the entrance; had he discovered something? Or had he just given up? It was getting darker in the courtyard, the sun having dipped behind the cliffs. Maybe Rafi had the right idea.

"It's nearing sunset, and we haven't seen anything. Let's head back."

Nadim must have seen them turn around, because he started toward the entrance as well. Hopefully, one of them had discovered a clue as to what they should do.

As they worked their way back, the sky slowly darkened. The

clouds turned pink, then red, and then more of a deep blue and violet. Somehow Amir looked even more handsome in the fading light. She wanted to reach out and hold his hand. That she, a mere servant, had even had such a thought, still surprised her. *Would it be so bad?*

She forced herself to look straight ahead toward the entrance, where Nadim and Rafi were converging. Before she and Amir could make it back, the last of the sun's rays disappeared from the cliffs.

The ground beneath them shifted.

"What's that?" Amir said sharply.

A low rumble rolled through the air, and the earth shuddered again. The dirt all over the Garden began to move. Pointed green shoots protruded from the earth, pushing upward and growing taller. The process increased in speed, and soon the entire landscape within the cliffs was filled with bamboo-like spears rising from the ground, some small and some reaching twenty feet or more.

"What's happening?" Zahra asked, backing away from a nearby shoot and bending low to maintain her balance.

Before anyone could answer, every single shoot unfolded in a great big *whoosh*. Thick, deep-green leaves unfurled in a rush near to her, brushing against her cheek. She stumbled back as plants quickly grew to full size, complete with mature leaves and flowers. A large tree with broad-reaching branches stretched overhead. All around her, every conceivable form of greenery she could imagine sprouted in the same instant.

The Garden of the Moon had come to life.

As the sky darkened further, vines similar to the ones they'd encountered in the Cave of Balihar spread throughout the garden. They produced the same glowing orb fruits, bathing the scene in a delicate, entrancing light.

"Unbelievable," she whispered in awe.

From the niches high along the cliff walls, a myriad of small creatures flew into the air. A songbird zoomed past her ear, chirping merrily before alighting on a branch above. Bees buzzed as they zipped from flower to flower, and luminescent butterflies of every color drifted down and flitted among the leaves, adding to the astounding beauty of the Garden.

Amir's jaw hung open. "Wow."

Zahra strolled among the flora in an enchanted daze, marveling at the wonders around her. Each section of the garden contained dazzling new plants and flowers she'd never seen before, their scents finer than any perfume she'd ever smelled.

Nadim intercepted them on their way back to the entrance. "Is this not extraordinary!" he exclaimed. "Ah, Zahra, I had grown jaded and weary of your world, but I must say that this is a joy to behold."

The three of them stood and slowly turned, taking in the marvelous scenery. She basked in the beauty and the fragrance, until Rafi's approach reminded her of their task.

"If the Midnight Lily is anywhere," Zahra said, "it must be here in this Garden. As much as I would love to spend the entire night here, we need to find it."

"I think we have to," Rafi said, running up to join them. "Spend the night, I mean."

"Why do you say that, little one?" asked Nadim.

"When the sun set and the plants came up from the ground, the door rolled shut. I couldn't get out."

"Oh..." Amir said. "I seem to remember my father saying something about spending the night in the Garden of the Moon."

"*Now* you're telling us this?" Zahra said.

"I didn't realize he was *forced* to stay the night. I thought he *chose* to."

Nadim inhaled deeply, with a satisfied smile. "I don't mind wandering this garden until morning."

"What if you fade away entirely?"

The jinni waved a hand dismissively. "I'll be fine through the night."

He projected confidence and nonchalance, but how truly concerned was he about their plight? This was the first time he'd shown a particular interest in anything since they'd summoned him. Maybe he was fascinated enough with the Garden to set aside their mission, even if it meant returning to his own realm. After all, it would likely mean he wouldn't have to grant their final wish, and thus avoid being, as he called it, stuck in their world.

Even if that was the case, did it matter? What were their options? "Looks like we don't have a choice. Let's enjoy it, but remember we're here to find a Midnight Lily."

She walked along, near to Amir, but not quite touching him. She stopped at a bluish-green plant with reflective veins along its leaves and bright flowers the color of a rich sunset. The leaves were soft, almost fuzzy. She sniffed and soaked up the flower's honey scent. "It's all so beautiful."

Amir brushed his hand lightly along her hair. "Just like you."

She stared into his eyes and smiled. *Will he still feel this way after we break the spell?*

What was Amir even like without the influence of this enchantment? They'd spent mere hours together beforehand, and for much of that time he'd had her running errands. Did he even like her at all? Maybe he would be insufferable, even obnoxious, as Maliha had called him. Was she right?

Zahra thought back to her short time with the prince in the palace. How had he treated her? At the time, she'd thought it was only playful banter and teasing. Now she had to admit she couldn't be sure.

Still, at this moment, in this place, she let her worries go.

She offered her hand to Amir. His fingers slipped between hers and they proceeded hand-in-hand amid the extraordinary landscape.

They meandered aimlessly for a few hours, mostly in silence, Zahra content to admire the stunning beauty around them. Dozens of plants were foreign to her, yet somehow familiar—violet acacias, blue spotted lilies, palm trees with a metallic shiny bark, a cactus with needles soft like fur, and ironwoods with twisted leaves that whistled in the breeze.

The air seemed to come alive as they progressed, and Zahra's ears were stimulated as much as her eyes. In a moist region, frogs croaked; in a grassy area, cicadas and crickets chirped; and a section filled with thin dangling bell-shaped flowers was accompanied by the whizzing of hummingbirds. She and Amir tried to emulate the sounds, but Rafi proved best at it, croaking and squeaking and buzzing in excellent mimicry.

As they passed a column of multicolored rose bushes with platinum-fringed petals, she nudged Amir to tread carefully through a patch of delicate striped toadstools. He tiptoed away and pulled her into a maze of plants with enormous, waxy leaves shaped like the ears of an elephant, Rafi and Nadim following along. Walking beneath the green canopy, holding Amir's hand, she felt sheltered from the world. Relaxed. Safe.

When they emerged from the thick growth, Rafi pointed excitedly. "Is that the lily?"

It was. The plant itself was taller than her, and from its sprigs were draped at least a dozen of the dusky translucent flowers. Zahra leaned in and held one to her nose. The sweet scent transported her to her youth, bringing to mind a long-forgotten memory: her mother had lifted her to her shoulders so she could see over a crowd of people and watch a troupe of dancers from a far-off land. The memory wasn't much more than that, other than her mother laughing and clapping. It was enough to fill her heart with warmth.

Nadim broke her reverie. "Would you like to cut one loose?" he asked, holding a knife out to her.

"Where did you get this?" she said.

"I took it off the guard we clashed with in the bazaar when I knocked him over." The jinni flashed her a mischievous grin.

Zahra held its blade below the base of a lily. She paused, relishing the moment. They'd found it—after this, they only needed one more component. A drop of the ifrit's demon blood. *No problem.*

"This is for you, my prince," Zahra said.

She sliced the flower free, and the world became chaos.

The remaining lilies snapped shut and the whole plant furled together and shot back into the earth. The other plants around her followed suit, plant after bush after tree. Radiating outward from their position, every single piece of vegetation wrapped itself up and squeezed tight before jerking back underground. The vines with their glowing fruits likewise retreated and disappeared.

The air was filled with a blur of light and motion as the bees and the butterflies and the birds and every other little creature zipped away, and flew back into their niches. A mad rush of rustling and swishing and buzzing and flapping roared through the garden, as everything that had shown up so quickly retreated just as suddenly.

The air settled, the sounds faded, and an eerie calm settled over the now empty garden. Zahra stood completely still, shocked. Her heart was pounding, but she held her breath, waiting to see if something else would happen.

In the moonlight, there was a soft blur of motion against the sky. Other things had come out of the holes. Flying, buzzing things, glowing a faint red—lots of them, swarming straight toward their position.

"What are those?" Rafi said, worry etched on his face.

"I don't know," Zahra replied, "but I don't think they're friend-ly."

They soon found out as the creatures advanced on them—mosquitoes. Large, angry mosquitoes.

They swatted at the droning insects, but they were surrounded by a cloud of them, all eager to drink their blood.

"Oh, Flame! Run!" Zahra sprinted toward the entrance. "Maybe the exit opened up."

But it hadn't.

CHAPTER 33

As the first light of day fell upon the Unbreachable Cliffs of Ka'Run, the round entrance door rolled open and Amir and his three companions stumbled through, covered in puffy red welts. They itched like he could never have imagined. His skin was becoming raw from so much scratching.

"That's why my father said the Garden is meant to be observed and not disturbed."

"You keep bringing up these facts a little late, young prince," Nadim said, scratching at even the increasingly translucent parts of his body.

"I know that," Amir said, frustrated. Obviously he would have warned the others if he'd known what would happen when they cut the Midnight Lily. "Believe me, I also wish my father had been a little more specific."

"This itches horribly," Zahra said, "but I'm so tired. I need to sleep." She pulled a pack off one of the horses and set it on the stone near the entrance, lying down and resting her head on it. She continued to scratch, but soon fell asleep.

"I'm..." Nadim yawned, "with her." He'd barely plopped himself on the sand before he was out and snoring loudly.

Rafi nestled up against Zahra, and Amir settled in on her other side.

The prince had dreams of being eaten by huge metal flowers and bitten by snakes, and woke up hours later still nearly as itchy as when he'd fallen asleep. He rose and stretched, and couldn't keep from scratching some more.

He nudged Zahra and the others awake when he saw a group of travelers in the distance coming their way. "We should get moving."

Shortly after they'd left, they neared the approaching visitors.

"A fine day to you," Amir greeted them.

"And to you, my friend," the man in front replied. "I must say, you look to have run into some trouble." He pointed to the mosquito bites that covered them.

"Yes, well, whatever you do, don't disturb anything you see in there."

"Ah... That is good to know. Would you be so kind as to tell us," the man said, looking puzzled as he stared at the entrance door, "how one gets inside?"

"Oh, you—" Amir hesitated. How *had* they gotten inside? Strange; he couldn't remember. He looked at Zahra and Rafi and Nadim, and their brows were furrowed in the same bafflement he felt. He glanced back toward the entrance. "I ... don't remember. I think it has something to do with the phases of the moon."

"Well..." the stranger said, in an incredulous voice, "blessings upon you."

As Amir and his friends rode off, Nadim said, "Wonderful! Magic that wipes the memory of how to get in. Truly fantastic!"

Amir didn't understand why the jinni was so pleased with it all. He, for one, would like to return without having to figure out how to get back in all over again. At least he knew now never to injure any of the things inside the garden.

"That reminds me," Nadim said. "When we undo the spell on you, Prince, you will most likely have trouble with your memory as well. You cannot simply undo an effect on the mind without consequences. Being forced to feel one way, and then pushed in a completely different direction will certainly dislodge or blur some of the memories associated with those feelings."

Though the warning initially sounded concerning, Amir wasn't too worried; counteracting the spell probably wouldn't have much of an effect. He already knew how he felt about Zahra, and he doubted much would change. If anything, he'd probably remember things that were murky in his mind from the previous application of the spell.

"We must hurry now," Nadim said. "I haven't much time left before I'm pulled off to my realm. I'm all but fading away."

"Does it hurt?" Zahra asked. *Always thinking of others, this girl.* It was one of the reasons he adored her.

"No, it brings no pain," the jinni answered. "The same thing happens each time at the end of the ninety-nine years I am gifted to be in your world."

"'Gifted'?" Zahra said. "I thought you didn't want to be here." She poked Nadim in his round belly.

The jinni took her action with mild surprise. "Ah, that was true. But I have to admit, I've gotten some amusement out of traveling with the three of you."

Amusement? Amir thought. "I'm so pleased that our life and death struggles have entertained you."

"Oh, they've done much more than that. I have a whole new set of tales to tell now. Like the Tale of the Besotted Prince and the Mosquitoes."

"Funny." Amir didn't find it at all amusing.

Rafi and Zahra erupted in laughter, and soon he couldn't help but join in, too.

"See? Amusement," Nadim said. "Now we must go."

They quickly created a plan for what to do when they returned to the city, and where to meet if they became separated, and began their journey back. They traveled as fast as they could without consuming their remaining water too quickly, and made it back just as the sun peaked in the sky.

When they approached the city gate, they tried the same under-the-horse technique one more time to sneak past the guards. The indignity of it! He—the Prince of Alhad—had to cling to the underbelly of a horse to enter his own city. At the same time, there was a certain thrill to the clandestine infiltration.

Nadim wrapped himself up completely in his clothes to hide his fading form, only his eyes showing. They proceeded up to the guards.

"Are you diseased?" a guard asked.

Oh, no. Rafi's covered in welts. Will they turn us away from fear that we might spread something?

The jinni was quick with a convincing tale: "My friend, it is a long story. To keep it simple, we passed near a rank pond, mistaking it for an oasis in the desert, and were set upon by a ravenous swarm of mosquitoes. We've ridden for hours and itch like a demon's tongue speaking the truth. Please, if you would allow us entrance and permit us to soak in your hot baths to keep our scratching at bay, I would owe you a hundred blessings and more."

"I see," the guard said, his tone betraying that he didn't believe the story. "You upset something in the Garden of the Moon, didn't you?"

The other guard laughed.

"I've seen it a dozen times before. Move along, traveler. May you find solace inside."

The guards stepped aside and allowed them entry. That was almost too easy.

As they trotted through the gateway, Amir recalled Zahra's sneezing the last time they had tried this. He chuckled.

Uh, oh. He'd made a sound. Had they heard him? He shifted his grip to look back and see, but one of his hands lost its hold and flopped down toward the ground. As he tried to recover, his other hand came loose too, and he collapsed to the earth below the horse, which scampered around to avoid him.

"Halt!" the guard yelled.

Before the guard had even finished shouting the word, Amir was already jumping to his feet and calling to Zahra. "We're spotted. Let's go!"

"Oh, prince, prince, prince," Nadim said. "You couldn't hold tight for one more minute?"

Amir joined Rafi on his horse as the guard reached out for them. He kicked at the horse and they lurched away, while Zahra hopped up to join Nadim.

Amir covered his face with a length of cloth. "Split up. Meet where we discussed."

They bolted in opposite directions. Amir and Rafi took a roundabout path toward the Palace of Light, keeping to main roads used by other travelers on horses or camels. Heading briefly away from the palace, they dismounted and quickly traded their horse for a few dinars—much less than it was worth, but they didn't have time to haggle. They slipped among the city crowds and made their way undetected to the winged lion statue at the Fountain of the Beasts.

Nadim and the beautiful Zahra arrived only a minute later.

They all stared up at his home, the Palace of Light. It felt good to be back, though odd to have to sneak inside. Amir stood up straight. He was home. He was in charge again. "I know a secret way in."

"Good," Zahra responded. "Remember, we have two tasks here: complete our spell by getting a drop of the ifrit's blood, and remove the ambergris from the Golden Scarab."

"I think we should do that one first," Rafi said, pointing to Nadim.

The jinni's head had almost fully faded away. "I concur," Nadim said.

Amir couldn't disagree. "Here's the plan, then. I'll sneak in with Zahra, we'll change into servants' clothes, and then we'll go straight to my father's chambers and hold the Scarab over the Eternal Flame. We'll summon you," he nodded to Nadim, "and you can use your powers to get us a drop of Ghazi's blood."

"Excellent," Nadim said. "This reminds me of the Tale of the Servant Girl and the Cave of Balihar."

"That was me," Zahra said. "And that just happened a few days ago. We all remember it."

"Ah, that is good. Do you remember the lesson from it?"

"Lesson?" she said. "I remember that we barely survived."

"Ah, yes. That was funny, wasn't it?" His voice sounded hollow.

Uh, oh—the jinni was rapidly fading. How could they undo the spell without him?

Zahra wrapped her arms around Nadim. "Hold on," she said. "Don't go yet."

Even the jinni's eyes were disappearing. "Oh, my. I'm feeling very weak. I think I've run out of time. Please succeed at freeing my Scarab—I want to see how this turns out. I need to complete the tale." His voice was barely a whisper. "It's surprising, but I find that I'm enjoying my time in your realm, with the three of—" And then he was gone, and his clothes crumpled into a heap on the ground.

CHAPTER 34

Z ahra's jaw slackened.

Rafi gasped. "Nadim?" The boy picked up the jinni's clothes and looked beneath them. "Where did he go, Master Zahra?"

They'd lost Nadim. As frustrating as Zahra had found the jinni at times, he was the only one who could help them. And he was their friend.

She held back tears. They could still free his scarab and summon him again. Besides, she needed to be strong for Rafi.

"He went home for a while, but we'll get him back. Won't we, Amir?"

Amir put on a comforting smile. "Of course we will," he reassured the boy.

Zahra vowed to herself that they would. "Where is this hidden secret entrance?"

"Follow me." Amir scampered over an unwatched area of the palace wall and onto the royal grounds, guiding them stealthily around the back. He ran his hand along a seemingly ordinary section of stonework. "Here."

There was nothing but an empty wall. What was he looking at?

"See the grooves here? I just reach into this small hole..."

There was no hole, but his hand passed straight through the rock.

Had Amir not previously found an invisible cave in the Sands of Fire, Zahra would have been astonished, but this clearly was another example of the magic of his royal blood. He pulled something and there was the sound of a bolt sliding along rock. Amir pushed at the wall and it swung inward.

"Wow," Rafi said.

Amir ushered them inside. Closing the door left them in near total darkness, but Amir knew his way and quickly found another door on the inside wall. Another small hole in it was visible this time, letting in a tiny amount of light.

He reached to unbolt the door.

Zahra touched his hand. "Wait."

They didn't need to risk Rafi as part of their plan. "Wait here," she told the boy. "I know it's dark, but you'll be safe."

"What if you don't come back?" Rafi asked, with a slight tremble in his voice.

"Don't worry, we'll come for you. Here, hold these and keep them safe until we return." She handed Rafi the satchel containing the Midnight Lily and the other spell components.

Amir peeked out the door—the way was clear. Zahra kissed Rafi on his forehead and told him to keep quiet and stay safe, and she and Amir slipped into the palace.

Even though Amir knew a few of the palace's secrets, Zahra knew far more about the lower levels than he did. She guided them carefully through the halls, acquired new servant clothes for the two of them, and led them up the least-used stairways.

When they approached the upper levels he took over, following the passages he'd used to sneak out to see Ulnar the Foreteller so many days ago. He retraced his path until they approached the entrance to the sultan's chambers. Two guards stood in front of his father's door.

"How will we get past them?" Zahra whispered.

"I know these men well. Hopefully, they're not under Yaseen's influence."

"We'd better not assume that. We should try to distract them and sneak in."

Amir frowned. "These men will not be distracted."

He was probably right, but what choice did they have? "Do you have another idea?"

Maybe Nadim would have told them a tale that could have helped, but she at least couldn't think of anything clever. They were both wearing servant clothes now, and servants weren't allowed unattended on this floor, so anything they did would be suspicious. It would be impossible for both of them to enter the sultan's room. But only one of them needed to get in...

"I have an idea," she said. "I'll run out screaming that someone is chasing me, trying to kill me, and I'll run past them down that hall. At least one guard will follow me. And maybe the other one will go and look for the person chasing me."

"But you'll get caught. And if the other guard does come looking, he will run right into me. No, if we're both going to end up facing them anyway, we should do it forthrightly."

Zahra didn't like where this was headed, but she knew her idea was ridiculous as soon as the words had come out of her mouth.

Amir continued, "I propose you wait here. I'll go to them and tell them I've returned from a trip and have something important to report to my father. They won't refuse me entrance, even dressed like this."

It was a terrible plan, but she could think of nothing better. She closed her eyes. After everything they'd gone through, it now came down to whether these guards would believe Amir. She wasn't optimistic.

Amir removed the covering from his face and strode up to them. "Hakeem. Mahdi. I have returned from a journey outside the city, and I wish to see my father."

"It pleases me to see you alive, my prince," Hakeem said, casting a bemused look at Amir's welt-covered face, "but I am afraid I have orders from the vizier, approved by the sultan, that none are to enter these chambers, and you are to be held for your own safety and well-being."

Hakeem approached Amir.

This was going exactly as Zahra had expected; she knew they'd both be caught now, but she had to plead their case. She stepped out of hiding and advanced on the men. "Hakim. Mahdi. Please, listen to us."

Mahdi shook his head. "No, I'm afraid not." The big man grabbed hold of her.

"Unhand her," Amir ordered.

"Please, my prince, come with us," Hakeem said.

"You don't understand," Zahra said to the guards. "The prince is under a spell."

"Oh yes, we've been told," Hakeem said.

"Yes, you devious she-ghoul, they know of your nefarious plan," Yaseen's voice came from around the corner. "Mahdi, clamp a hand over that wily girl's mouth. I've heard enough of that traitor's lies."

"Traitor?" Zahra said before her mouth was covered. "Mm nod dhaa wnh whmms dhaa tradr!" She struggled in Mahdi's grip, but the man was twice her size. He easily held her arms pinned behind her back with one hand, and kept her from speaking with the other.

Amir stood tall, jaw clenched. "Release her. She's done nothing but try to help."

"Ah, my prince," Yaseen said, "it is wonderful to see you returned, though I worry at your condition." He indicated Amir's face, covered with mosquito bites. "I fear you have been beset by some malady, obviously caused by the machinations of this treacherous servant girl."

"Yaseen, I—"

"Please, my prince." Yaseen held up his hand. "Worry not. We will undo what this villainous tart and her demon have done to you.”

Amir gritted his teeth. “No, Yaseen, you are the one who’s been manipulated by a demon—the ifrit has its own plan.”

“Hakeem, gently subdue the prince. I have prepared a counter-spell that will free him from this girl’s bewilderment. It is not his fault he spouts her lies. Make him consume these.” Yaseen handed the guard a handful of ripe dates. “It is the beginning of the process to dispel the enchantment.”

Hakeem pressed the fruits into Amir’s mouth, and the prince had no choice but to bite down on them. The vizier’s words were nonsense; forcing the dates upon Amir was obviously intended to keep him from speaking.

“And now stand back, please.” Yaseen wrapped a sash around Amir’s head, covering his eyes.

Why was he blindfolding Amir? The vizier stepped behind the prince and produced another Midnight Lily. So *this* was Yaseen’s plan. He was going to perform the spell again, and this time ensure that Amir didn’t see anyone else when the spell took effect.

Yaseen held the flower to Amir’s face, right under the prince’s nose. “And now, to wipe away the spell and clear his mind.”

Amir inhaled and his body relaxed in the guard’s arms. Upon Amir’s sniffing of the flower, the lily crystallized, the same way it had the last time the vizier tried this spell on the prince.

No! It couldn’t be happening again, after all they’d done.

Yaseen stowed the flower in his satchel and called, “Maliha.”

Maliha rounded the corner. Yaseen would ensure she was the first person Amir saw. Zahra couldn’t believe his audacity, to per-form his sorcery right in front of the sultan’s chambers.

Maliha eyed Zahra warily as she approached her father and Amir. The vizier’s daughter’s face was a mess of confusion, hurt, and nervousness. “Father, something isn’t right here. I don’t be-lieve Zahra would do what you’ve said.” She met Zahra’s eyes. “Would you?”

Zahra was clamped firmly in the hold of Mahdi. She tried to shake her head, but could barely budge. *I didn’t do it.* “Ah nnt nh ih," was all she got out.

"Nonsense," Yaseen said. "This one has been causing trouble since I foolishly agreed to take her in as a child—and now she's gone too far. The evidence is clear."

"Zahra, why? Why would you do this?" Disappointment weighed heavily on Maliha's face, but there was still a trace of disbelief there.

I didn't do it. Zahra tried to scream with her eyes as she strained against her captor. *You know I didn't! How could I have?*

What lies had Yaseen filled his daughter's head with? Had he used magic on her as well? Or had she decided she had no reason to doubt her own father?

"Behold, my prince, my beautiful daughter and the girl you truly love, and be rid of the cursed spell placed upon you." Yaseen held Amir's head facing straight toward his daughter and undid the sash from around his face.

Amir opened his eyes and his gaze fell upon Maliha.

Zahra's heart broke.

She could see his transformation instantly. She stomped on Mahdi's foot, catching him by surprise. His grip around her arms slackened. She threw an elbow at his gut, pushing herself away. "No! The vizier is the traitor—he just put the prince under another spell."

"Silence that wretch!" Yaseen yelled.

Amir's eyes had glazed over, and Zahra saw his lips shape into the familiar stupefied smile as he gazed into Maliha's eyes. And then when he looked at Zahra, confusion and then anger formed on his features.

The door behind them burst open, and the sultan stormed out. "What is this yelling all about?"

"My king," Zahra said, trying to think of a way to explain this before the vizier had her silenced again. The problem was, she had no evidence on her side now. The only thing she had was ... the Golden Scarab! She quickly pulled it out and held it before her. "I was trying to undo a spell Vizier Yaseen placed on your son the prince, and we found the Golden Scarab of Balihar to—"

Yaseen shouted over her words, and Mahdi restrained her once more. "You see, my king, it is as I have said. This foul girl acquired the Golden Scarab and used the power of the jinni within to bespell Prince Amir. I have disrupted her sorcery and returned the prince to his right mind."

"My son, you are alive!" The sultan pulled Amir in for a hearty hug. Upon noticing the prince's welts, he added, "What happened to you? What has this girl done? Does my vizier speak the truth—were you under an enchantment?"

"I ... was, father. I ... believe he is correct. I'm ... confused, but things are becoming clearer now. Father, this girl, Zahra, she did summon a jinni with that Scarab." Amir shook his head, as if trying to accept that his view of the world had just changed.

No, Amir. Fight it. Zahra thrashed fruitlessly against Mahdi's grip.

"I ... I love Maliha. That is one thing I have no confusion about. That ... that is why I was hesitant about the other girls you invited into the palace. I was already in love with Maliha, but I didn't know how to tell you. This girl..."—he gave Zahra that angry look again—"she befuddled my mind and made me believe I loved her."

Fight, Amir! You know that's not true. She turned and twisted to try to get the words out, but was held firm. *How can you forget all that we've been through?*

Nadim's warning came back to her, that feelings can't be forcibly changed without consequence, that memories would be distorted as well. She thought, too, of how differently Amir had behaved by chasing her from the palace all the way to the Hafiz Oasis. Some part of her had hoped it wasn't just because of the spell. Now it couldn't be any clearer—it had been.

The sultan took Nadim's ambergris-coated beetle from her hand, looking it over. "The Golden Scarab of Balihar," he said with a sense of wonder.

"Rendered inert and ineffective now, my king," Yaseen said proudly.

"A shame, perhaps," the sultan said. "In any case, it will make a fine addition to my private collection of rarities. As for you, my son, you should have spoken to me of your feelings earlier; it would have saved us much time, not to mention a great deal of unnecessary travel for a number of hopeful princesses and their retinues."

"I was not sure how you would have reacted, father," Amir admitted. "I thought you had your heart set on finding me someone from afar."

"It was my plan, yes, but how could I say no to a union between my son and my own vizier's beautiful and capable daughter? As for you, Maliha, is this also your desire?"

"I..." Maliha looked back and forth between Amir and Zahra.

Tell him the truth, Maliha. Zahra pleaded with her eyes. *We can still fix this.*

Maliha's frown cast at Zahra made it clear that she had chosen to follow her father's wishes.

"I ... would be overjoyed to be wed to your handsome and..."—*No, don't do it*—"charming..."—*Maliha, you don't even like Amir*—"and witty son."

Flame! What are you doing, Maliha?

Zahra wanted to shout, but all she could manage was a muffled rage that made her look guilty and jealous.

"It is settled, then," the sultan proclaimed. "Tomorrow shall be a day of celebration, for the prince will marry the lovely Maliha. Yaseen, make preparations immediately."

The vizier's broad grin made Zahra sick. She had to try to do something to stop this. She let her body go slack and slid out from the guard's grip.

"No, my king," she cried, rolling to the side. "It's the vizier. He summoned an ifrit and put a spell on your son, and the kingdom is in danger because the ifrit wants to—"

Mahdi once again caught her up and subdued her.

The sultan said, "I'm afraid you've caused enough discord, child. Take her to the dungeon."

She thrashed against Mahdi's grip as he hauled her away. "Amir, wake up! Remember! Maliha, you know I wouldn't do this. Tell them!"

They turned away from her as she was dragged around the corner.

I've lost Nadim, and now Amir, and even Maliha. And if the jinni was right about Ghazi's plan, possibly the kingdom as well.

Tears of frustrated anger and helplessness streamed down her face.

CHAPTER 35

Zahra slumped against the dungeon wall in a state of shock. They'd been so close! How could this have happened? Why had nobody believed her? They hadn't considered her words at all, not even Maliha.

From the cell next to her, the acrobat thief, Selene, tried to engage her in conversation, but Zahra was in no mood and ignored the woman.

She wanted to scream. So she did. The prison guard, Firuz, stormed to her cell and banged on the thick wooden door, yelling in through the small opening at head-height, "Keep it down, enchantress!"

"Get Maliha," Zahra said. "The vizier's daughter. I need to speak with her."

"I'm sure if she wants to speak with you, she knows where you are. Since you're here, locked up in a cell, I'm thinking she doesn't care."

He was right, but she had to try. "Then get Prince Amir. Tell him I want only a moment of his time."

"Oh, sure. Or maybe you'd like me to call the sultan down to share some wine with you." He threw a glop of mashed-up food through the opening and into her face. "Now keep your mouth shut or I'll gag you." He stomped away.

Zahra wiped off the food and leaned against the wall in defeat.

"Servant girl, is that you? Zahra?" Selene called from her cell.

Zahra put her head in her hands. She was now in the same position as the thief—she knew the vizier's secret, and nobody would listen to her. The weight of the day bore down on her; the last thing she wanted to do was commiserate with the woman, especially because she had been right all along and Zahra hadn't listened.

She banged a hand against the wooden platform that served as a bed. The vizier had won, and if Nadim was right, the ifrit might win, too. And she was trapped—in a dungeon. Her mind flashed again to the day her mother had dropped her off at the palace. How worried, and scared, and utterly alone she'd felt. Much like now.

And poor Rafi! Her chest tightened when she remembered how they'd left him. He too was alone, and in the dark. He'd be waiting for them to return. His concern would be growing by the minute. How terrified he'd be, as the hours passed and nobody came for him. She'd done the one thing she swore to him she'd never do—left him all alone to fend for himself. Abandoned him.

Would Amir remember to go to him? Probably not.

Zahra collapsed onto the stiff bed and cried herself to sleep.

She woke to a shout by the other guard, Aman. "Time to face the glory of a new day, prisoners."

He thumped on the heavy oaken cell doors as he traversed the dungeon hallway. At Zahra's, he slid a bowl of food through the small opening near the floor. Was this to be her life now? Living in a dark, dank, disgusting cell, eating revolting food served by a repulsive guard?

How had she come to this point? She'd only been trying to improve her life. She'd just wanted to gain respect, to earn the affection of the prince. And then she'd tried to do the right thing and free him from the vizier's foul plan, and this was her recompense.

She'd suspected the prince wouldn't have feelings for her when freed from the spell, but she hadn't expected to be summarily tossed in prison and completely ignored. It brought up the question she'd been wrestling with since the start of their journey together: who *was* Amir? How much had the spell changed him? Was he so different now that he couldn't even come to visit her?

Zahra frowned, realizing she shouldn't be surprised. She was nothing—just a servant. Of no importance, having no power, and no sway in the minds of others.

"It's a great day," Aman shouted. "The prince is getting married. The entire palace will be celebrating."

Thanks for the reminder. A sense of failure and despondency weighed upon Zahra.

"If you're all nice and quiet today, maybe I'll bring you some grapes after the wedding."

How kind.

Zahra sat and gnawed at the loathsome food, depressed. Up in the palace above, Amir was going to marry Maliha. As much as Zahra wanted to be angry at both of them, she couldn't be—Amir was once again enchanted, and Maliha was a victim of her father's machinations, too. She was in love with the architect's son. From the way Maliha had looked outside the sultan's chambers, Zahra was sure her friend had had no inkling of her father's collaboration with the ifrit.

Didn't she believe Zahra at all? Maliha had clearly felt that something was amiss. Unfortunately, Zahra had no case to present other than an outlandish story about the vizier summoning a demon. And she had to admit that running from the palace had only made her look guilty of something.

But what else could she have done?

Zahra ground her teeth in frustration. If she'd been a noble-woman or a princess, they would have believed her, and Yaseen wouldn't have been able to get his way. But she was a nobody, and he was the vizier.

The return of Aman interrupted her thoughts. "Wedding's over, criminals. The prince is married. Sorry to say they couldn't spare any food." He chuckled and settled onto his stool.

Amir and Maliha are wed, and now it's over.

Or was it? She'd heard that once the official ceremony conclud-ed, the festivities lasted into the night. How long would it be before the ifrit enacted whatever dark revenge it had planned?

After some time, Aman started to snore. Great. Everyone else was completely oblivious to the impending destruction of the kingdom.

"Zahra," Selene whispered from the adjacent cell. "Are you here because you know about the vizier's demon?"

That's right, there was one other person who might know the danger they were in—Selene. "How did you know of the ifrit?" Zahra asked. "And what did you steal from Yaseen?"

"It was a small thing, but of great significance. I took the Ring of Inara, which summons the wicked ifrit, Ghazi."

"We've run into him. I think Yaseen is being duped by that ifrit. Everyone in the kingdom is at risk."

Selene groaned. "That confirms the worst of my fears. We must stop them."

"What can we do from here? They won't even let me speak with anyone who can help."

"Speak with another servant, perhaps? If someone came to clean, like you did, and both of us told the same story, maybe they'd listen and warn the sultan."

"I already spoke to the sultan myself, but he believes his vizier."

No, the only way they could help was if they got out of this dungeon. She couldn't count on Maliha coming to get her out this time, yet she had no other way to get free. As she contemplated her situation, it felt like the walls of the prison cell were closing in on her. Her frustration and anger edged into hopelessness and despair.

What must Rafi be feeling? She'd left him alone, in the dark. He was counting on her to return. She'd promised. Amir needed her to save him, too, though he didn't know it.

She didn't have time to wallow in self-pity. "We need to escape."

Selene snorted. "If I knew how to do that, I would have already done so."

"Now there are two of us." Maybe they could create a plan together. Zahra pressed her face against the small, barred opening in her door. Aman was still passed out on his stool.

"If only I had something to pick this lock," Selene said slowly.

Did Zahra have something she could use? She scanned the room as well as she could in the dim light, her eyes settling on a spoon. Scooping it up, she lowered herself down onto the filthy floor. This was the cell she'd been cleaning when Maliha had pulled her away. She had never finished scrubbing it, and it was obvious nobody else had come after her. She wrinkled her nose in disgust, but gritted her teeth and slid forward to reach her hand out through the small food slot at the base of the door.

"Here," she called to Selene as loudly as she dared. "Catch." She flicked the spoon over toward Selene's door.

It clanged along the floor and Zahra froze. Aman kept snoring.

"What am I supposed to do with a spoon?"

"Pick the lock?"

"Maybe if I could melt it down and shape it into a lockpick. Do you have a blacksmith in there with you?"

Zahra shook her head at her dumb idea. Of course; Selene would have been given a spoon with her own meals. If she could have used one to escape, she would have already. So much for that.

If only there was something else... *Wait. Nobody has cleaned this room after me.*

Holding her breath, she bent down to a puddle of sludge on the floor. She stuck her hand into the goop and reached all around, trying to feel for—there it was! Selene's hairpin.

Using a bowl of water left by Aman, she cleaned her hand and the pin as best she could.

"Try this." She again got to the floor and reached through the food slot, flinging the pin to the acrobat's door.

"Ah. This looks familiar." Selene pulled it into her cell.

"Will it work?"

Selene gave no response, so Zahra rose to peek through the barred hole in her door—and saw Selene's face staring in at her. That was fast.

"Quick, let me out."

Selene smiled and whispered, "First, apologize for getting me imprisoned in here."

What? "Now's not the time for this."

"Apologize."

"How would I have known what you were..." Zahra trailed off. "Fine. I beg a thousand pardons for your capture. You were right and I was wrong and I should have listened to you, O wise one."

"Even with your insincerity, I'll graciously accept your apology." Selene pulled open the cell door.

Together, they tiptoed past Aman to the dungeon entrance and peered through a window in the door. The first guard, Firuz, was leaning against the wall outside eating a piece of cardamom ranginak, no doubt from Amir and Maliha's wedding. They wouldn't be able to sneak by him as they'd done with Aman.

"We'll have to deal with them one at a time," Selene whispered.

Zahra came up with a plan. Selene wasn't enthused but couldn't offer a better idea.

They locked the door to Selene's cell, and then hid in Zahra's.

"Guard!" Zahra startled Aman awake.

"Huh?" Aman wiped drool from his lip. "What do you want now?"

"Something has happened to the thief in that cell."

"What are you talking about?" Aman walked over and banged on the thief's cell door.

Of course, there was no answer.

"She was there talking to me and then she just disappeared."

"Aha—sure." He leaned in and peered inside. "What demon's magic is this? Where is she?"

He retrieved his keys and slid one into the lock. Zahra and Selene eased their door open.

The guard pushed in Selene's cell door, standing in the doorway as it swung open. He leaned forward to get a view inside.

Now, Zahra mouthed to her new cohort.

They rushed forward and slammed into Aman, forcing him into the cell. But the guard was faster than they'd expected, and before they could get him far enough in to shut the door on him, he spun and blocked it with his foot.

"Nice try, girls."

They pushed against him but couldn't shove him farther back. Aman grabbed Zahra around her left wrist. Mistake on his part—Zahra tapped the head of the snake wrapped around her right forearm.

It sprang to life.

Aman lurched backward. "Foul witch!"

Selene gave the man another nudge, even as she deftly snagged the keys from him. Before he could react, the door was closed in his face and locked from the outside.

He banged on the wood. "Open this door now!"

"Stay quiet, or I'll unleash my snake on you." Zahra waved her arm in front of the door's tiny window.

Aman backed away, scowling but silent.

"That's a neat trick." Selene appraised Zahra as if seeing her anew. "Just a servant girl, huh?"

"I've had some ... experiences ... since we last met." She tapped the snake again, and it coiled back onto her arm and became inert.

The acrobat smiled. "So I see."

They returned to the dungeon entrance. "We can't count on that ruse working again," Selene said. "Luckily, I have the keys now. I say we just open the door and use your snake to force the other guard in here."

"I like that plan." Zahra readied herself to unleash the serpent.

Selene stared blank-faced at the exit. "Uh-oh."

"What?"

"There's no keyhole on this side of the door."

CHAPTER 36

A mir was amazed at his luck. He'd convinced his father to let him marry Maliha, the girl whom he loved. The ceremony had taken place in the Fathi Garden. Yaseen had done a wonderful job with his preparations, decorating the garden with satin banners, silk draperies, and ribbons embroidered with Moroccan gold. Blue and green parakeets flitted about and chirped above, and women played soft melodies on chang harps, accompanied by a dozen maidens in joyous song.

He guided his bride along a trail of rose petals that led from the courtyard and through the palace, all the way up each winding staircase and into his royal chambers. She glowed as she followed him in her sunset-inspired gown, her seventh and final dress of the day. She was radiant. Her long, luxurious hair flowed back over her shoulders, with one deep violet crocus flower wedged above her ear to complement her ceremonial makeup.

Amir's attendants had adorned his room with tulips, roses, and lotus flowers, and hung fine silks around his canopied bed. A platter of pomegranate seeds conserved with almonds and sugar rested on a table, along with a flagon of wine and an array of cheeses and other fruits.

A line of male servants stood to the left, and a line of female servants to the right. Amir dismissed them all, and the last boy to leave closed the door behind him.

Amir pulled his adorable, intoxicating, magnificent Maliha in for a kiss. Their lips met, and he was transported to the first time he'd held her in his arms like this, back when he'd rescued her from the waterfall after they'd survived the assault of the sand warriors.

Maliha pushed away from him lightly. He pulled back and gazed upon her with confusion. That first kiss hadn't been with her, had it? No, it was with that servant girl, Zahra, the one who'd used magic on him.

"Are you well, my prince?" Maliha asked.

"Yes, I'm ... I was remembering something. A moment from a different ... time."

"That's generally what memories are." She turned away from him and went to the wine.

"Have I upset you, my love?" he asked.

"No—my prince."

Was that hesitation? She *was* upset. "Please, call me Amir, my love. What is wrong?"

"I'm just a bit ... overwhelmed. Amir." She poured herself a glass of wine and moved to the window to look out upon the city. "I know this is our wedding night, but I can't help thinking of Zahra. I don't think she did what my father is claiming."

"But she put me under a spell. You saw it with your own eyes, my love."

"I'm not sure what I saw, but I've never known her to be anything but honest. Often to her detriment. This makes no sense; we should go speak with her."

Amir waved a hand dismissively. "You're being silly. She's a criminal." Saying that felt uncomfortable, but Amir wasn't sure why. She *was* a criminal, wasn't she? Why should he feel bad about saying that? "But I know she's your friend. We'll speak with her tomorrow if you so wish."

The door to Amir's chambers creaked open behind them. A young male servant walked in, uninvited.

Amir glared at the interloper. "How dare you disturb us, boy!" The boy stared at him, surprised. "Prince, it's me, Rafi."

"Rafi?" It took a moment for Amir to remember him. The boy he'd traveled with—at the oasis, and the cave, and... His memories were hazy and elusive, like fog in a breeze. "Yes, of course. You're the one who helped Zahra. Are you here seeking revenge for her, now that her plot has failed?"

"What do you mean? I'm here to help you. Neither of you came back, so I knew the plan didn't work. Were you able to free the Golden Scarab?"

Maliha stepped forward. "Amir, who is this boy?"

"Zahra found him in the Hafiz Oasis. He..." Amir pushed through his fuzzy memories. "He acted as her servant. He caused no end of trouble, from what I recall."

"That's not true. The part about being Zahra's servant is true—she's my new master. But I didn't cause trouble, I only helped. Don't you remember how I led you to the Sands of Fire? And I helped you fight the giant scorpion. And how I swam after the Golden Scarab?"

"I..." Yes, the Sands of Fire. And a scorpion—now he remembered the scorpion. Rafi *had* helped, but was he part of Zahra's scheme?

"What happened, Prince?" Rafi asked. "Where's Zahra? And who is this girl?"

"Excuse me, little boy," Maliha said. "I'm the daughter of the vizier, and now I'm Princess Maliha, so you'll show me some respect."

Rafi squinted. "Of course, Princess Maliha. Much respect to you."

Amir saw his princess bristle at the boy's dismissive tone. "This is my love, the one Zahra tried to keep me from marrying. And she's correct—you must show her respect."

"Oh, no." Rafi shook his head back and forth. "Did you smell a

Midnight Lily before you saw her?"

Midnight Lily ... Midnight Lily... That sounded familiar.

Maliha's brow furrowed. "A lily? A Soul Lily?"

"Yes," Amir said. "Yaseen had me smell a lily. To clear the spell, he said."

"Prince Amir, you're sure?" Maliha asked, visibly upset. "A dark lily? Like the one I presented to you in the garden, that Zahra knocked from your hand?"

"I had a blindfold on, so I didn't see it clearly, but it smelled similar."

"See?" Rafi said. "He's under a spell again—he doesn't love you. No offense. Much respect, Princess."

Under a spell again? What was Rafi talking about? "No, I'm free of Zahra's spell now. That's the point, boy. She had me under a spell, and Vizier Yaseen released me from it. Now I've finally married my love, Maliha."

Rafi smacked his forehead. "Oh, rotten dates! Wake *up*, Prince."

Maliha rubbed her chin. "Are there other components to this spell?"

"Of course," Rafi said. "You have to mix acid from some beetle with cobra venom, and ... uh ... poppy seeds, kohl..."

"And frankincense," Maliha finished for him.

"Yes, that's right. See?" The boy produced a sack he'd concealed beneath his loose-fitting shirt, showing them all the items he'd mentioned. "And a drop of the ifrit's blood, which we couldn't get. And then soak it all up into the Midnight Lily."

Dismay washed over Maliha's face. "He ... he *did* do it. Zahra was telling the truth. My father was the one who put you under a spell." She looked sick. "He made you fall in love with me."

"No, he didn't." Amir grasped her hands in his. He loved her. She had to know that.

"He did." Maliha gripped his hands back and shook them. "Don't you see? He did—he cast a spell on you."

"Even if that's true, it doesn't change anything. The magic just made me accept the feelings I already had for you. I've always felt this way; spell or not, I love you."

Rafi stamped his feet on the floor. "That's exactly what you said to Zahra, too!"

No, he hadn't. Had he? "I would never have told Zahra that, because I didn't feel that way toward her. I love Maliha."

"Ohhh..." Rafi plopped down onto the bed. "This is crazy. You don't remember? You were always telling her how much you loved her, and how you were meant to be together. Then you kissed her by the river after we almost died going over the waterfall."

"You kissed her?" Maliha said.

"I..." Was that what he'd remembered when he kissed Maliha a moment ago? There were the sand men, and the bandits, and Rafi on the rock at the edge of the waterfall, and then he'd pulled them up, and ... yes, he *had* kissed Zahra! "Yes, but that's because I was under—"

"A spell?" Maliha said. "Just like you're under one now."

He tried to bring back his memories. An image came, of Zahra latching onto the tail of a scorpion ... and grabbing the head of a striped snake ... and wishing for an ugly, smelly camel ... and snipping a beautiful flower in the Garden of the Moon ... and nearly falling from a window in the palace, and... He smiled. That girl was a mess, but exciting to be around. And she was so strong, with determination and a good heart. And ... wait, was it truly Zahra he was thinking of?

"I'm so confused." He shook his head. "I have to acknowledge that my thoughts might not be trustworthy."

"Ugh, finally." Rafi hopped up from the bed.

"What do we do?" Amir asked.

"We have to tell your father," Maliha said.

That wouldn't work. "No, we have no proof. He'll just be angry with us for accusing Yaseen again."

"Think, Prince," Rafi said. "We have to bring back Nadim."

CHAPTER 37

"Remember?" Rafi said. "Nadim—the jinni in the Golden Scarab. Remember, he was in the cave that flipped us upside down?"

"A *cave* flipped you upside down?" Maliha asked.

"It was fun," Rafi said. "We rolled along the ground and then along the walls and then I climbed up—"

"Stay focused, Rafi," Amir interrupted.

"Okay. Do you remember, Nadim cut off his finger because you lost yours, and then he grew it back? He grew yours back, too."

Maliha looked shocked. "You lost your finger?"

Amir held up his hand, the memory pushing through the fog in his mind. Oh, right. He *had* lost his finger, because of the scorpion. Zahra had wrapped up his hand. "My ... pinkie finger."

"Yes," Rafi said. "You remember!"

"The jinni made fun of me, telling me I should just regrow it."

"This is the jinni we're supposed to summon again?" Maliha said.

"He's funny sometimes," Rafi admitted. "But he knows things, like the spell. To break the spell, we need the ifrit's blood, and

Nadim's the only one who can get that for us."

Maliha looked upset. "I can't believe my father summoned an ifrit. You're right—we have to undo this, and if that means summoning this jinni, then let's go."

"The Scarab's in my father's collection of rare treasures; it's a small room in his private chambers. If he's still hosting the celebration below, we can slip in and get it now."

"Let's go," Rafi said.

"No, Rafi, you stay here. Nobody should enter these chambers on our wedding night, but just in case, stash those spell components under the bed." Turning to Maliha, he asked, "Will you help us?"

"Of course, my—Amir." Maliha's face wrinkled up. "I can't believe I didn't trust Zahra. We have to set this situation right."

He should have trusted her, too. Or was he incapable of that while under this new spell? From the memories that had come back to him, he felt horrible that he'd so quickly discarded Zahra and left her to rot in the dungeon. What kind of person was he? He considered his current situation, and what he could remember over the past week, and he couldn't honestly answer that question. Regardless, he had to do something to make up for his earlier inaction.

"Rafi, we'll be back in a moment." Amir took Maliha's hand—which now felt awkward—and led her from the room.

As they exited, Rafi added, "Oh, congratulations on your wedding, Prince. And Princess, much respect to you."

"That boy is impertinent," Maliha said.

"I know." Amir remembered that Rafi could be as irritating as sand under the fingernails.

Maliha grinned. "I *like* him."

Outside of the sultan's chambers, they encountered Hakeem and Mahdi standing guard once again. Amir glanced at Maliha and a memory of Zahra standing here with him flashed through his mind.

"Congratulations, my prince," Mahdi said, and then nodding to

Maliha with a smile, "and princess."

"Mahdi," Amir said, "we wish to speak with the sultan."

Mahdi's eyebrows rose. "So soon after your wedding?"

"I..." Amir started, trying to think of what to say. He hadn't expected to be questioned, but didn't want to raise any suspicion by asserting his authority.

Maliha helped out. "We wished to speak with the sultan about some of the guests."

"Ah," Mahdi said. "The sultan is in, though in fact he's only here for a few moments to refresh himself."

Amir had expected his father to be enjoying the festivities down in the gardens. As the guards parted to allow them entrance, he thought furiously. How were they going to get the Scarab now? Or clear it of its ambergris coating using the Eternal Flame?

The doors closed behind them.

"What should we do?" Maliha whispered.

It was a good question. An image of a snake striking at him as he fell backward came to mind. "Distraction."

"What?"

"You distract my father, and I'll sneak off and get the Scarab."

Maliha bit her lip, her eyes squinted in thought. "Alright, I can do that—leave your father to me. You get the Scarab, but be quick."

They walked further into the sultan's chambers, but still hadn't seen or heard him.

"Oh!" the sultan shouted as he came from his room and spotted them standing there. "You startled me, my son. What are you doing here? Is your room not prepared to your liking?"

"No, that's not it at all, my king," Maliha said. "Or should I call you Father now?" She smiled. "Please forgive our intrusion; the blame falls on me. You see, I was talking with the prince and I told him I'd never once seen the Eternal Flame, and so I asked him if I could see it now that I'm a member of the family."

Quick thinking, Maliha.

"Of course, of course, my dear," the sultan said, smiling at Maliha's request. "Follow me."

Amir lingered behind, saying, "I'll meet you there in a bit, Father, I'm just going to..." he let his voice trail off, realizing the sultan wasn't even paying any attention to him. His wife was a charmer. How he loved this girl—or did he? He couldn't be sure.

He crept off noiselessly into the sultan's Room of Wondrous Treasures, as he liked to call it. Where was the Golden Scarab? His memory of exactly what it looked like was hazy, but a gold scarab covered in a waxy substance should be easy to spot.

Only it wasn't.

His father had a hoard of items, many crafted from ivory and silver and platinum, but most were made of gold. Where was it? He searched high and low, from shelf to shelf, pillow to pedestal. Maybe Yaseen had stolen it for himself. But then he spotted it on top of a column, next to a jade figurine of a spear-wielding soldier on a rearing stallion.

Grasping it in his hand, more memories solidified. He recalled Yaseen's man Ghazi coating the scarab in ambergris. Ghazi—the ifrit! How could Yaseen have entrusted an evil demon with his daughter's future? Amir didn't think too highly of the vizier, but he hadn't believed him to be a bad person. Were his actions born of malice, or was he simply so misguided in his desire to see his daughter rise to royalty that it had blinded him to the danger?

Amir stuffed the Scarab into his waist sash and rejoined his father and wife. She looked dazzling in the dancing, reflected light of the Eternal Flame, the way its colors glinted off her silky hair... He had to stay focused. His father was wrapping up his story.

"This is amazing," Maliha said. "It truly burns forever, and just as brightly?"

"Always," the sultan said.

"Now I feel yet one more privilege of being part of your family," she said. "You are as wonderful as this flame, my king."

Now Amir needed to stay behind to use the Flame to remove the ambergris from the Scarab. He caught Maliha's eye and tilted his head toward the exit.

She inferred his intent and moved to leave, holding out her arm to the sultan. "Are you returning to the celebrations, my king?"

"Yes, you are welcome to rejoin us yourselves if you wish," the sultan invited them.

"I think it's time for us to retire to our own chambers for a while," Maliha said with a wink.

"Ah, quite so," the sultan said.

Amir lingered as the other two headed for the exit. "I want to spend a moment at the Eternal Flame myself, my love. You go ahead and I'll be right over."

"Of course, my darling," Maliha replied, leading the sultan from his chamber.

Amir ran straight to the Eternal Flame, taking out the Golden Scarab as he went. The column of flame was blindingly bright, but it generated little heat. Amir doubted the jinni's plan. Would the Flame really be able to burn the ambergris coating from off the Scarab? How long should he hold it in the fire?

Amir retrieved the lengthy tongs his father sometimes used when burning things in the Flame himself. Grasping the Scarab with the tongs, he covered his eyes against the intensity of the light and held Nadim's scarab in the fire.

There was a brief sizzle and then a pop. *That was fast.* He swung the tongs out to avoid damaging the Scarab. The ambergris coating had cracked apart.

He tapped the Scarab on the stone tile floor and the waxy shell broke into pieces before completely dissipating. In only a few seconds, the magical artifact was cool to the touch. Snatching it up, he hastily made his exit and joined Maliha outside, and together they returned to his—to their—chambers.

"Alright, Rafi," he said. "We did it. Here's the Scarab. Now, how do we summon the jinni?"

Rafi took the Scarab from him, turning it over in his hands. "I'm not sure. I think Master Zahra pushed the wings or squeezed it or something." He pressed at the sides of the Scarab, and *poof*, a column of smoke burst forth and swirled around.

Maliha stepped back in surprise. "Wow, it's actually real."

The smoke dissipated, leaving behind a familiar, bedraggled, paunchy little man standing before them—the jinni Nadim.

"That took a while," Nadim said, looking between the three of them, his brow furrowing upon noticing Maliha. "I'm guessing things didn't go according to plan."

Rafi pointed to Amir. "It's the prince's fault."

CHAPTER 38

Amir wanted to smack the boy. "It wasn't my—"

"No one is to blame except for my father," Maliha interrupted them.

"You must be the vizier's daughter, then," Nadim said. "Don't underestimate the wiles of Ghazi; he's one cunning ifrit. But tell me, where is Zahra?"

"Yes, where's Master Zahra?" Rafi asked.

"She's..." Amir hesitated, embarrassed to answer.

"She's in a dungeon cell," Maliha said. "She was imprisoned for my father's crime."

Rafi's mouth opened wide in horror. "She's in a dungeon? We've got to get her out."

"I agree with the boy," Nadim said. "Let's go."

Maliha held up her hand to halt them. "Shouldn't we free the prince from the magic spell first?"

Nadim's eyes locked onto Amir's. "Do you have a drop of Ghazi's blood?"

"Not yet," Amir said.

"The counter-spell is incomplete without it. To try would be inviting catastrophe, like in the Tale of the Falconer and—"

"We need you for that," Amir said. "What chance do we have of making the ifrit bleed?"

"Not much. But here, within the sultan's palace, I cannot use my magic." Nadim's eyes widened. "Unless I am released from the ancient contract by a member of the royal family, and that person—"

"Fine," Amir said. "I release you from the contract."

"You didn't let me finish," Nadim said. "That person must be the one I am bound to, and right now that is Zahra, who is not here and is not of royal lineage."

"What?" Amir said. "I thought a jinni could do anything!"

"Not quite anything; limitations were placed on the powers of those from my realm by an ancient pact between my father and your ancestor, Alhad. Believe me, Prince, they are for the benefit and protection of both you and your people."

What other rules and limitations were there that would stymie them?

Maliha hung her head low. "I am ashamed that I ignored Zahra's plea. I should have listened to her."

Her shame only amplified Amir's. What had he promised to Zahra? How often had he told her he loved her? And he'd kissed her—the first girl he'd ever kissed. Had he promised to marry her? How could he have so easily forsaken her?

Maliha continued, "But now our path is clear: we must go free her at once."

"That's what I said before," Rafi said. "With much respect to you, Princess."

"Would you stop that!"

"Don't bother," Amir said, "it only encourages him."

"Encourages what?" Rafi said, trying to look innocent.

"Let's go," Amir said. "Rafi, follow behind us as our servant. Nadim, you should probably—"

The jinni disappeared in another cloud of golden smoke.

"—do that." Amir stashed away the Scarab and took the others on a winding path down through the palace.

"Why are we going so far out of the way?" Maliha asked. "We can take the eastern staircase and go by the wall along the lawn."

"I'm taking a less traveled route to reduce the chance of running into people. I know a special way."

"Yes, I understand," Maliha said, "but I know every inch of this palace, and the lawn will be nearly empty, especially today. Much respect to you, my prince."

"No, don't you start with that now."

Rafi chuckled behind them.

"And you watch yourself back there, servant boy. You're one mocking quip away from becoming my slave."

The boy *was* impertinent. But Amir had to admit that he was helpful, and he was always supportive of Zahra. Zahra—there she was again in his thoughts. He squeezed his wife's hand, feeling guilty about thinking of a servant girl who'd tried to steal him away from Maliha. Or should he feel guilty about having married Maliha? A thousand curses on Yaseen for using this magic on him.

Amir agreed to go with Maliha's route. They ran into a handful of people who congratulated them on their marriage, but afterward they slipped unnoticed down the stairs leading to the dungeon.

One guard stood outside the dungeon's entrance door, at full attention, a pomegranate honey glaze visible on his lips. "Prince Amir and Princess Maliha." The man stood straighter. "Such a pleasure to see you."

Maliha met the guard's eyes and dabbed her lips gently with a finger.

"Oh," the man said, quickly wiping at his mouth. "Apologies, Mali—uh, Princess."

"No need to apologize, Firuz," she said. "I'm glad the treats from our ceremony were enjoyed throughout the palace."

"What brings you to such a dreary place on your happiest of days?"

"We wish to see the traitor, Zahra," Amir said.

"Ah." Firuz bit at his lip. "I'm under orders to allow nobody into these cells other than the vizier or the sultan himself."

Who did this Firuz think was standing before him? "I'm your Prince; this is Princess Maliha. Son and daughter-in-law of the royal sultan. You will open the door and let us in."

If Firuz had looked uncomfortable before, now he looked positively distressed. As well he should. "Please, my prince, a thousand pardons," he said, eyes and head down. "It was the vizier and your father themselves who issued me them orders. Nobody goes in here but them, they said. And he added—your father did, the sultan, I mean—he said especially not the prince or the princess. For your own safety, they said, on account of the magic and craftiness of the wicked girl locked up there."

Maliha sighed. "That girl is not wicked, nor is she a danger. She's our friend and has been wrongfully accused and we need to see her."

"Even still Mali—Princess. My orders come from the sultan himself."

"Firuz, I've known you for how long?" Maliha said. "You know I'm not some simpleton easily fooled by trickery."

Amir saw movement behind the window into the dungeon. A woman's face peered out for a brief moment, to be quickly replaced by Zahra's. So she'd freed herself?

Zahra held up a ring of keys and pointed to them. They would be able to get her out of there if they could lure this Firuz away.

"I know you're a sharp one, Princess—" Firuz said.

Apparently, Rafi had noticed Zahra too, because before the guard could finish his sentence, Rafi dashed between Amir and Maliha, grabbed the set of keys from the man's waist, and bolted up the stairs.

"You desert rat!" Firuz chased after the boy.

As soon as the guard had topped the stairs and chased Rafi around a corner, Zahra shouted, "Catch," and tossed the keys out to them.

Amir snatched them from the air and hurriedly unlocked the

door, freeing Zahra and the other woman. A part of Amir thought he should hug her, but he realized that feeling was gone. Wasn't it?

Maliha did hug her. "I owe you a huge apology, Zahra. You were the one who was trying to do the right thing all along. I feel horrible."

"I, too, must beg your forgiveness," Amir said. "My memory is still cloudy, but I should not have so easily dismissed you."

The woman who'd exited the prison stepped forward. "Well, if anyone had listened to me, all of this could have been avoided from the beginning."

"Who are you?" Amir asked.

"This is Selene, but we can catch up later," Zahra said. She threw both Amir and Maliha a stern look. "We can talk about forgiveness then, too. Right now, we need to get Rafi."

She was right—they needed to move.

Zahra followed Amir up the stairs. "Did you undo the spell?" she asked.

"Not yet. We needed to free you first."

They turned another corner and ran into Firuz, who was pulling Rafi along by the scruff of his neck.

"Guard," Amir said. "Let the boy go. As you can see, we've gotten what we came for, so you can return to your post."

The guard's face went white. "Prince, you should not have let her out. Your father was very clear about how dangerous she is."

"We'll be fine. And don't worry, this won't reflect poorly on you."

Zahra whispered into Amir's ear.

"I'm told that your fellow guard, Aman, is locked in a cell. Please release him and resume your duties. I will speak with the sultan and explain everything."

Firuz stood there dumbfounded for a few moments before slinking off down the stairs and into the dungeon without uttering another word.

Zahra wrapped her arms around Rafi. "I'm so glad you're alright."

"I can't believe the prince sent you to the dungeon." Rafi smacked his palm to his forehead. "And now he's under another spell."

"Yes, he is," Maliha said. "Thanks to your servant boy, we now understand the truth of what happened."

"He's not my servant boy."

Rafi frowned. "I thought we'd settled this, Master Zahra."

"Rafi." Zahra shook her head in frustration. "Never mind, forget about that. Do you still have the items needed for the spell?" She held out her hands.

"Yes. They're in the prince's room."

"What?" Amir said. "Why did you leave them there?"

"You told me to hide them. Then we left, and you didn't tell me to bring them with us."

"It doesn't matter," Maliha said, already starting back to the main hall. "We have to go back up, anyway. We need to confront my father and have him call out the ifrit."

"You'll do no such thing," Yaseen said, coming around the corner, accompanied by a cadre of his guards. "Ah, Maliha, I tried to keep you from seeing your servant friend again. I see now that what I feared has come to pass, that you have allowed yourself to be twisted by her lies. And my prince, have you so easily fallen back under the sway of this treacherous girl?"

Zahra jabbed her finger at the vizier. "I'm not the treacherous one, *Yaseen*."

She'd defiantly addressed him without his title. *Good for her.*

"I should have had you exiled from the city for speaking falsehoods about me," Yaseen said, his voice icy.

"No, Father, we know what you've done. *I* know what you've done. What I don't know is why. Why did you do this? You were already the sultan's vizier, his chief adviser and administrator. Your dreams for my future can't have been worth all this mayhem."

"Because we are royalty, you and I, my child. Or we should have been. I am only correcting a wrong from decades past. Now I have set the world right, and you, my daughter, are exalted."

"That was worth imprisoning my friend? Chasing her down and trying to kill her? Forcing the prince to marry me against his will? Against *my* will? Consorting with a demon in the sultan's own—"

Yaseen bristled. "You mustn't listen to these wild tales trying to besmirch my—"

"Stop it, Father! Enough. I know what you've done. I know about the Midnight Lily, and the kohl, and the cobra venom, and the drop of demon's blood. It's ... it's ... horrific. It's abhorrent. You ... you shame me."

The vizier spread his arms before him. "Maliha, my dear daughter, I have only ever wanted the best for you. Now you have what even I have never achieved. Please, you are—" Yaseen advanced toward her, his attitude beseeching.

Amir stepped between them. *Enough of this.* "No. We're going to speak to the sultan. Right now."

"Guards." Yaseen returned to his men. "The prince and princess are confused, their minds addled by this girl's sorcery. Take them and hold them in my chambers so I may undo the magic upon them. Execute the others."

CHAPTER 39

The guards surrounded and took hold of them, and once again Zahra found herself a captive. But one guard at the back of the group remained where he was—Ghazi.

Ghazi, the ifrit in human form, turned and faced Yaseen. "I think, good vizier, it is time for you to uphold your end of our agreement."

"Not now. We will complete our dealings in my chambers at an appropriate time."

"I prefer that it be now. Your daughter is wed; she is the princess. Royalty, as you desired. As a member of the royal family, she now has the ability to grant that which I seek."

Yaseen's right eye twitched. "Ghazi, this is not the time."

"Oh, but it is." Ghazi's voice took on a menacing tinge. "This plan has taken long enough." He spoke louder now. "And I have been patient."

"If you'll suffer only the additional delay of a walk to my chambers," Yaseen said.

"No, vizier. Our bargain will be satisfied now. My restraint is at an end." He grew before their eyes, skin changing color, tattoos spreading across his body, and horns sprouting from his head as he retook the horrible form Zahra had witnessed in Yaseen's chambers.

Everyone but Zahra and the vizier gasped.

The guards released their captives and drew their scimitars. Rafi scurried behind Zahra, clinging to her waist.

Amir glared fire at his father's vizier. "Yaseen, have you gone mad?"

"Silence!" the ifrit roared. "There is a transaction to be completed."

Ghazi's gaze shifted to Maliha. "And now, dear girl, I believe your father has a request to make of you."

"I ... I ... Ghazi, what are you..." Yaseen stammered.

"Spit it out, man, and let us be done with this. Tell her my request; fulfill the terms of our agreement."

"I..." Yaseen started again. "He wishes..." He looked around the room, now evincing the shame he'd brought upon his daughter. "You must free him of his binding, Maliha. It is the bargain I made with him. That you would release him from his bonds so that he may again experience the world with freedom."

"No," Maliha said. "Father, I'll not do it. He's a demon; you can't trust him."

Of course Ghazi couldn't be trusted—how could Yaseen be so blind as to not see this? Zahra recalled Nadim's dire warning. "She's right. The ifrit seeks only revenge, and plans to exact it upon the royal family, your daughter included."

"You know nothing, girl," Yaseen said. "Keep your unsolicited thoughts to yourself. Maliha, it is alright. We will be fine."

Ghazi loomed over Yaseen. "You fail to uphold your end of the agreement?"

"No. Here." The vizier removed a ring from his finger and handed it to Maliha. "I pass my control of the ifrit Ghazi to Princess Maliha. Now, daughter, do it. Free him from his magical bonds."

"My love," Amir said. "Hold strong against this."

It was strange for Zahra to hear Amir refer to another as "my love." She knew the spell had been transferred, but she wondered if Amir did, in fact, love Maliha. Whatever his feelings, she knew they would be tested now.

Maliha, horrified, stared at the ring in her hand. "I won't do it."

The moment she uttered the last syllable of her defiance, Yaseen gasped, and his eyes bulged. He fell to his knees. His hands came to his throat—he was struggling to breathe. Veins stood out on his forehead, his skin turned a purplish hue, and blood trickled from his nose. He looked pleadingly at his daughter.

Two guards closed on the ifrit, but the demon's massive arms tossed them away with ease.

"Stop this," Maliha shouted to the ifrit. "Stop it."

"It is not my doing, Princess. It is a deep, irreversible magic—he has made the Oath of Bahamut, bound in blood, offering his own life as collateral to our agreement. By failing to deliver on his promise, his life is forfeit. This is the bargain he made."

Maliha rushed to Yaseen. "Father, what have you done?" Her voice quavered as tears rolled down her cheeks.

Yaseen reached for Maliha, his head lolling forward as pain clearly wracked his entire body. Blood dripped onto his daughter's wedding dress. Yaseen's arms tensed, his hands balled into fists. The muscles on his neck stretched taut and his jaw clamped shut.

"His life is not yet over," Ghazi said. "You, my dear girl, beautiful princess of the royal family of Alhad, have the power to save him. Simply grant me my freedom and his oath will be fulfilled."

"Oh, father." Maliha held the vizier close. Her tears dripped on the back of his shoulder, even as his blood trailed down hers.

Zahra couldn't imagine the turmoil raging within her friend at this moment. Even though she herself was disgusted with the vizier and reviled him, did his actions warrant a torturous death? She thought about her own selfish reasons for wanting to marry the prince and found it hard to pass such a harsh judgment on the man.

Maliha looked at Amir through tear-soaked eyes, and choked out through her sobs, "I ... can't ... let him die."

Amir kneeled beside her and rested his hand on her shoulder.

"It's alright, Maliha," he said softly. "Do what you must."

They really needed Nadim—right now.

"Amir," Zahra whisper-called to him.

The prince turned stiffly to face her.

"I release you from your bonds," Maliha said.

"Maliha, wait," Zahra said. They could still stop the ifrit.

Amir had a vacant look, as if accepting their fate. Zahra clapped at him to snap him back to the moment. She made an explosive gesture with her hands, trying to mimic the jinni's appearance. "The scarab." Then she mouthed, not wanting to alert Ghazi, *Did you free it?*

Amir squinted in confusion.

The ifrit stood tall and bellowed a question to Maliha, "Now and henceforth?"

Amir's eyes widened—he finally understood. He reached into his broad waist sash.

"Now and henceforth. You are free." Maliha cried as her father collapsed, a look of relief washing over him as his muscles all relaxed.

The ifrit stretched wide his arms and inhaled a loud, deep breath. "So ... many ... years..." His voice echoed loudly through the halls. "Finally, I am free!" The ifrit looked to Maliha, who held her father propped up against her. "You, princess, and your pathetic father, will be spared my wrath."

"But you..." Ghazi said to the prince. "You and *your* father will watch as I tear this so-called Palace of Light to pieces around you and unleash the power of your precious Eternal Flame." The ifrit snapped his finger and there was a clap of thunder.

Both he and Amir disappeared in a thick cloud of red smoke, leaving behind only the strong, repugnant stench of sulfur.

CHAPTER 40

"Amir," Zahra reached out for him, but he was gone.

"Father," Maliha cried, a haunted look on her face. "By the Flame, what have I done?"

"Not you," Yaseen gasped. "This is all ... my doing. I put you ... in a terrible position."

For the first time ever, Zahra completely agreed with the vizier. This was all his fault, but there would be time for laying blame later. Hopefully. In the meantime, they needed to stop the ifrit. "We must get to the sultan and rescue Amir."

Yaseen struggled to rise. "Zahra's right."

The guards stood nervously, waiting for orders. Zahra was done waiting. "Go to the sultan's chambers and see that he is safe."

The men looked briefly at Maliha, who was still in shock. Surprisingly, all but one guard obeyed Zahra and ran off. The remaining man moved to Maliha, saying, "I'll stay and help the princess."

"What do we do now?" Rafi asked. "The prince had the Golden Scarab."

He'd been so close to giving it to her.

"Did you clear the seal from it, the ambergris? If so, he can summon Nadim."

"Yes, it's free," Rafi said, "but Nadim can't use his magic within the palace."

"Flame! That's right. But Amir has royal blood—he can release that constraint."

Rafi shook his head. "You have to transfer your bond with Nadim to Amir first. Like when the vizier handed the ring to Maliha."

Zahra's head was spinning. She hadn't known it would be so complex; she'd thought the jinni would be able to do anything he wanted.

The ground rumbled beneath them, sending a statue and a large vase smashing to the floor.

"What was that?" Rafi's brow scrunched up with worry.

"*That* was a sign that we need to go," Zahra said.

The acrobat Selene walked up to face Yaseen. "Curse you, vizier." She spat at his feet. "You've brought destruction upon us all."

Another tremor shook the palace, and stone tiles clattered down from the ceiling above. Now wasn't the time for curses and complaining.

"Selene," Zahra said, "do what you can to raise the alarm and get everyone out of the palace."

The thief ran off to follow Zahra's instructions, but paused at a junction in the hallway. She reached up, undid her hair, and tossed her gold hairpin back to Zahra. "If you ever find yourself in Egypt." She winked and bounded away.

What exactly did that mean? It didn't matter; Zahra didn't have time to ponder the acrobat's oddities. She shoved the pin into her own hair.

"Are you able to walk, father?" Maliha asked.

"Don't worry about me; you must flee the palace. Guard, take her to safety."

"No, father—I released the ifrit. I'm going to do what I can to stop it." She turned to the guard. "Help *him* from the palace."

"That's madness," Yaseen wailed. "You can't hope to stand against..."

Maliha placed her hand over his mouth and kissed him on the forehead. Zahra grabbed her by one arm and pulled her along. "Come on, Princess. Rafi, let's go."

They raced through the main hall. Wedding guests were running in all directions, bewildered and terrified and looking for the exit. Zahra pointed the guests toward the way out, asking if they knew where the sultan was. None had seen him recently.

Maliha spotted Hani, the royal architect's son—the boy she was in love with.

"Maliha!" He rushed over to her. "What's happening?"

"Something terrible; a demon is destroying the palace. Have you seen the sultan?"

"He—he disappeared into smoke. One second he was there, and the next—"

"We'll find him. You get outside." She grabbed him by the shoulders and pulled him to her. "I love you." She kissed him softly on the lips.

Hani looked shocked. "You're married to the prince. We can't—"

"We'll talk later, if we survive. Now go."

The palace shook again, and more sculptures toppled over and shattered. Braziers fell clanging to the floor, hot ashes and burning coals sliding along the tile. The palace residents and guests alike screamed and fled in terror.

Think, Zahra, think. "Where would the ifrit take them?"

Rafi scrunched up his face. "Maybe they went to the prince's room?"

That seemed unlikely. Why would it take them there? But where *had* he gone? What was his goal? To destroy the palace, obviously... He'd wanted to make the sultan and the prince watch. He wanted to release the power of—

"Not the prince's chambers. The *sultan's* chambers!"

The ifrit had said he wanted Amir to watch the destruction.

Zahra clung to the hope he might still be alive.

"Hold on, Amir. Hold on." She remembered him saying those words to her when she was dangling over the edge of the waterfall. Now it was he who was on the precipice of death. She only hoped she could save *him* this time.

The floor bucked beneath them as they ran, knocking them off their feet more than once, but they rose each time without suffering serious harm. They passed a row of windows. Outside, rain lashed down against the night sky. A blinding flash of lightning caused a deafening blast; the base of the northeast minaret shattered and exploded outward. The whole tower tilted, then crashed to the earth with a tremendous boom.

Zahra couldn't imagine the rage it would take to revel in the destruction of such beauty.

"We have to hurry," Rafi again stated the obvious.

They at last reached the top of the palace and rushed to the sultan's chambers. The doors lay splintered in pieces in the hallway. Two of the king's guardsmen lay dead at the entrance, and in the sultan's expansive inner room, more guards were strewn about, some lying motionless and others writhing in pain.

A large section of the outer wall had been blown apart, and wind and rain blew into the room. Amir and the sultan both floated a few feet off the ground, suspended by Ghazi's magic, forced to gaze in horror at the ifrit's destructive rampage.

"Another of your precious towers falls," the ifrit gloated over the devastation.

"Stop this," the sultan said. "We've done nothing to you. You cannot hold us responsible for injustices we did not commit."

"Silence, filthy human."

Amir caught Zahra's eye as she approached. He surreptitiously retrieved the Golden Scarab from his sash. As the ifrit caused another part of the palace to collapse, he flicked his wrist and tossed the Scarab back toward her. The sound of it tumbling along the floor was entirely masked by the ruin the ifrit was causing.

Zahra scooped it up and wasted no time in calling forth Nadim.

The burst of golden smoke and motes of dust that accompanied the jinni's return caught Ghazi's attention.

"The great jinni, Nadim!" the ifrit shouted in surprise. "Welcome back. You've come to witness the fulfillment of my revenge?"

"No, Ghazi. I've come to put a stop to it."

Comparing the short, unkempt, paunchy jinni, wearing only a loin wrap and sandals, to the towering, muscular, fiery ifrit, Zahra's heart sank. What hope did they have against this monstrous demon?

Ghazi shook his huge, horned head. "Nadim, Nadim. I'm free. There's no stopping me now. This justice I unleash is long overdue; you know what was done to me. You know the centuries of enslavement and abuse I've had to endure. This is only righteous."

"This is not right at all, brother. *These* humans did nothing to you."

"Their ancestor took from me everything that mattered. And why—because I had the audacity to love? Because I wanted to have a deeper connection to this world?"

"It was more than that, and you know it," Nadim said. "You disobeyed the dictates put forth by the Father of Jinn."

The ifrit let out a booming laugh. "Ah, yes, our noble father. I'll be going after him next."

Ghazi scanned the room, his eyes falling on the Golden Scarab in Zahra's hand. "Girl, I see my brother Nadim is bound to you. He is limited in his powers, constrained by the ancient magical covenant between Alhad and my father. I no longer suffer such fettering, and so he no longer presents a threat to me."

"Ghazi, please," Nadim said. "See reason."

"Listen to the jinni," the sultan said. "We can work this out."

Ghazi ignored them. "Girl, you are a servant here, made to wait on this family. I have sympathy for that; you need not be a part of this. Drop that scarab and your connection to this annoying jinni and I will let you live."

The ifrit's offer was absurd. Even if Ghazi could be trusted—which she highly doubted—she would never abandon her friends for her own gain.

She walked toward the ifrit, who stood near the hovering sultan and prince, holding the artifact before her. The ifrit smiled, reaching out an enormous hand in expectation of receiving the Golden Scarab.

"I pass my bond with Nadim the jinni … to Prince Amir." Zahra stood tall and placed the Scarab in the prince's hand.

Ghazi frowned in contempt. "Foolish."

Amir, still held floating in the air by the ifrit's magic, turned as best he could to face Nadim. "I grant you the right to use your power anywhere in our kingdom, Jinni Nadim."

CHAPTER 41

"You think this feeble jinni can stop me?" Ghazi laughed. He stretched his arms high and grew massively.

The sultan and the prince were released from the ifrit's magic and fell to the floor, Amir yelping in pain as his ankle twisted on impact.

"Stand back," Nadim said as he stepped between them and Ghazi.

Zahra hurried to pull Amir away from the enlarging demon, while Maliha saw to the sultan.

Ghazi continued to grow, now towering twenty feet high and still getting larger. The ifrit slammed his fists upward and smashed through the domed ceiling. Stone crashed down into the room.

"Ghazi, halt your madness." Nadim raised his arms and he, too, became taller.

"Halt? I am only getting started. I shall not stop until the palace is razed to the earth and this kingdom is destroyed. At the end, when they've watched all that I've done, the descendants of Alhad will be my slaves."

Ghazi reached to the skies. Dark clouds formed and swirled

overhead. A twisting funnel descended and whirled toward the city, raging through the outer wall. Stones and humans alike were swept like debris into the air.

Nadim now matched the enormous height of the ifrit. "Stop this," he shouted over the whipping winds.

Ghazi was already moving on to his next assault. Lightning danced within the thick, ominous sky; winds howled throughout the city, matching the chaos of the maelstrom above. The air tingled, and all the hair on Zahra's body stood up, while more and more lightning arced among the clouds. The ifrit raised his hands and called down the pent-up energy from the skies.

Nadim bellowed, "I said stop!" And in a blink, he transformed.

Gone was the disheveled, potbellied man. The jinni now stood resplendent—golden-skinned, massively muscled, with four arms, long swirling hair, and glowing magenta eyes. Truly a wonder to behold.

Now *this* was the jinni Zahra had expected from the legendary Golden Scarab of Balihar.

Nadim intercepted Ghazi's blast. Lightning had indeed shot down from above, but the jinni redirected it into the ifrit.

Zahra covered her eyes against the bright flash. A thunderous crack boomed through the sultan's chambers.

The mighty Ghazi shrieked in pain, and when Zahra looked again, smoke was drifting from his body. Nadim's visage was fierce like she'd never seen.

"Ghazi," a voice called from the entrance behind them. "Stop this."

Everyone turned to face the newcomer, Yaseen. The vizier limped into the room.

The ifrit merely laughed; any control the vizier had over him was gone.

"Yaseen," the sultan called to his vizier. "You shouldn't be here. Get my people to safety."

"My fault, my king." Yaseen lowered his eyes. "All of this. Daughter,"—he turned his attention to Maliha—"the ring. Call the ifrit back inside by rubbing it."

Maliha tried, but nothing happened. Yaseen's head sagged. "Then we're lost," he said.

Zahra refused to give up. They must be able to do something. What did they have to work with? The Golden Scarab? That wouldn't help—they'd already called forth Nadim.

The jinni was doing his best to stymie the demon's destruction. Nadim slammed Ghazi's enormous body against the remains of the sultan's chamber wall. "This is why we have rules in this world. Look at what you're doing."

"You are right," the ifrit said. "I should make this punishment more personal."

There was a flash, and the ifrit had returned to his previous size, now looming above them at only eight feet. "I agreed to leave your bride out of this, prince, but not your other friends. Since they seem so intent on being involved, let's have them join us."

An invisible magic force pulled Zahra from her feet, with Rafi likewise held in the air next to her. "Do you care about these two mortals, Prince?"

Zahra felt something tightening around her throat. She tried to pull it away, but there was nothing there. The pressure increased, and she struggled against it, arms reaching up and her legs flailing to find support. She couldn't breathe. Her eyes locked with Rafi's and she saw his terror.

Giant Nadim's leg arced past her, his foot slamming into the ifrit and sending the demon flying through the wall of the sultan's anteroom and into the chamber of the Eternal Flame.

"No, not the Flame," the sultan cried, dropping to his knees in helpless fear.

Zahra and Rafi were released from the magical grip and fell to the floor. She sucked in a deep breath.

Nadim shrunk back to his normal size to check on them, but Zahra waved him toward the other room. "We're fine. Get to the ifrit."

Nadim stormed over, but Ghazi had recovered. The ifrit blew

out the rest of the wall, fully exposing the antechamber to the Eternal Flame. Nadim intercepted the flying bits of stone and flung them with his magic out into the howling night.

Ghazi stood tall, silhouetted by the vivid glow of the Eternal Flame. He stretched out a hand and called down lightning, this time aiming it full force straight at Nadim. The jinni was ready, flicking his wrists and again redirecting the energy at the demon.

The impact smashed the ifrit back into the column of mirrors above the Eternal Flame. Glass shards flew everywhere. The intense light of the Flame bounced off the remaining mirrors, bright reflections spinning wildly around the room.

"Yes!" Rafi yelled. "Get him, Nadim!"

The ifrit sneered. His malevolent eyes flitted to Zahra and Rafi. She and the boy were yanked across the floor toward the demon, while simultaneously, shards of the broken mirrors came flying toward them.

Nadim stretched out his four arms, blocking all the deadly glass with an invisible barrier.

"Jinni!" Ghazi growled. "You've interfered enough." He leaped across the room and onto Nadim, wrapping his hands around the jinni's throat.

Nadim grappled with him and they thrashed about the room, crashing into walls and furniture. Ghazi again sent debris hurtling toward Zahra and Rafi. The jinni defended them, but he was sufficiently distracted for the ifrit to get behind Nadim and wrap an arm around his neck.

Nadim wrestled against the demon's grip, but none of his four arms could dislodge him. He maneuvered Ghazi's arms from his neck just enough to squeak out two words: "Inara's here."

"What?" Ghazi said.

"Your lover. She's here," Nadim said.

"What foolishness do you speak?"

The flying debris dropped to the floor, and the flashes of lightning faded.

"Inara," Nadim said again. "Your lover is here. The immortality she sought—to be young and beautiful forever—it was given to her. That was her punishment for betraying her king."

Ghazi looked around. "I don't understand. What trickery is this? What are you playing at, brother?"

Even the skies above had calmed down, and the winds wailing around the city had stilled to a slight breeze.

"I do not lie, Ghazi. Inara is right here. There she is: your love." Nadim pointed over the ifrit's shoulder. "You were blinded by your love for her. Now behold her blinding beauty. She is immortal. She is the Eternal Flame, the source of the power of Alhad."

The Tale of the Demon and the Sultan's Wife, Zahra realized. The queen who'd wanted to live forever.

Ghazi released Nadim and walked toward the Eternal Flame, mouth agape. The clouds above roiled, faster now, and darker. "No. It cannot be." The light from the Flame flickered in Ghazi's eyes. "What perversion is this?"

Lightning arced again and cracked down around the city. A light drizzle turned into rainfall and then a heavy downpour, with balls of hail clacking into the stone floor.

Ghazi roared, thrusting out an arm and clapping Nadim against the wall with his magic.

"I will destroy ... everything! Starting with *them*."

Eyes full of menace and fury, Ghazi glared at the jinni. "Now you and your precious royals of Alhad can watch as I crush the life from these mortal friends of yours."

An immense pressure closed in upon Zahra, as though her whole body were being squeezed by a giant hand. Her arms were forced against her sides and the air was compressed out of her lungs. She strained against the crushing force, but only managed to wiggle her toes.

Rafi squealed as he was constricted next to her. "Master Zahra," he squeaked, "are we going to die?"

She wouldn't say what she was thinking.

Amir watched in horror as Zahra and Rafi were about to have the life squeezed out of them, and Nadim was clamped firmly against the wall by Ghazi's magic.

Someone had to stop this. His father might be able to call upon the magic of the Eternal Flame, if that was even possible, if their ability to use its power was any more than a vague story passed down through the generations. The sultan lay weak and injured on the floor—he was in no condition to help. If the vizier possessed any magic, it was clear he had nothing that would work against the ifrit.

Nobody can help us.

Nobody could save Zahra and Rafi. Nobody could save the kingdom.

But Amir had to do something.

Ignoring the pain in his ankle, he rose to his feet.

Zahra managed to say, "It's okay, Rafi. Look at me." She met his gaze with compassion, and as much strength and confidence as she could muster.

Rafi cried out, "I'm scared. I don't want to die."

But then Amir was there. "Don't worry, little one—I'll handle this."

"How?"

Amir flashed a quick smile. "I'm the prince."

He lifted a mirror shard and held it up to the Eternal Flame. An intense beam of light reflected off the mirror, and he aimed it directly into the demon's eyes.

For a moment, it appeared as if the ifrit basked in the light, as if he truly saw and welcomed his long-lost love. Then the sheer brilliance of it overwhelmed him, and he threw up his arms to cover his eyes.

The crushing force around Zahra eased and she slumped to the floor, cradling Rafi to her.

Nadim was also free and wasted no time—he leaped onto the ifrit's back. The jinni stabbed a knife into Ghazi's side and then wrapped all four of his arms around the demon.

"Zahra," Nadim called. He glanced once toward her right arm and shouted over the rain and hail and thunder, "the scarab. Destroy it!"

Zahra's mind raced. Destroy the scarab? Why would she do that—and how? Thoughts flashed through her mind like the lightning around the city, and her mind latched onto one memory. The Cave of Balihar, with the Golden Scarab held above the coiled snake, its mouth open. And then she knew how.

But if she destroyed the scarab, that meant destroying ... Nadim.

A golden cloud of smoke drifted off the jinni, unaffected by the pouring rain and pelting hail. It expanded and surrounded and obscured both him and the ifrit. A reddish cloud joined it and the colors swirled around as if each was trying to dominate the other. The twin trails of smoke roiled and expanded to fill the chamber. Ghazi let forth a loud roar from within the murky vortex.

"Do it, Zahra," Nadim called.

He was right; she had to do this. Her heart felt like it was being stabbed. She'd never see the jinni again. "Amir, the scarab!"

The prince didn't hesitate. He tossed it toward her.

Zahra tapped the head of the serpent wrapped around her arm. The snake came to life, its eyes immediately locking onto the scarab arcing through the air. It snapped out—

In an instant, the Golden Scarab of Balihar was gone, swallowed by the serpent.

Goodbye, Nadim.

The smoke around Nadim and Ghazi had turned to an inky

black. It twirled and spun and was sucked inward, shrinking. Zahra heard Nadim's voice call out one more time, "Take this and use it..."

The smoke collapsed in on itself, and just before it disappeared with a loud *pop*, a blood-soaked dagger clattered to the floor.

CHAPTER 42

T he rain subsided to a drizzle, the raging wind became a
breeze, and the storm clouds turned to wisps.

Zahra crawled along the floor to pick up the knife Nadim had
dropped. Amir hobbled over to his father, and they shared a massive hug. Maliha hurried to check on Yaseen.

"Is it over?" Rafi asked. "Are we safe?"

"Yes," Zahra said. She sure hoped so.

She brought the bloody dagger to Amir.

"What do you intend to do with that?" the sultan asked.

It was too complicated to bother explaining to him; best if they
just got on with it. Rafi clearly thought the same. The boy ran
out and returned a moment later with the spell components they'd
collected.

"Nadim—the jinni—his last act was to make sure we could
undo the spell placed on your son," Zahra said. She looked at
Yaseen, who frowned and hung his head in shame.

"I'm going to need an explanation for all of this," the sultan said.

"Of course, my king," Zahra said. "First, there's something your
son must do."

Zahra mixed the ingredients of the spell with trepidation. They'd been working toward this for so long. What if it didn't work? She held her breath and dipped the flower into the potion.

"Hold that shard of mirror and close your eyes," she instructed Amir, who complied.

She held the flower out before her, placing it under Amir's nose. For the third time, the prince inhaled the scent of an enchanted Midnight Lily. Then he lifted the mirror, opened his eyes, and gazed into his own reflection.

A blank look passed over his face, and the mirror fell from his hands and shattered on the polished travertine floor. He bent over, the blank look turning to strain. He groaned and listed to the side.

The sultan caught him and held him upright. "What is happening? What have you done?"

"The spell—" Amir said. "It's unwinding; I can feel it." He pressed his hands to his temples. "Dizzy."

Amir reached out to Zahra and his father, who helped him take a seat on the floor.

"The memories. So confusing."

He squeezed his eyes shut and wobbled for a moment. When he opened them again, they were bright and aware.

The prince took a deep breath and looked from Zahra to Maliha. "I don't know what to feel."

"It's okay, my son. There'll be time to work everything out. Now why don't you catch me up on recent events? I'd very much like to know why an ifrit has almost destroyed my kingdom."

Amir told his father the long story, Zahra chiming in with the details as necessary.

"So now you see we made a great mistake," Maliha said. "The prince was under a spell all along, as Zahra tried to tell us. While I respect your son and I hope he feels similarly toward me, I suspect he doesn't love me, and never truly wanted to marry me."

"I … I agree." Embarrassment clouded his face. "Maliha might make a fine wife and princess, but I had no thought of marrying her prior to being under the influence of that spell. I humbly request and beg of you, my king, that our marriage be—"

"Yes, yes, of course," the sultan said. "Maliha, do you swear that you did not in truth wish to wed my son, but only did so at the behest of your..." he cast a withering look at Yaseen, "...traitorous father? And do you further swear that you wish the wedding to be annulled?"

"Yes, my king."

"And do you, my son, Prince Amir, swear that you did not and do not wish to marry Maliha?"

Zahra held her breath. She already knew the answer, of course, as they all did, but she still wasn't certain how she felt about it.

"I do, my king."

The sultan nodded. "Very well. Your vows are now undone and you are no longer, nor were you ever, husband and wife."

Zahra exhaled in relief. Regardless of how Amir felt about her, at least he was finally free from the madness of the enchantment and from a coerced marriage.

The sultan again glared at Yaseen. "This happy day has become a miserable mess." He shook his soaked head, droplets of water spattering to the tile floor. "To think it nearly ended up even worse."

He looked over at his guards. Only two of the men who'd come to protect their sultan were still alive. He ordered them to stand watch over the vizier. "Now, son, I must ask you—was the vizier's daughter, your former wife Maliha, complicit in this treachery?"

Yaseen lifted his head. "My king, she—"

"Silence!" the sultan commanded. "Or I'll have your tongue cut out."

"No," Amir said. "She knew nothing of her father's plan."

Relief flooded Yaseen's face.

The treacherous vizier had indeed fooled everyone, even his own daughter. Zahra looked upon Yaseen with the same disgust visible in the sultan's gaze.

"In fact," Amir continued, "when this boy here stole into my chambers and tried to convince me as to what had occurred, she

271

was the first to believe him and act to remedy the situation. She helped free the jinni, and then Zahra as well. And although she released the ifrit Ghazi from his bonds, she did so with my permission. I would have done the same in her place to save your life. When the palace was being shaken, she ran not out into the streets, but here to help us. Maliha is honest, and true, and loyal. I believe she should be praised, not punished."

Zahra had never heard Amir speak so highly of someone else, and he wasn't even under a spell. He looked at the vizier's daughter and flashed that goofy smile of his, and Zahra wondered if maybe it wasn't a lingering effect of the enchantment.

The sultan lowered his head and remained silent for a moment, considering his son's words. "I've been a fool. I've had my focus on the wrong things, looking outward to the world when I should have been paying more attention here at home. Trusting the wrong people, ceding control where I should have kept it, and controlling too much,"—he looked at Amir—"where I should have relaxed my grip and listened more. Your mother would be ashamed of me, my boy, and I'm not too proud to say it. It's time to set things right."

The sultan turned to face Maliha. "Maliha, I cannot disagree with anything the prince has said. You have certainly proved yourself more loyal and worthy than your father. I have been led to believe, by my *former* vizier's own words, that you have in fact handled many of the daily operations of the palace yourself on his behalf. Is this so?"

"Mostly the general pool of servants and the lower levels of the palace, my king."

"I think perhaps you are the best of your family, my dear girl. I find myself in need of someone with your intelligence, bravery, integrity, and perhaps even some of your charm. I am in want of a new chief adviser, and so I name you my vizier."

"I..." Maliha's face showed the shock that Zahra felt. "I ... I will serve you with my utmost ability."

"Better than your father, I trust. Speaking of which, your first act will be to advise me on the punishment of my former vizier.

What would you have me do with the man?"

"If I were in your position, my king, I would have him executed publicly for his crimes."

What? She would execute her own father?

"I see." The sultan nodded.

"But," Maliha continued, "as your vizier, I would beg that you show mercy and instead confine him to the dungeon for the remainder of his days. I ask this so that I may learn what knowledge he possesses in regard to handling your affairs, and also, humbly, as a gesture of kindness to your new vizier. Know, my king, that I will accept your decision, whatever it may be, and remain steadfast and loyal to you and to your kingdom."

"I have decided. Guards, take him to the dungeon, as my vizier advises."

I hope they put him in the same cell I was in, Zahra thought.

Yaseen never even looked up or stood to walk on his own as they dragged him away.

The sultan now turned his attention to Zahra. "Now we get to you, girl, the one Yaseen told me was disloyal, and villainous, and plotting against me. Yet you are the one who has risked your life to save my son on numerous occasions. Without you, our kingdom would have been destroyed, and my son and I would be facing a life of torture at the hands of a demon. It could be that no reward is too great."

He looked again at Amir and winked. "But I see that perhaps I can offer you one. I've noticed the way my son looks at you. And though you have been but a servant to our family in the past, I am reminded that one's heart and deeds are more important than mere happenstance of birth. You have also shown yourself to be loyal. More than that—brave, clever, and noble of spirit—worthy of my family, more so than any princess I've invited to meet my son. If you so desire, you may wed my son, and a princess you will be as well."

A princess. Zahra had been running and struggling so long now just to survive and prevent the next catastrophe that she'd almost forgotten why she'd sought the Golden Scarab in the first place. Now here she was, being offered the very thing she had fantasized about.

She looked at Amir and smiled. He was devastatingly handsome, and strong. He'd saved her life just as she'd saved his. They'd been through harrowing situations and survived, and they'd formed a bond that would never be broken.

The memory of their kiss brought another grin to her lips.

It was really happening—the sultan standing before her, offering everything she'd ever dreamed of.

Only now she realized it was no longer what she wanted.

The thought of marrying Amir had filled her head with lofty fantasies of a fairy-tale life, but she had never considered what that really meant. She hadn't looked at it in terms of being a partner to Amir, but had only focused on the feeling she thought she'd have being a princess. Perhaps that was what had concerned her during their journey together. The idea was great as a fantasy, but what did it mean to really be partnered with someone? And in particular, with Prince Amir?

Yes, he was a prince, and he was attractive, and she liked him. But she couldn't say that she truly loved him. How much of the person she'd traveled with had even been the real Amir? Was the true Amir the one who'd saved them at the edge of the waterfall, or the one who'd frequently expected Rafi to put himself in danger at his behest? Both? Neither? She couldn't be sure.

Did it matter at this point? Looking back on her experiences, she knew she didn't need the life of a princess to be happy. She wasn't even sure she wanted it. She reflected on the adventures she'd had, and the people she'd met and the places she'd seen. Walking through the Sands of Fire; escaping from a dust demon; surviving a living cave that had tried to kill them; acquiring a magical pet snake; making friends with a jinni, with Josef and his brother, and, most importantly, with Rafi and Amir. She hadn't needed to be a princess to do any of that.

She'd experienced things nobody in the palace had—even the

nobles. The events she'd longed to be a part of seemed insignificant now. Dances? No dance could compare to a stroll through the Garden of the Moon with loyal companions. A magic show, with clever illusions? She'd found the Golden Scarab of Balihar, and summoned a jinni from another realm. Feasts fit for royalty? The fanciest palace meal could never be as fine as the gift of a freshly picked date from a new friend.

Zahra held her head high. "I am honored, my king," she said, nervous about telling him how she felt. "Truly, I am honored. Your son is wonderful."

"I don't know about that," Rafi mumbled.

Zahra ignored Rafi and continued: "I thought this was exactly what I wanted. But now I think..." Before leaving her with the vizier, her mother had told her to always be true to herself, and to be honest. She wouldn't back down from that now. "Well, I think I would like to explore more of the world. If you are still inclined to grant me a request, I would be grateful for a sturdy horse, some supplies, and a little money for my journey."

Zahra looked at Rafi. "For *our* journey, if that's what my young friend here wants. He helped every bit as much, and deserves to share any reward."

Rafi beamed, but Amir's face was solemn, maybe even disappointed.

The sultan, pensive, nodded his head. "I think you have a rare wisdom, Zahra. You shall have anything you desire for your journey—speak to my new vizier and you will be provisioned as you wish. Know that you will always return to a hero's welcome."

The sultan turned to Rafi. "What about you, little one? You've proved yourself brave and loyal. But you're young; perhaps you should stay with us here at the palace for a while. Would you like to be trained to be one of my guardsmen? Or to be educated at the royal academy?"

Rafi didn't hesitate. "No. I want a horse, too, so I can go with Master—with my friend, Zahra."

Zahra beamed and held out her arms to welcome the boy into a great hug.

CHAPTER 43

Zahra wasted no time the following morning in meeting with Maliha to gather their supplies for the road. She sent Rafi to wait for her outside as she spoke with her friend one last time before heading out.

Maliha sighed in mock exasperation. "You're still here?"

"To think, both of us almost became the Princess of Alhad."

"And neither of us wanted to be." Maliha shook her head. "At least, I didn't want to be. I have a feeling you might change your mind someday."

"I made my choice; I'll live with it. What about you and Hani, the architect's son?"

Maliha flashed her a half-smile. "We'll see. I'm the vizier now, and I'll be quite busy. Especially without my favorite servant to handle things for me. You know, I might actually miss you."

"Don't try to fool me. You're going to be glad I'm not causing trouble anymore, especially now that you're the vizier."

"Maybe." Maliha poked Zahra's belly. "But I think it's going to be less fun around here." The new vizier's face soured as her eyes shifted to someone standing behind Zahra. "Speaking of less fun..."

Zahra turned to see Dalal approaching. "That's my hint that it's time to be going," she said quickly.

She had barely made it out Maliha's door when Dalal reached her.

"Zahra, what are you doing in those clothes?" the girl asked, disbelief all over her face.

Because Maliha now wore garb befitting a vizier, she had given Zahra a few of her old outfits.

Zahra experienced only a brief twinge of annoyance at Dalal's comment; of course the girl would be upset that Zahra wore the clothes of someone that far outranked her, clothes that had color and layers and style beyond those of even the highest-level servants. Zahra was proud Maliha had felt her worthy of her outfits, and it amused her that Dalal took offense.

She had a brief temptation to shoot off a mocking reply to Dalal, but to what end? She had no need to respond to the girl's silly concerns anymore; she might never even see her again. So instead, Zahra pulled the servant girl in for a hug, enjoying the shock in her eyes.

Poor Dalal—she was stuck in her world of meaningless competition. Zahra could sympathize. Not too long ago, she herself had wanted nothing more than to advance in the palace ranks. At least her world had opened up, while Dalal's remained small.

Zahra released her from the embrace and held her at arm's length, offering a genuine smile. Who knew? Maybe with the recent catastrophe, Dalal would change. She hoped so.

"I'm leaving now," Zahra said. "Say farewell to the others for me."

Zahra turned away from the open-mouthed servant girl, left the palace, and met Rafi outside.

They mounted up and made their way leisurely through the city, navigating around piles of rubble and workers. The gates to Alhad stood open, with laborers, artisans, and merchants already streaming into the streets to help in its reconstruction. But Zahra was leaving. A flash of guilt ran through her at the thought that she was abandoning Alhad in a time of great need. She suppressed that feeling; she'd helped save the city. Was that not enough?

That wasn't the only reason she felt uneasy, though. She *had* helped Alhad, and they would rebuild and recover. No, that wasn't the true source of her guilt—it was Amir.

When she'd turned down the sultan's offer to marry the prince, she'd seen the look on his face. He'd been hurt by her decision not to marry him, and her request to be set free. Free to leave both the palace and the city.

Since that moment in the sultan's chambers, she'd spoken only with Maliha, her fellow servants, and Rafi, and had studiously avoided Amir. How could she face him? Just thinking about having to speak with him roiled her gut. But had that been fair to him?

She told herself they really didn't know each other, that the prince she'd traveled with was someone else and not the true Amir, free of the spell. What did she owe this prince? Again, hadn't she done her part?

Her stomach churned. It was an excuse, and it didn't sit well. The truth was that she didn't know what to say to him, and was terrified she'd only make it worse.

Amir had gotten little sleep, but was it any wonder? After everything he'd been through in recent days, culminating in the near destruction of his kingdom, it was surprising he'd slept at all. It wasn't the terror of confronting the ifrit that kept him awake, or the devastation wrought on the palace and the city, or even having faced his own mortality. It was thoughts of Maliha and Zahra and his father. And of himself.

He'd been so in love with Zahra, and then with Maliha. Now he didn't know *what* to think. What did he feel? Confusing and conflicting emotions pulled him in different directions.

He remembered everything that had happened now, including what he'd felt for both of them. Some of that desire was still there. How could he trust his feelings? Would he ever be able to?

He'd known Maliha for years. She was attractive, and she was always polite to him, but prior to the spell, he hadn't had any particular interest in her. She'd never really caught his fancy, and he'd mostly seen her as the vizier's daughter. Plus, he hadn't been under the love spell with her for long, so it was easier to let those feelings go than it was with Zahra.

He had to admit to himself that when he'd first spent time with Zahra, he'd seen her as little more than an amusing distraction, someone new to toy with. Her straightforward attitude and honesty were things he'd not encountered before in a servant. They'd jarred him from his normal routine.

He was ashamed of how he'd treated her.

Of how he treated all his servants—everyone, really.

He thought of who Zahra was as a person. She was the only one in the palace other than his father who'd ever spoken plainly to him. When the vizier had tried to place a spell on him the first time in the Fathi Garden, she'd been under no obligation to stop him, but nevertheless she had. When she'd been forced to flee the city, she could have left and started a new life. When he'd found her in the oasis, she could have taken advantage of his enchantment and returned with him to the palace to become his bride. Instead, she'd chosen to seek a mystical artifact that they hadn't even known existed to try to free him from the spell.

She had risked her life, many times, to save him and the kingdom. For her efforts, she'd been falsely accused, hunted down, vilified, and thrown in prison. And betrayed—by Yaseen, by her sultan, by Maliha—

And by himself. The man who'd professed to love her.

After she'd saved the kingdom, when his father had offered her anything she wanted, she'd asked to be free. She could have been a princess, but she'd turned it down.

Amir completely understood.

Even so, it hurt.

The girl he'd once teased for his amusement had worked her way into his heart. And she'd shown him how utterly unworthy he was of her affections.

He was the Prince of Alhad, and most would think he wanted for nothing. They would be wrong.

Zahra and Rafi exited the city gates, others on horseback galloping past them, in more of a hurry than they were.

"Where are we going, Mas—" Rafi began, before catching himself. "Where are we going, Zahra?"

"I don't know." Anywhere but here, for now.

But something had stuck with her, literally. She removed the hairpin the acrobat thief, Selene, had given her and considered the symbol—a stylized outline of an eye, with a teardrop and an angled swirling line. As she'd thought when she first examined it in the dungeon cell, it looked familiar. Where had she seen it before?

Then it hit her: it was the same symbol on the necklace her mother had been wearing when she'd left her at the Palace. What did that mean? Was this a common design? Or did it have a special significance? She shoved the pin into her satchel.

"What do you think about Egypt?" she asked Rafi. "I hear they have great pyramids, taller even than the Palace of Light."

"As long as they don't have demons, or warriors made of sand."

"I am told there is a giant sphinx, but it's carved from stone."

"What's a sphinx?"

"A big cat, I think."

"I like cats," Rafi said.

A horse trotted up behind them. "Me, too," Amir said, reining in his steed next to Zahra's.

"Zahra, look. It's the prince!"

"I can see that, Rafi." Now she was facing the very encounter she had tried to avoid.

"You left without saying farewell," Amir said. For a fraction of a second, Zahra thought he was going to add "my love" to his statement. Instead, he stared at her until she was forced to look him in the eye.

Why had he come out here? Did he want an apology? "So you came out to see us off? To wish us well?"

His lips compressed and turned down briefly. "Listen, Zahra, I know I messed things up. I understand why you would be mad at me, and disappointed. I'm disappointed in myself."

She supposed he had reason to be. There had certainly been moments during their journey where he could have been kinder to Rafi, or when his princely arrogance had shone through. And abandoning her to the dungeon had simply been cruel after what they'd been through. How much of that was the entitlement of being the prince, how much the spell, and how much his true nature? Could she hold that all against him? In any case, none of that was why she had decided to leave.

"No. I'm not mad at you. It's just that ... I was caught off guard when the sultan..." she let her words drift off. "I meant what I said. My view of the world and what I want has changed. If I hurt you, I didn't mean to. I apologize."

"How can you not be mad? I did nothing when you were sent to the dungeon. I married Maliha, after ... after all that time telling you..."

"That you loved her?" Rafi said.

Amir nodded.

"Amir, I know it wasn't your fault—none of it was. Yaseen and that demon are to blame for everything. When it came down to it, even when you were under the second spell, you got me out of prison, and you saved me and Rafi from the ifrit. You did the right thing."

"That's generous of you to say."

It was true. Some of the tension in her was released as she realized that. "Before the spell, we'd barely even met, and you were just telling me what to do because I was a servant and you were the prince. You didn't love me, and a huge part of me didn't want to accept it. I was struggling with that the whole time."

Amir dabbed at his eyes. "I know. I didn't make it easy."

Zahra took a deep breath. It felt good to put words to her thoughts and feelings, to get it out into the open. She needed to get everything off her chest now. "I also realized I'd had enough time being in the palace. Before all of this, I'd only wanted to take part in all the great things there, things I'd only seen at a distance or heard about afterward. Now I realize there's so much out here, in the world outside of Alhad. It took me a while to realize it. I didn't know how to tell you; I didn't know what to say. I'm truly sorry if I offended you or hurt you."

Zahra's whole body relaxed, like a huge weight had been lifted.

The prince laughed. "I'm not offended—in fact, I feel the same way. I've been trapped in that palace my whole life. As for us, I admit I'm still figuring out my emotions. I realize now I didn't love you," he held up his hand as Rafi was about to interject, "as embarrassing as that is to admit. But I do *like* you. I know that you don't know me, the person I am without the influence of the spell. Honestly, I feel like I'm in the process of figuring that out myself. Maybe we can get to know each other better, if you'll allow me to join you."

He wanted to come along? *I wasn't expecting that.* But... "Aren't you needed in the palace for the reconstruction projects? And to look after your father?"

"My father's healing quickly, and he and Maliha are already on top of everything. Really, I was just getting in the way. They probably won't even realize I'm gone."

"You didn't tell them you were leaving?"

Amir shrugged. "I left a note."

Rafi buried his face in his hands. "That's not very responsible, Prince."

"I'm kidding, silly boy. Shockingly, my father gave me his blessing. So, what do you think, Zahra? May I join you on your trip?"

A lingering part of her feelings for him leaped at the thought that he wanted to join them. But which version of him would this be? "If you wish to come along, it must be as our equal."

"Agreed. As friends." He added with a wink, "For now."

A feeling of warmth washed over her at that. "Then I welcome you to ride with us." She was curious to see who the prince would turn out to be, away from the palace and his servants, and free from any spell. And if traveling as friends would turn into something more.

"Wait a minute," Rafi said. "I didn't get a say in this."

"My apologies," Amir said. "What do you think?"

Rafi looked him up and down, as if weighing his merit. "Of course you can come along. You're the prince."

"Not on this trip. I'm coming as your friend, Rafi."

Rafi gave Zahra a wide-eyed look of surprise. "He called me by my name."

Amir chuckled. "Don't get used to it, little boy."

Zahra smiled. It felt good to have Amir along, that he wanted to join them. "Then it's settled. Let's go see the pyramids of Egypt."

"We're back together for a new adventure," Amir said. Then he grew solemn, probably thinking the same thing she was. "I just wish Nadim was here with us."

The sand swirled around them and there was a great *poof*, followed by a burst of golden dust and smoke. When it cleared, the jinni Nadim was riding next to them, on an ugly, smelly camel with a stripe down its neck. A broad grin spread across the jinni's face. "And here we are, out on the road again."

"Nadim!" Zahra, Rafi, and Amir all shouted at once.

"I thought you were gone for good," Zahra said. "How are you here? The Golden Scarab is gone."

"Ah, yes. My poor scarab. That was my portal into your world, and because of its unfortunate destruction—and I don't blame you at all for that, my dear girl—my only way into your realm was through another portal."

"Another portal?" Rafi said.

"Yes. If you recall, a portal between our worlds can only be formed from an item of significant emotional value to the human I'm bound to. I was last connected to the prince here, remember."

"What are you carrying that has such an emotional value to you?" Zahra asked Amir.

The prince pulled something from his robes and showed it to them—the Midnight Lily.

"It reminds me of everything we've been through together, good *and* bad," Amir said. "To me, it represents my freedom. This is the one that cleared me of the spell; it opened my eyes to truth, in more ways than one. And it links me to all of you, who helped to set me free."

"Your portal can be a flower?" Rafi asked the jinni.

"It can be anything, young one. Jewelry is common, like Ghazi's ring. I've also seen many other things used, like an oil lamp, a royal sash, and even a small rug."

"Wow," Rafi said.

"This lily is meaningful to me now, too," Nadim said. "It's the culmination of all our hard work. I'm glad the counter-spell was effective; I was about 60 percent sure it would be. Luckily it was a one-time use, so it's perfectly safe now. The flower's not as much fun as my Golden Scarab was, but I like it."

"It's good to have you back, Nadim," Zahra said.

"I must say," the jinni said, "when you first discovered my Scarab and summoned me forth, I would have cursed the lot of you for bringing me back to the realm of humans. But as I grabbed hold of Ghazi, as smoke swirled around us and I was being pulled back into my realm, I hoped that you would remember your last wish and bring me back. And so you have, my friends—so you have."

"Are you crying?" Rafi said.

"No, of course not! I am the great jinni, Nadim."

Zahra wiped a tear from her own eye and laughed.

"So," Nadim said, "now that I'm here for ninety-nine years,

where are we going first?"

"To see a sphinx!" Rafi said. "It's a huge cat."

"Ah, have I told you the Tale of the Emperor and the Cat...?"

Zahra smiled and undid her braid, and let her hair blow freely in the warm breeze.

Nadim rambled on, and they rode off into the unknown, toward the glow of the rising sun.

AUTHOR'S NOTE

T hank you so much for reading my debut novel, *The Golden Scarab of Balihar*! I hope you enjoyed reading it as much as I enjoyed writing it.

Zahra's journey will continue in *The Wrath of Sekhmet*.

I am an independent author, so I heavily rely on word of mouth and reader reviews to spread awareness for my books. That's why support from people like you means so much to me. It would help me a lot if you would be so kind as to leave a rating and review for this book.

Also, I'd love to have you join my newsletter group so you can get updates on my writing, see concept art, read bonus scenes, and more!

Head to my website to sign up:
www.MichaelGrayford.com

Thank you, dear reader, and I'll see you next book!

.

Printed in Great Britain
by Amazon